A Fair Prospect

A Tale of Elizabeth and Darcy: Volume III

Desperate Measures

A Fair Prospect:
A Tale of Elizabeth and Darcy
In Three Volumes

Volume I: Disappointed Hopes
Volume II: Darcy's Dilemma
Volume III: Desperate Measures

ISBN-13: 978-1482357400

ISBN-10: 1482357402

This book is dedicated to

Julian

Without whose constant love, patience and support

This story would never have been written

Author's Note

A Fair Prospect is a story inspired by Jane Austen's *Pride &* *Prejudice*. It begins at the point in that story where Mr Darcy makes his first, ill-fated proposal of marriage to Miss Elizabeth Bennet.

For the purpose of this particular story, the Gardiners have no children of their own and the Militia left Meryton before Elizabeth travelled to Hunsford to visit her friend, Charlotte Collins.

Acknowledgements

I would like to repeat my heart-felt thanks to the Pinkers, the readers at *Pen & Ink* and *The Derbyshire Writers' Guild*. For their encouragement, support, suggestions and/or invaluable advice, I also thank again Mel, Jan, Renée, Abigail, Sybil, Roxey and also, for the same in recent months, Ioana and Janet.

Adrea, Diane and Rebecca – thank you once more for another beautiful cover.

Finally, I must also, at the end of this incredible experience, say a special thank you to four other people:

To Adrea and Tara, for always being there; for guidance, support, feedback and, above all, friendship;

To Wendy, my friend for 35 years, without whom I wouldn't have had the courage to take my first nerve-racking steps into publishing;

And to Julian, who has, over the past seven years, read countless newspapers and books during holidays as I sat scribbling away at scenes in my notebooks, has cooked, ironed, cleaned and tidied the house as I sat typing away at the PC, who has taken me to almost every location used in the 1995 and 2005 adaptations of *Pride & Prejudice*, who, even when the story was complete, then had to tolerate nearly three years of my saying '*I just need to do another edit*' and who, throughout it all, kept a smile on his face and acted like living with someone who spent half her waking hours in Regency England with a host of fictional characters was all he could ever want in a wife!

Thank you!

Chapter One

RESTORED SAFELY TO GRACECHURCH STREET from Bellingham House, Elizabeth Bennet climbed the stairs to her chamber with a sombre air. Having declined joining her family in a cup of tea before retiring, she made good her escape on the pretext of weariness, quite out of countenance with all and everything, the last thing she desired being a conversation around the ball they had so recently attended.

Muttering under her breath, she pushed open the door to her room, then let out a startled "Oh!" as someone inside flew across the room and flung themselves into her arms, which instinctively closed around the small figure now hugging her tightly.

"Serena! When did you arrive?"

Releasing her friend, Elizabeth hurriedly closed the door before turning to study her friend in the dim candlelight. Serena Seavington was of slender build, not dissimilar to Elizabeth herself, but she lacked the latter's height, reaching only to her shoulder, and though they shared hair of a similar hue, Serena's grew straight as a rod, and no amount of rags or hot irons would persuade it otherwise.

"I have been here these three hours. Oh Lizzy, how I have longed for your kind face!"

Elizabeth reached out and squeezed Serena's hands in hers, smiling. "Your patience will have to endure. If I am not mistaken, word of your arrival must have reached your sister."

Footsteps could be heard moving rapidly along the landing, and Elizabeth flung the door wide to reveal her aunt and Jane, both of whom hurried into the room with wide smiles upon their faces.

"Serena! My dear girl, we did not expect you so soon! I hope you did not overtire Papa's horses!"

Returning her sister's hug, Serena shook her head, then rested it familiarly against Mary Gardiner's shoulder, reaching out to squeeze Jane's hand in greeting.

"I was fully prepared before your letter arrived; it was but a matter of hours before we were on our way. Papa sent Ethel and Samuel to accompany me; they are quartered above the mews."

"Well, I am glad you are safely come, but you must be tired. Come down and greet your brother and then you must rest. We can catch up on all your news on the morrow."

Serena caught Elizabeth's eye as she set herself up from the embrace with her sister. "Indeed, Mary, I am anxious to see Edward. I will come now as you suggest, but I must beg for a few moments with Lizzy before I retire."

"You shall have as long as it takes us to drink our tea – then I insist upon your resting. It is a long journey from Derbyshire, and you have been travelling to and fro about the country for some weeks now. It would not do to over-tire yourself."

Exchanging a quick glance with her friend, Serena nodded and followed her sister out of the room and, excusing herself to finish drinking her tea, Jane went after them.

Impatient for Serena's return, Elizabeth walked over to the window and released the drapes, quickly shutting out the darkness. The lowness of mood that had descended upon leaving the ball she disregarded for the moment, her interest solely focused upon what enlightenment she might glean from her friend.

As she turned around, however, her eye was caught by something sticking out from under the bed, and she walked over and picked it up. It was the built up Patten that Serena habitually wore when out of the house. Doubtless she had kicked it off soon after her arrival, for Elizabeth knew how much she hated having to wear it.

With a sigh, she sank back onto the bed, the Patten still held in her hand, her heart aching for her friend. Serena felt her disablement keenly and rarely socialised, choosing to keep herself to herself and permitting but a select few to become close to her. As such, her attachment to

Nicholas, when she had found affections engaged, had remained steadfast. Thus, what could have led to her rejection of him?

Before Elizabeth could dwell further on the matter, she heard a sound out on the landing, and replacing the Patten on the floor she hurried to open the door.

"Has he spoken?" Serena's voice was low and urgent as she came into the room.

"Yes – though he has fought for the moment." Elizabeth ushered her friend over to the bed before settling beside her. "I do not understand. I cannot believe that you are so altered."

Serena clasped her hands in her lap, shaking her head. "I am not. Oh Lizzy!" She turned anguished eyes upon her, and Elizabeth bit her lip in consternation. "I never dared to dream that such a thing could come to pass, and thus I had neither considered the implications nor thought upon my response."

Elizabeth studied her thoughtfully for a second. "Thus you said "yes" and then "no" to cover all eventualities?"

Despite her obvious distress, Serena managed the glimmer of a smile at this, but it soon faded.

"I accepted without considering the consequences." She sighed and her gaze dropped to the floor.

"Is that why you rescinded?" Elizabeth frowned; it seemed a singular motive for such a reaction.

Serena shook her head, her air quite despondent.

"No. Indeed, Lizzy, there are two reasons why I could not allow it to persist." She glanced at Elizabeth, and at her friend's encouraging nod, she continued. "Perchance had he remained as he was – a second son who must make his way in the world, in a profession, anonymous – then, had he taken up the church, for example, I might have been able to accept him. As a clergyman's wife, I would not be expected to be out in society, and never in Town. We could be sequestered in a rural community, and my disability would be overshadowed by the good I might affect towards those less fortunate than myself."

Getting agitatedly to her feet, Serena limped over to the fireplace and stared into the dying fire. "Now he is made a gentleman, and I am not fit for a gentleman's wife, especially one who has such a love of company."

Elizabeth shook her head. "Nicholas must consider you suitable, or he would not have made you the offer."

Serena spun on her heel. "He pities me."

"Why would you say such a thing?"

"I believe he thinks of his mother; she has oft claimed I am the daughter that she lost. He is a good man, a dutiful son…"

"He would not do this for his mother's sake alone." Elizabeth patted the bed and Serena returned to perch at her side, a soft sigh emanating from her as she sat. "He is devastated. A man who offers marriage out of pity would not suffer as he is."

Serena threw Elizabeth a startled glance. "He suffers?"

"Indeed he does. He hides it well – you know Nicholas – but now he has spoken to me, I can sense his pain. I have never seen such…" Elizabeth's voice faltered as she realised the falseness of what she was about to utter.

"Oh dear." Getting to her feet once more, Serena began to pace to and fro, hobbling as her skirts dragged on the floor. "I knew he was displeased when I retracted, but I thought… I – he cannot be in love with me."

"Was it not touched upon?"

"No; he had barely spoken when James happened upon us, and all was left to hang."

"And then?"

"My mind was in turmoil; I had reacted without thought, astonished by his application." Serena turned to face Elizabeth, her face a picture of sorrow. "Then, I heard – oh, Lizzy, 'tis too maddening."

"What did you hear?"

"I was coming back down the stairs – I did not think that James needed Nicholas for any lengthy business; my intention was to seek him out, explain my concerns, but before I could, I heard voices coming from Aunt Alicia's day room."

Serena sighed. "She and her husband were in conversation. She was sad – she said that she had sensed my reluctance to visit this time, and that as soon as I had arrived, she had realised that I was no longer a child, but a woman, that I would marry one day and be taken from her – despite Nicholas' approach to me earlier, I could hardly credit her words, never having any suspicion such a fate could befall me."

"And then?"

"Then – Uncle reassured her. He said…" Serena put a hand to her throat. "He said that she should not fear; that they had three intelligent sons and that one of them would surely have the good sense to secure me for her, make me a daughter by marriage. Oh, can you not see, Lizzy? This is what happened. Uncle clearly knew of Nicholas' intent – *this* is his purpose in offering for me."

Elizabeth studied her friend with compassion. "But his affections are engaged; of this I am certain!"

Serena shook her head. "Not in that way. I know of his affection for me; it is his warm, loving heart that makes him offer for a cripple that no one else would have. He thinks to save me from a lonely spinsterhood, but he does not think of what it will do to him, and he will repent it. He will regret his association with me and that would be even harder to bear than this sorrow now."

"I believe Nicholas is stronger than you are giving him credit for. He would defend you to the hilt."

Serena met Elizabeth's eye with a frantic look on her face. "But he should not have to! He should not be burdened with a wife who… whom people may scorn." she stopped and swallowed visibly. "I have lived with this – with *this*," she gestured at her leg, "all my life. You know how those with a disfigurement are viewed. I cannot pretend it is not so, that I do not have a physical debility by which people judge me and find me wanting."

Elizabeth felt so sad for her friend; there was nothing she could do to aid her, yet she would do anything to make her happy.

"How can you turn your back on a future with Nicholas when you love him so dearly? It will surely break your heart, and his too."

"My heart has long been broken. As for Nicholas," her voice softened. "He will find someone far more suitable to be his wife."

"He will not let it pass so easily."

"I cannot face him, Lizzy."

"Not face him! Dear Serena! Besides the fact that he is a frequent visitor in Gracechurch Street, he knows you are expected any day, and he is most anxious for your arrival, so that he might speak with you."

Raising her chin, Serena's face took on the stubborn look that Elizabeth was well acquainted with. "We have said all that there is to say upon the matter."

"Serena! Stop this! There must be a solution, some hope of…"

"*No*, Lizzy. I cannot allow myself to hope. It is entirely a situation *without* hope. We cannot be wed. I would bring dishonour upon him and his family. I would not have them suffer the stigma of being associated so closely with me."

"You do Nicholas a disservice."

"I know I do!" Serena hung her head. "I am ashamed of myself, and I am saying words I do not mean. It never occurred to me that I might be in such a situation."

Elizabeth sighed and got up to put an arm about her friend's shoulder, and Serena turned into the comfort of her embrace.

"Your feelings – you have not confessed the truth to him?"

Serena shook her head.

"You did not wish to tell him?"

"I had no chance, there being so little time before we were disturbed." Her head shot up and she paled. "Pray, Lizzy, tell me you have not told him?"

"No, I would not disclose it – it is not my place."

A sudden sound of footsteps approaching alerted both girls to someone's presence and, seconds later, Jane entered the room.

"Aunt Gardiner says you are to rest now, Serena." Jane smiled at them both and turned towards the dresser, laying her reticule on top of it and starting to unpin her hair.

Elizabeth and Serena exchanged a look and the former nodded. "It has grown quite late. Go and sleep; we shall be able to talk further in the morning."

"Dear Lizzy," Serena gave her a quick hug, repeated the action with Jane and hurried to the door. She slipped through it, but her anxious gaze met Elizabeth's as she glanced back before closing it gently.

Chapter Two

HAVING DISPATCHED THE NOTE containing the pertinent facts to his commanding officer, Colonel Fitzwilliam left London with Darcy in the early hours of Tuesday morning to ensure arriving at Longbourn by dawn.

Once admitted to the house by a rather startled housemaid, and shown in to an equally astounded Mr Bennet where he lounged in his banyan in his library, they wasted little time in laying before that gentleman the purpose of their call. Taking it in turn, they related Wickham's history within their family and revealed his current situation, interspersed with occasional questions from Mr Bennet, and in conclusion advised him of the likelihood of an arrest within hours; yet once the tale was told, a profound silence settled upon them all.

Mr Bennet eyed his visitors thoughtfully. He was of an inclination to shoo them out of the door and on their way, trusting to hope that he might never cross paths with either of them again, or their delinquent acquaintance who threatened to disturb the even tenor of his life.

Yet his interest was piqued, he could not deny, by Elizabeth's letter from the previous day. The content of it had surprised him, disturbed him even, but whether he would have acted, had not this strange visitation taken place hard upon its heels, he could not say.

Hindsight was a blessed thing: he may have been both wise and pro-active, but in his heart of hearts, this was questionable. Yet it was not in Thomas Bennet's nature to dwell upon what might have been. The fact was that he now knew the full background of the blackguard who seemed to be venturing an alliance – or worse – with one of his foolish daughters, and though the task laid before him was minimal, he could carry it through with all the conviction of one who had drawn that conclusion himself if he so wished.

Yet the letter intrigued him. Though she had disclosed very little in yesterday's *Express*, it was evident that Elizabeth was fully cognisant of the facts he now possessed. How could she have learned of such deeds? If the gentlemen were to be believed – and he had little reason to doubt them – much of it was held in the utmost confidence for the protection of Miss Darcy.

Conscious that Darcy and his cousin were now eyeing him with some puzzlement, he sat up in his chair and waved a dismissive hand.

"Forgive my distraction, gentlemen. You have given me much to ponder."

Darcy inclined his head, but the Colonel said nothing, merely keeping his eye upon Mr Bennet, something that the latter found somewhat disconcerting, and he shifted restlessly in his seat.

"Yes, well, quite. I thank you for the intelligence; it is timely and valuable beyond measure. For that you have my gratitude. But I would have my curiosity satisfied before you depart."

Both men exchanged a quick glance at this, but then returned their attention promptly to him.

"I am hoping for some enlightenment – from one, or both, of you." Darcy blinked and sat up straighter in his seat. "This information you have shared with me is disturbing, but I must own that I had received some inkling of there being some difficulty with the person we have been discussing. I received this yesterday," and he leaned over to the pile of papers on his desk and lifted the letter that lay on the top.

"It is an *Express* advising me to be on my guard against Wickham. It discloses a certain amount of accusation towards the young man, but gives little by way of proof as to the assertions within it. I will own to being somewhat sceptical upon first reading it, but two things made me wonder if there may be something of import here." He placed the parchment on the desk before him. "Firstly, this letter is from my daughter, Elizabeth."

Neither gentleman seemed surprised by this. If he did not mistake the matter, they both knew that she had written to him and, moreover, the content of that letter.

"Lizzy is no slouch when it comes to expressing her opinion." Mr Bennet paused as Darcy stirred in his chair. "Though it is merely that – her opinion, and therefore not necessarily fact – I do pay it a certain amount of mind because, unlike some of my daughters, she has good sense and knows how to use it."

He got to his feet. "Secondly, the *Express* was sent with my sister-in-law's approval. Now, admittedly Lizzy says that her aunt knows little of the content of the missive, but that she supports her sending it speaks volumes. You might well assume that I do not fare well for sisters, Mr Darcy, having made the acquaintance – as I know you have – of my brother Philips' wife; nonetheless, I do have one of whom I am proud in Mrs Gardiner."

"Indeed, Sir," the Colonel said. "We have made the acquaintance of both Mr and Mrs Gardiner and have much respect for them."

A wave of annoyance swept through Mr Bennet, and he turned his back on his company and walked over to the window. This was ludicrous. First Elizabeth wrote of confidences that could only have come from this family, and now *this family* had become acquainted with more of his own.

"You must be wondering, Sir, how it is that Miss Elizabeth Bennet was aware of Wickham's proclivity for base behaviour."

Darcy's voice roused Mr Bennet from his speculations, and he turned around to find both gentlemen also on their feet.

"Must I? You presume to know this family extraordinarily well." The frustration in his voice was apparent, and Darcy glanced at his cousin before continuing.

"I would not wish to imply anything of the sort, Sir. If you have no desire for enlightenment on that score, then let us have the words unspoken. You will excuse us, I am sure. We have intruded long enough upon your good nature."

"Oh no no no. Not so fast, young man." Mr Bennet shook his head at Darcy as he made to turn away. He walked over to where they both stood and eyed them carefully. "My good nature be damned, if I ever had one. Come, be seated. Here," he walked over to the tray of spirits and poured them all a measure before walking back and handing the glasses over. "It is early, let us not deny, but I believe that one shot will not harm our perceptions and it may well oil our tongues. Let us get this out in the open."

He knocked back his drink and the others did likewise. Darcy grimaced, but the Colonel gave no reaction, merely removing his cousin's glass from his hand and placing them both on the desk.

Mr Bennet leaned against his desk and studied them both thoughtfully. Then he waved a hand at them to resume their seats and walked round to take his own.

"Explain to me, then, gentlemen – and I care not which of you takes the stage – how it is that my daughter understood such intimate detail that she could, though carefully worded, seek to raise my awareness of Wickham's true nature. I am certain that your explanation will cover all manner of ills that remain a void to me: how it is you have managed to become acquainted with the Gardiners; how it is that you have arrived here but one day after Lizzy's letter, bearing the same intent – a warning; how it is that you discovered Wickham's presence in the neighbourhood at all?"

There was silence for several seconds, the only sound being the ticking of the long-case clock in the corner of the room. Darcy stirred in his seat again, but whether he was about to speak or not, Mr Bennet never discovered, for his cousin stood and with the succinct manner of one used to responding to orders, spoke up.

"If you will permit me, Sir, I will tell all I am able: we had the good fortune to meet with Miss Elizabeth Bennet this Eastertide when she resided in the home of our aunt's parson in Kent. Darcy, as you are full aware, was known to the lady and Mr and Mrs Collins and during the course of their renewed acquaintance, a situation arose during which my cousin felt it his duty to enlighten your daughter as to Wickham's true nature. However, as we all believed him gone from this neighbourhood that seemed the end of the matter. Then, Miss Elizabeth advised Darcy last evening that one of her sisters had informed her by letter of Wickham's return. Knowing what she now did, she admitted that she had sent word by *Express* to Longbourn in an attempt to protect her family. Darcy and I – cognisant as we are of the depths to which Wickham can and will stoop – felt it incumbent upon us to ride out to reinforce your daughter's word. She had informed Darcy that she had not disclosed anything in support of her accusations, and we felt it essential to add our voices in order to secure the protection that is required from a cad such as he."

Having finished this statement, the Colonel gave a short bow and retook his seat.

"I see." Mr Bennet leaned back in his chair, his hands steepled upon his chest as was his habit, and his gaze moved from the Colonel to his cousin. "I shall not press to know what situation you refer to, Colonel, but you, Sir, astound me." He frowned at Darcy. "I was not aware that you were on a level of acquaintance as to discuss such matters with my daughter."

"We were much in company in Kent. The two parties from Rosings and Hunsford met on a regular basis, Sir."

"And my brother Gardiner? How is it that you met? And how is it that you saw Lizzy last evening in London?"

Darcy met his interrogator's eye firmly. "We – I – encountered Miss Bennet and Miss Elizabeth by chance in Town, which led to an introduction to Mrs Gardiner. There were several occasions when we were all frequenting the same events, culminating in a ball last evening at Bellingham House. Miss Elizabeth advised me there of her sister's letter and the sending of the *Express* whilst I had the pleasure of dancing with her."

At this, Mr Bennet raised a mocking brow. "You had the *pleasure* of dancing, Mr Darcy? With my Lizzy?"

Looking somewhat uncomfortable, Darcy nodded.

"Unfathomable. I was under the impression – erroneously, it would seem – that you took little enjoyment at all from the exercise, and that you do not often find partners you can – tolerate?"

A suppressed snort from the Colonel seemed to rouse his cousin, who got to his feet followed swiftly by the others.

"We are all victims of other people's perceptions, and opinions, I find, are changeable." Darcy acknowledged him and the Colonel followed suit. "We must make haste, Sir; thank you for your time so early in the day."

Mr Bennet eyed them both gravely, his initial frustration and intrigue fading away. He owed them a gesture of some sort, and he offered his hand to first one, then the other.

"It is I who thank you. Forgive my abrupt manner. No man likes to have his shortcomings brought to the fore in such a way. I can assure you I shall act as you have directed and, on behalf of my family, you have my gratitude."

They made for the door, but as the Colonel strode down the hallway towards the servant holding their outdoor garments, Darcy stayed Mr Bennet with his hand.

"Sir – I would request that you say nothing of our having visited to Miss Elizabeth Bennet."

Mr Bennet frowned. "Why ever not?"

"I – I would prefer anonymity. Let her believe that her warning alone was sufficient."

"Aye, and I wish that I could say that it would have been, but I would likely be lying, would I not, Darcy?" He eyed the taller man thoughtfully for a moment. He had little intention of acceding to his request, but Darcy had no need to be made aware of that.

"Well, be off with you. You have both left me plenty to dwell upon and no doubt you have things to be about in turn."

Darcy nodded, and with that the visitors were on their way, and Mr Bennet turned and went back into his library, shutting the door with a firm snap.

Chapter Three

THE UNMISTAKEABLE SOUNDS OF the household stirring as the servants began their day roused Elizabeth from her curled up position on her uncle's armchair in the drawing room at Gracechurch Street.

Unable to sleep, she had given up the attempt some hours earlier and removed herself downstairs that she might not disturb Jane whilst she attempted to occupy her interminable thoughts by becoming engrossed in her book. The story had been unable to capture her attention, however, and for some time now she had been sitting with her head leant against the back of the chair, the closed book upon her lap and her hand absent-mindedly stroking the reed book marker, its place in the pages quite disregarded.

At first, when she had earlier laid her head upon her pillow, her thoughts had remained with the quagmire that her two friends seemed to have become immersed in, and she had endeavoured to set her mind upon the best manner of aiding them. Once sleep had fully eluded her, however, and she had taken herself downstairs, she had dwelled instead upon the previous evening and what had happened between herself and Mr Darcy.

With a sigh, she shifted her position in the chair, tucking her shawl about her feet in an attempt to warm them, the fire having long died in the grate. The alteration in that gentleman's demeanour from the beginning of the set to the end she could only attribute to her revelation of her family's latest venture into the realm of the ridiculous. This had to be the disturbing news that the Colonel had suggested led to his cousin's sudden departure, and she had cursed herself for indulging in the confidence. That this evidence of poor behaviour might reinforce his earlier opinion and, even worse, lower herself in his eyes, smote her to the core, and she was hard put to identify what troubled her most: that Mr Darcy's regard for her had been diminished, or that she could care so much that it was so.

However, reminding her as this did of the potentially perilous situation in Hertfordshire, she was soon consumed by a succession of questions for which she had no answer. What was Wickham's purpose? How was it that he was in Meryton when his regiment was sequestered in Brighton? Were his intentions honourable? Did he even comprehend the meaning of such a word?

Releasing a pent up breath, Elizabeth stirred restlessly in her seat. Which would be the worse fate? Having the permanence of Wickham within the bosom of her family as a brother or having a sister whose reputation was in tatters?

Though it was perfectly obvious that the latter was the greater evil, their ruin as an entire family being complete should such a thing come to pass, she could not help but shy from the ignominy of the man being her kin. That in other circumstances he might have become brother-in-law to Mr Darcy – and poor Miss Darcy likewise – was a thought she quickly shied away from. Dwelling upon any of that family or Mr Darcy's former intentions towards her was pointless.

Getting to her feet, Elizabeth dropped her book onto the seat and walked over to the window to draw back the drapes. The sun had risen; the usual bustle of trades people and early walkers were about in the street and soon a maid would be coming in to set a fire in the grate. She raised a hand to reach for the rope, intent upon fastening the curtain, when she realised that she still held her marker, and for a moment she studied it with more interest than it had heretofore warranted. There was something reminiscent about it, with its neat weaving, and with sudden clarity she recalled the faded reed stick in the cabinet in Mount Street.

The thought of that house and their delightful evening there only reinforced her sadness, and frustrated with herself for such self-indulgence, she turned quickly away from the window, gathered up her book and shawl and made haste to return to her chamber.

⁓✲◦

Thomas Bennet sighed heavily and ran a weary hand across his forehead. He had little time for the follies of other men, and even less for untimely intrusion upon his leisure, especially when the disturbance left him with an intense sense of disquiet that his normal apathy could not quite dispel. He also did not like having his shortcomings forced upon his notice, and though that had not been the intention of his visitors, it was, nonetheless, the outcome of their call.

Turning at last from the view afforded by the window, having watched the gentlemen depart – one making use of the carriage, the other on horseback – he surveyed his domain, a warm, cluttered room, three walls shelved from skirting to ceiling, housing all manner and size of books and two long windows fronting onto the main driveway. He had always relished this time of day, when the rest of the family was at slumber. No voices reached him, no footsteps clattered up and down the stairs, no shrieks of laughter pierced the thick wood of his door, nor did the strident tones of his wife.

Walking over to his desk, a large leather-topped piece of furniture inherited from his father, he threw himself disconsolately into the high-backed chair that accompanied it, swivelling to and fro for a few minutes, his fingers steepled upon his chest in silent contemplation.

That he needed to take action, and swiftly – two things that were somewhat alien to his nature – caused him to sigh again. His wife… his *wife* would be of no assistance. He grunted. When was she ever? Well, he was obliged to proceed and thereafter endure her caterwauling, something he eschewed at all times.

His shock at the calamity that might have befallen his family had taken full hold now. Hearing the Colonel's theory – that Wickham, in his desperation, would likely believe in the protection of the Bennets – had astounded him. If married into them, either by intent or by default through his having had his way with his foolish daughter, he would likely count on the release of some assets, that Mr Bennet would pay to secure his release rather than bring shame upon the family with the penalty he was sure to attract otherwise for his desertion.

With a rueful grimace, Mr Bennet reflected upon the ease with which a family's financial well-being could be established these days. Darcy's suggestion that Wickham was well aware of Mr Bennet's pecuniary status and what he may or may not be able to do for him made it perfectly clear that the gentleman himself likewise clearly understood the full situation.

He let his gaze roam about his library. It was common enough knowledge in the neighbourhood that, though the main house and acreage that comprised the estate of Longbourn were entailed away, he had some fifteen years earlier acquired some extensive land in his own right, along with several farmsteads. These acquisitions had been funded in part by a small sum he retained from his mother's passing and further enhanced by a welcome inheritance from an elderly neighbour who had no family to speak of. The gentleman farmer had greatly appreciated the care and support offered to him during his final ailing years by Mr Bennet and had amply rewarded him with the bequest of his own farmstead and acreage. Though all these now held a significant value as assets, the price of land having risen so precipitously, the income generated by them was negligible, mainly down to Mr Bennet's lethargy and disinterest over the years. Shifting uncomfortably in his seat, he blew out a slow breath.

He was a good landlord in many ways, and amongst his tenants, he was universally liked. Yet he fully understood his own failings as a business man. Had he paid more interest over the years to raising the rents payable by those leasing his farms and land, or considered other, better ways to exploit the substantial hectares he owned in his own name, he might have managed to put some money by.

Out of countenance with this train of thought, he let out a grunt of self-disgust, and glancing at the clock on the mantel, he got wearily to his feet. Speed, according to Colonel Fitzwilliam, was of the essence. He must away to his Brother Philips' home and do his duty to his family. Perhaps if he redeemed himself in that way, he would be able to rid himself of the niggling sense of shame that nudged at his conscience.

Colonel Fitzwilliam had watched his cousin's carriage fade from sight as it rounded a bend in the lane that led to the turnpike heading west before turning in his saddle to gaze once more upon Longbourn. He had been quietly impressed with the fair-sized manor, for though allegedly of little capital, it was a substantial property and, in the circumstances, appeared well tended. Turning away and encouraging his mount forward, he mused upon its patriarch. Mr Bennet was an enigma; his apathy at first was palpable, as Darcy had forewarned, but in complete contrast to his blatant paternal protectiveness over his second eldest daughter. It was, however, a comfort to see the man's serious intent by the end of the interview, and the Colonel hoped he could trust to his instincts and that Mr Bennet would be the necessary guard required for the next few hours.

The Colonel urged his horse into a canter, but had gone no more than two furlongs along the lane before he pulled on the reins once more and slowed the steed to a halt. Tethering his mount to an obliging stump, he extracted his leather water pouch and walked over to the stone trough that had caught his attention, nestled against a stable belonging to a nearby steading. Pleased to see that the trough was fed by a clear flowing stream that filtered in at one end and trickled out of the base at the other, he served himself several cupped handfuls of water to confirm its purity before quickly filling his container.

Getting to his feet as he secured the stopper, the Colonel stretched his back, his eyes scanning the undulating farmland with appreciation. The scenery lacked the drama of the northern counties, but it was a satisfying vista. He flexed the arm holding the pouch in preparation for his lengthy ride, but suddenly the opening of one of the stable doors caught his eye, and a couple emerged caught in a fast embrace, their dishevelled appearance testament to their recent activity.

Wickham was quite clearly too engrossed in his companion to sense the presence of company, but with no means of escaping detection, being but paces from them, the Colonel realised he would be taking justice into his own hands after all.

The couple soon took their leave of each other, the maid collecting a milking stool and disappearing inside the nearest cowshed, and the Colonel stepped forward, conscious that Wickham had turned his attention to making himself presentable, tucking his shirt into his trousers and attempting to brush the straw from his coat. Before this advantage could be put to effect, however, some instinct must have alerted Wickham, for he turned suddenly, and they were face to face not three paces apart.

Wickham froze at first, but one horrified glance at the Colonel was sufficient for him to realise his predicament, and he was off across the farmyard, his would-be captor hard upon his heels. Though the younger man, Wickham had never been particularly active in the military, and his advantage lay only in that he knew the terrain. Thus it was that he had soon scaled a stile to race across the open grassland in the direction of Meryton. Yet the Colonel wasted little time in clearing the same obstacle, setting off across the field in keen pursuit.

"You run like an old goat," Wickham shouted as he reached the far wall. "Must be the company you keep."

Saving his breath in order to put on a spurt of speed, the Colonel finally caught up with him and, grabbing his leg as he made to scramble over the wall, pulled him to the ground.

"And you run like a wench, Wickham. What says that of you?"

Struggling to his feet, Wickham swung his fist, but the Colonel merely dodged aside.

"Give it up, man. The game is over."

"The game is never over. *Never!*" Wickham bent quickly and grabbed a handful of lose stones from the foot of the wall, flinging them at the Colonel who instinctively raised his hands to shield himself, and Wickham took the seconds of respite to renew his attempt to clamber over the wall, this time succeeding.

Blowing out a resigned breath, the Colonel scaled the wall, his water pouch yet in his hand, and took chase as Wickham ran down the lane that he had only minutes earlier ridden along.

"Come here and fight like the man you wish you were!" he yelled after him.

"Go hang, Fitzwilliam!"

The Colonel was out of breath, but determined not to lose his quarry, pleased to note that the hedgerows on either side of the lane were both too dense to pass through and too high for a man to scale. Had Wickham looked back over his shoulder with a little less frequency, he might have made more progress. As it was, the Colonel gained on him; within seconds he was behind him and, sticking out his leg, he tripped him so that Wickham fell in a heap on the dirt road.

For a moment, Colonel Fitzwilliam stood with his hands on his hips, inhaling some much needed air before leaning down and grasping a winded Wickham by the upper arm.

"Get up, you scum."

He dragged him to his feet, but his prey was not about to succumb so easily, stamping hard on the Colonel's foot, who let out a distracted yell of pain as Wickham launched himself at him, knocking them both to the ground. They rolled in the dirt, landing what blows they could, each taking the upper hand for a moment before Wickham, his face taut with malice, pinned the Colonel to the ground and grasped him about the throat with both hands.

The Colonel had a fleeting recognition of being surprised at the man's muscle, a strength likely borne of his fear of the outcome should he not make good his escape. It was still insufficient, however, to successfully close his wind pipe, and with a surge of force, he raised his knee sharply into Wickham's groin.

With a howl of pain, Wickham recoiled and rolled into a ball on the ground, whimpering, and the Colonel leapt to his feet and rubbed at his throat for a second, before turning away to pick up his leather pouch from where it had been cast aside. Before he could straighten, however, he was laid flat by a glancing blow to his head from behind.

Chapter Four

STRUGGLING TO CLEAR HIS HEAD, the Colonel pushed himself onto his knees, cursing his inability to get quickly to his feet. A sudden noise behind him made him tense as he anticipated a further blow, only to perceive Wickham crashing to the ground beside him, a deep gash across his forehead and quite clearly stunned senseless.

"Had I not made your acquaintance earlier, Sir, you may well have been the one on the receiving end of my crop."

Sitting back on his knees, the Colonel squinted up at his saviour before taking the proffered hand and struggling to his feet.

He gave Mr Bennet a wry grimace as he dusted down his coat. "There is a lot to be said for gaining an early start, Sir."

"Indeed, indeed." Mr Bennet nodded. "I was on my way to Meryton when I perceived the commotion. I assume your encounter was a matter of chance?"

"Indubitably. Though I suspect our captive would deem it a poor rather than happy one."

Mr Bennet frowned. "You are not injured? He does not have much of an aim for a military man, it has to be said. I think the rock gave you merely a glancing blow."

The Colonel grimaced as he put a hand gingerly to the sore spot on the back of his head. There was blood on his fingers when he removed them, but nothing conspicuous, and he shrugged. "It will mend. I have suffered worse."

They studied Wickham's motionless body where it lay sprawled on the ground, and the Colonel bent down to check that he still lived. With a grunt, he straightened and turned to the man at his side.

"He will need to be under lock and key until the Militia arrive. Loath though I am to suggest it, do you have any such place on your property?"

Mr Bennet shook his head, his gaze fixed upon Wickham's prone figure. "Not sufficiently safe – but I do know the perfect place: the lock-up on the Green. Never yet known an escapee, so I am told. "

"How far is it?"

"But a mile further down this road," Mr Bennet indicated with a hand. "I shall summon a horse and cart from my stable; it will make it easier to transport him."

The Colonel shook his head. "I can think of a more fitting way, and the sooner he is secured, the safer for all. If you ride but half a mile further back you will find my mount; could I charge you to bring it to me? I shall guard our prisoner."

Mr Bennet nodded and regaining his own mount he set off down the lane, and the Colonel looked around for a moment before shrugging and settling himself as comfortably as possible on Wickham's prostrate form. Flexing his bloodied hand, he reached inside his coat for his hip flask and took a hefty swig before wetting his fingers with the alcohol and patting some on the wound on his head, wincing at its sting.

Before long, he heard the sound of hooves approaching, and soon he was reunited with his mount and made haste to extract a coil of rope from his pack and a sharp pocket knife. It was a matter of minutes only before Wickham was safely trussed up by ankle and wrist, and the two men stared down at his inert body for a moment before the Colonel stepped forward.

"Come, I will lift his legs, you take his head; if I have hold of that end, I may be tempted to punch his worthless face."

Together, they man-handled the lifeless form until it was slung across the Colonel's horse with all the ceremony of a sack of potatoes and, gaining his seat, he thanked Mr Bennet for his assistance.

"It is the least I can do in the circumstances. Come, let me accompany you – I know the key-holder and it will ease your path." He gained his own mount and waved the Colonel forward and they set off in procession towards Meryton.

⁂

Struggling to shake off the oppression that had taken a firm hold, Elizabeth's lowness of spirit did not go undetected, and Mrs Gardiner, who attributed it to the exertions of the ball and the late night that ensued, instructed her to make an easy morning of it. Thus it was, whilst her aunt and

Jane went out to carry out the commissions that Mrs Bennet had asked for in her letter of the previous day, Elizabeth settled in the drawing room, attempting to continue her letter to Charlotte and waiting for Serena to rejoin her, her friend having returned to her chamber for a book.

She glanced about the room, in no mood for her own company. Though she could detect Jane's pleasure in preparing for the journey home, Elizabeth could not help but feel some regret over it. Her sister had been her sole confidante, the only person who knew of what had happened between Elizabeth and Mr Darcy. Last night, when Jane had shared the Colonel's words regarding that gentleman's departure, her dismay had been hard to conceal, and later, as they had lain in their bed prior to sleeping, she had confessed to Jane the content of her conversation with Mr Darcy during their dance and her thoughts as to why he had withdrawn, both from her and from the ball. She would miss her sister sorely, for her interminable thoughts would henceforth remain churning around in her head.

At least Serena had come at last, but even that brought little comfort following their discussion of the night before, hard upon the heels of Nicholas' confession. Serena had remained equally adamant this morning that she had no future with Nicholas. Unable to accept that he could have fallen in love with her, her fear of his being made to suffer for aligning himself with her overrode any argument her friend could summon. The only counsel she would seek, now that she had confided what troubled her, was how best to avoid the man.

Elizabeth, knowing full well that Nicholas wished her to assist them to a resolution, was frustrated and torn over what to do to aid the troublesome pair. Their needs were completely opposed to one another. He would have her mediate and find a solution, and she would have her be a shield. Elizabeth shook her head. If it was her advice they sought, she was sorely tempted to simply box their heads together to knock some sense into them. How could two people who loved each other end up in such a tangle?

Elizabeth glanced down at the half-composed letter on the desk before laying her pen back on the blotter. Then, she pushed back her chair and got to her feet and began to walk about the room, trying to marshal her thoughts into some form of order. She had only turned about the room twice, however, when the door opened and Serena came in, her book in her hand. She eyed Elizabeth with some puzzlement as she took a seat by the fireplace.

"'Tis a strange way of writing a letter, Lizzy." Serena waved an arm at the unoccupied desk.

Elizabeth gave a short laugh. "Aye, that it is. I cannot seem to settle to it. I fear I shall have to put it off for another day. What are you reading?"

Serena turned the book so that Elizabeth could see the lettering on the cover, but as she walked over to read it better, sounds came from the hallway and, as a familiar voice drifted through the still open door, her gaze flew to her friend's face.

Getting clumsily to her feet, Serena threw Elizabeth a beseeching look and, before the latter could react, she hurried through the door and disappeared, the book still clutched in her hand.

"Serena! Wait!"

Elizabeth arrived in the hallway to see Nicholas staring down the corridor, a flash of skirts as she fled through the rear door the only sign of Serena.

He turned a shocked face towards her. "When did she arrive?"

"Last evening; she was here when we returned from the ball. Come, Nicholas, let her be for a moment." Elizabeth led him into the drawing room, concerned by his pallor.

"Did you speak with her about me?" He threw himself into a leather armchair, and Elizabeth walked over and sat opposite him.

"We spoke."

"Is there any hope?"

"I – I do not know."

He dropped his head into his hands, and Elizabeth eyed him with compassion. Then, he straightened up and sat back in the chair, running a hand through his hair distractedly before glancing about the room. With a rueful smile, he turned back to look at her.

"Days of desiring a moment alone with you, yet today we are granted it without question."

"Aunt Gardiner and Jane have gone shopping. They will be away for some time."

He sat forward. "Then help me to understand, Lizzy. Why will she not have me?"

Biting her lip, Elizabeth ruminated over what she could or could not reveal, but having come to the conclusion that *something* must be done, she decided she had little option but to tell him a little of her friend's concerns. "She believes she is not fit for a gentleman's wife."

Releasing a slow breath, Nicholas leaned back in his seat again.

"I feared as much. That is why I have been in earnest discussion these past days with my father over the estate. I have had to confess why I wished to refuse such kind generosity and take a family living. Papa was very understanding in the circumstances; he leaves me to make the final decision."

"Why do you not tell her?"

Nicholas let out a humourless laugh and waved a hand towards the door. "Chance would be a fine thing, would it not? Besides, I would have her take me for who I am, not who she would have me be."

"But she is frightened of your new status. She fears bringing you dishonour, of not being capable."

"Yet she does not fear bringing me pain."

"Nicholas, that is unfair. You are not the only one who is suffering."

He got to his feet and walked over to the window, staring out into the street. "My suffering is greater. I had set my heart upon spending the rest of my life with her – protecting her, loving her, treating her with all the respect that she deserves and rarely receives."

Walking over to join him, Elizabeth touched him gently on the arm. "Let us not argue over who suffers most. I see my two friends in distress, and I would do all that I can to alleviate it."

Turning to face her, he took her hand in his and gave it a squeeze before releasing it. "Do you see now why I proposed to take Crossways Court over Rowlands? It is well situated in gentle, undemanding countryside. Rowlands is built on the cliff tops of north Devon, where the pathways are difficult enough to traverse for one with able footing." He shook his head. "That is precisely why it is the principal seat of the neighbourhood, the area being such a distance from any sizeable town or city. The property is the centre of all society in the district, and the owner would have an obligation to entertain the local populace."

Finally understanding his decision, Elizabeth felt deeply for him, but knew not what to say. Then, she sighed, deciding she must offer what little she could. "She believes you pity her."

Nicholas grunted. "Pity? There are many feelings in my breast towards Serena, yet pity is not one of them. She was an infuriating child, and she has become an infuriating woman. She is ludicrously ill-named."

"Yet you are in love with her."

Nicholas turned to stare out into the street again. "Yet I am."

"Then you must convince her, for she does not know; open her eyes to the truth of the matter. You do realise that her selfless reasons for refusing you are proof of her affection for you?"

"Ironically, I find little comfort in such evidence."

"Bitterness does not become you, Nicholas; nor does it Serena. It is not in either of your natures, yet you both seem to be wallowing in it."

He turned back to face her, his countenance uncharacteristically solemn. "Then what do you propose?"

Elizabeth eyed him thoughtfully for a moment. "I wish I knew. Perhaps, in the circumstances, you should go for now and call back later. I will endeavour to speak with her on the subject one more time."

He sighed heavily, but gave a reluctant smile. "A walk will be certain to clear my head; perhaps you are right. But I shall return, and I *will* speak with her."

Elizabeth took his arm and walked with him through the silent house to the front door, and as she closed it behind him she put a hand to her head which had begun to emit a dull ache.

Chapter Five

WITH HIS RESTING PLACE FOR THE night yet some distance away, Darcy stared fixedly out of the carriage windows at the passing countryside. Determined not to allow thoughts of Elizabeth to consume him, he reflected instead upon her father and his reaction to their visit.

That Mr Bennet had been surprised by it was to be expected. That he had believed what they chose to tell him had not been guaranteed, but Darcy had been satisfied by his reception of their words, and he could not help but derive some comfort from the fact that, whilst Mr Bennet may not have held Darcy in much esteem prior to his visit, he clearly trusted the veracity of his information. He sighed wearily and shifted in his seat, attempting a comfier position. Fair play to his cousin, for without Fitzwilliam to support him and reiterate his point, he was not so sure that Mr Bennet would have been so quick to accept his word.

Leaning his head back against the leather seat, he closed his eyes. His mind was far from seeking repose, but staring at the constant flow of green fields and woodlands, steeped in the lushness and acidity of early summer, brought Elizabeth all too clearly to mind, something he knew he must not indulge. She was no longer merely his deepest regret; now, she was utterly lost to him, and of her he must think no more.

How he wished Fitzwilliam had been able to travel with him. Little though he would wish to give his cousin the satisfaction of learning how much value he had been to Darcy over these last ten days, he could not deny the compliment. Without his staunch support and his guiding arm, Darcy would have fallen at more than one hurdle cast in his way. Even today, it was his cousin who had put before Mr Bennet the wisdom of visiting his brother Philips and putting him on his guard, that someone in the household be aware of the situation in the hours until the Militia arrived to remove Wickham.

Having been so lately in Hertfordshire, however, and more so, at Longbourn, Darcy's endeavours to close his thoughts to Elizabeth were floundering. Frustrated, he opened his eyes again and stared at his booted feet. He could not cease from reflecting upon her altered circumstances and how soon the happy news would be received by her family. Harington could not fail to visit Longbourn – and her father – at the soonest opportunity; indeed, perchance he had even now set off to seek that gentleman's consent. With a sense of discomfort, Darcy speculated on how Mr Bennet might have received *him*, had he been successful in securing Elizabeth's hand. How singular it had been to sit in his library, privy to his daughter's change in situation, knowing her father had yet to be informed of it.

He pulled his watch out to study the time: Bingley would be anticipating his departure for Netherfield, no doubt somewhat mystified by their sudden journey. It was fortunate that Darcy could trust to the length of their friendship for Bingley's being placated by the hastily written note he had left. The reminder of his friend's return to Hertfordshire, however, brought the Bennet family to the fore once more, and he mulled upon how news of Bingley's return had been received. Such a reflection could not fail to bring Mrs Bennet to mind, and a sudden visitation of that lady at the Netherfield Ball was soon superseded by the notion of her gloating over Elizabeth's success with Harington. Feeling his chest tighten at the recollection of his own loss, Darcy sighed; how he was to banish her from his thoughts he knew not.

A sudden jolt of the carriage as one of the wheels caught a pothole roused Darcy, and he returned to his earlier study of the landscape, noting with some relief a milestone that indicated they were now but two miles from a watering stop.

⁂

Nicholas Harington had led a somewhat fortunate life until the age of two and twenty, if one could discount the sadness of losing two younger siblings when he was but a child himself.

He had been raised in a situation of comfort, wealth and of an old family name so as to gain admittance to much of society with nothing more than a winning smile. Both his parents, who had had the good fortune to make a match of lasting, mutual affection, were full of good sense, understanding and further enjoyed a healthy constitution, ensuring that their example of how to live a contented married life had sufficient time to fully influence their three sons.

As such, Nicholas had grown up confident that he would await marriage until he found the happiness of his parents. The recent change in his situation, which had propelled him from the position of second son into that of a gentleman (and happily not at the loss of an elder and much-loved sibling) troubled him little. He would, he was certain, with his father's excellent guidance, soon adapt from anticipating a life in one of the many professions.

Having yet to be thwarted, he was much affected by his present situation and uncertain of his direction, finding his rejection by Serena almost impossible to comprehend.

Determining that he would – he *must* – speak to her, he had yet to walk anywhere, and too impatient to heed Elizabeth's advice, he remained outside the Gardiners' residence, looking up and down the street for inspiration. Knowing full well that all houses had more than one entrance, and familiar as he was with this one, Nicholas straightened his shoulders, ran a hand through his hair and walked quickly along the pavement, heading for the mews that ran the length of the back of Gracechurch Street.

⁂

Serena sat on a stone bench in the garden, attempting to read. Yet no matter how hard she tried, her eye would scan the same line time and again, the words failing to penetrate, for her mind was in the hands of her heart – and her heart was sore.

A sudden sound caused her to start, and she turned in her seat to observe the figure of a man straightening whence he appeared to have landed, having scaled the wall of her brother's garden. As he faced her and his identity was confirmed, she paled and rose slowly to her unstable feet, clutching the book to her chest.

"What do you mean by this?"

Nicholas gestured impatiently with his hand. "The gate is padlocked." He sighed. "Serena – we must talk."

Her heart lurched at the very sight of him, but resolutely, she shook her head. "There is nothing further to say."

"How can you say so? You accepted my hand – I cannot comprehend..." he stopped. "Help me to understand, before I run mad."

"You? *You* run mad?" With a flash of her eyes, Serena turned and limped away from him, but she found herself quickly restrained as Nicholas grabbed her arm.

"How came you to say yes, Serena?"

Conscious of the heat of his hand on her skin, she swallowed, attempting to dislodge the lump that had risen into her throat. Her insides were clenching with despair and anxiety, but she turned around, and he released his hold upon her as she stared up at him mutely.

"Please – at least give me this much."

The torment quite clearly revealed in his eyes and his voice struck her forcibly. Elizabeth had spoken truly – whatever the cause, Nicholas did indeed appear to be suffering, something she could not ignore. With a slump of her shoulders, she realised she owed him the truth, and whispered, "Instinct."

He frowned and stepped closer to her, and she caught her breath. "Did you say instinct?"

Unable to speak, she nodded, her gaze held by his. She knew she should look away but for some reason could not.

"Why, Serena? What was instinctive about it?"

She could not answer, her throat so tight she could barely breathe. In an attempt to escape, she took an unsteady step backwards.

"I love you. Is that not sufficient?"

She shook her head and swallowed hard. "You love me as a sister." Serena's voice throbbed with suppressed emotion.

"Perhaps once, but not for some time."

"I heard your mother speak of her fear of losing me – you are a dutiful son, and I know that you would do anything to make her happy."

Nicholas let out a harsh laugh. "Would I? I believe you give me more credit than I deserve. I asked for your hand for my own happiness – and God willing, yours – I have to own that my family is the least of my concerns." He made an impatient gesture with his hand. "I wish you for my wife, Serena. I do not offer you marriage that you may be my mother's daughter." He reached out and took her hand. "Do not hide the truth from me. If I have to live my life without you, then at least give me this; if it was instinctive to accept me, then tell me why you changed your mind. Is it because you do not hold me in esteem?"

Serena shook her head again; then, she whispered, "Yet I cannot marry you."

The pain in her chest was so intense that she struggled for breath, and conscious of the welling of tears and determined that he should not see them, she wrenched her hand free and turned on her heel, going as fast as she could towards the house.

"Serena! Do not do this. *Please* – I beg of you." Her step slowed at the urgency in his voice, conscious that he had followed her.

"Look at me." Slowly, she turned to face him once more, her eyes widened to prevent the tears from falling. Nicholas reached out and grasped her hand again, refusing to let go when she tugged. "Tell me why we cannot be wed."

Swallowing hard on the constriction in her throat, Serena struggled to summon the words, that he might understand her.

"You are now a gentleman. You need a wife who can cope with the social status and pressures of being a good hostess, a good mistress to a manor with all its correspondent responsibilities. You need a partner in life who can fulfil that role, that position."

"That *position*? Do you know what position I would have for you? *This*."

Before she could perceive his intent, Nicholas pulled her into his embrace and kissed her fiercely. "This is where I would have you, all the days of my life. I adore you, and I would do all in my power to make you happy, and if being a gentleman's wife is what makes you refuse me, then I refute it. I will turn down Papa's offer, and I will take a profession; anything but lose you."

Shocked by his actions and struggling to assimilate his words, Serena stared up at him speechlessly. Her mouth throbbed from his assault upon it, and she would have raised a hand to touch her lips had she been able, but he retained his hold upon her. She could sense his heart beating against her chest, so close was he holding her, but then he seemed to become aware of what he had done, slowly releasing her and taking a step backwards.

She felt all at once bereft, perversely wishing to stay within the security of his embrace, and she wrapped her arms around herself by way of comfort.

"Did you hear me, Serena? I am in love with you. I wish to marry you for one reason only: the deepest of affection."

"But I am disfigured." She gestured wildly towards her affected leg. "People will…"

"The devil take those *people*. What do I care for them?" He stopped at her quick intake of breath and then let out a sigh. "Come, let us sit."

Weary of their argument, Serena allowed herself to be led to a wooden bench that nestled below one of the windows that overlooked the garden. Once seated, however, Nicholas possessed himself of one her hands once more and, when she continued to study the floor rather than look at him, he placed the other under her chin and turned her face to him.

"I do not mean to belittle how difficult it has been for you, nor to imply that there will not be hurdles to overcome in the future. All I ask is that you consider the lack of implications for *us* – how little it will affect our daily life."

Serena stared at him, trying to accept what he was saying, tendrils of hope beginning to weave their way about her heart, which was pounding fiercely in her chest.

"Think upon it, Serena. As man and wife, what is its detriment? Will it affect our happiness in each other's company? Is it likely to prevent us from sharing time as one, from doing the things that we love? Shall we not be able to go riding together, as we have in the past?"

He waited, and unable to summon words, she gave an almost imperceptible nod. "And will it preclude you from sitting by the lake at Crossways with your drawing pad and pencils whilst I make a pretence of being a fine angler?"

She gave a watery smile and shook her head. "And what of your music – will it hamper you from playing to your heart's content for me?" He paused and then swallowed visibly. "I cannot bear the thought of a life without you, Serena."

Incredulously, she stared up at him as the truth of his words struck her. It would seem she could dare to hope, and as the realisation came that this future could be hers, her defences began to crumble, and a solitary tear escaped and rolled down her cheek.

"And what of this, my love?" He brushed the tear away with his thumb and lowered his mouth to hers, kissing her slowly and gently, in complete contrast to his earlier assault upon her lips, and tentatively, she kissed him back. When he released her, she found herself unable to tear her gaze from his as she took in the expression in his eyes.

Then, she spoke hesitantly. "You – you do love me, truly? As a man loves a woman?"

Nicholas nodded. "Without question. And you? Do you hold me in affection? Will you permit me to take care of you?" He sighed and took one of her hands in his again. "Will you marry me?"

She studied his face, holding on tight to his hand as it gripped hers. Perceiving the strain upon his features and finally comprehending the truth of the matter, she felt some of the tension inside begin to seep away, and reaching out tentatively, she touched his face.

He placed his other hand over hers. "Make me the happiest of men, dear girl."

Swallowing the emotion that would rise into her throat again, Serena smiled, at first tentatively, then more widely as a reciprocal smile covered Nicholas' face, and she nodded. "Yes – I will" and with a whoop of joy, Nicholas leapt to his feet and swept her up into an embrace, holding her protectively against his chest.

Chapter Six

HAVING BEEN ABLE TO CLEAN himself up somewhat at the home of Mr Bennet's brother, Philips, where he was provided with a wholesome meal, the Colonel wasted no further time in making his farewells and setting out for Mount Street. Wickham was safely secured in the lock-up, and Mr Bennet had promised to send word once he was in proper custody. Furthermore, the Colonel was but eight miles upon the turnpike to London when he encountered the small company of soldiers that was on its way to Meryton to perform the detention that had by now taken place.

Quickly furnishing them with the necessary information, the Colonel continued on his way and, stabling his weary mount in the mews, he entered the house through the servants' entrance, intent upon reaching his room undetected.

A soothing bath was sufficient to ease his aches and pains whilst his manservant attended to his head which he confirmed to be merely a graze, well concealed for now by his hair but likely to produce a bruise of some tenderness and discolouring before long. The Colonel shrugged. It was but a small price to pay, as were his bloodied hands, for the outcome.

Once dressed, he headed down the main stairs, wincing slightly on his bruised foot, intent upon finding Georgiana and Bingley, pulling soft white gloves over his hands so as to conceal the evidence of his morning's activities.

Bingley had been a little disturbed by Darcy's note, which had told him little other than the need having arisen to make an unexpected journey. He was, however, quickly reassured by the Colonel that all was well, and he soon found his thoughts more pleasantly occupied as they waited upon his carriage to be made ready. In fact, so enticing did this step seem to be that he was taking, following hard upon the pleasures of an evening in Jane Bennet's company, that the Colonel suspected Bingley was probably hard put, barely an hour after expressing his concern, to recall that he even had a friend by the name of Darcy.

Such it was that by noon, Bingley's valet, Overton, and an assortment of servants, packing cases, trunks and other sundry items that a gentlemen must take with him whilst travelling, had departed from Mayfair. The gentleman had, in the meantime, paid a quick call to take leave of his family in Grosvenor Street, during which he had detailed his enjoyment of the ball on the previous evening and outlined his intentions for his estate in Hertfordshire, quite oblivious to the disgruntled expression upon his sister, Caroline's, features.

Soon after his return from this visit, Bingley was waved off by the Colonel and Georgiana, who had then repaired to the drawing room where the Colonel had advised his young cousin of her brother's intention to sojourn in Bath for a while and that they were to set off on the morrow with the intent of joining him.

Georgiana, reassured by her cousin that Darcy had sent Thornton on ahead to secure them lodgings that would ensure they did not need to stay with her aunt, was quietly determined to complete her preparations to join her brother without delay. Having observed the restrained way he attempted to conceal his distress from her the night before only reinforced her desire to be with him, so that she might offer what comfort she could.

Colonel Fitzwilliam, meanwhile, having despatched a note to his commanding officer advising him of his plans to depart for Bath and promising to forward his address as soon as it were known, had proceeded to his own chambers to instruct the servants in the packing of his belongings.

The afternoon was well progressed in Gracechurch Street, and the excitement generated by Nicholas and Serena's news, shared as it had been with first Elizabeth and then, upon their return some time later, Mrs Gardiner and Jane, had yet to abate.

Conscious that the engagement must be a matter for the family alone until formal consent could be obtained from Mr Seavington, Nicholas was at present attempting to compose a letter to that gentleman.

His attention, however, could not be held by the pen or the parchment, and Elizabeth, seated as she was by the fireplace in the drawing room, could not help but smile at the number of times he glanced over his shoulder from his position at the writing desk to where Serena sat opposite her, also attempting to write a letter, Aunt Gardiner's slope perched upon her lap.

Her aunt and Jane had, after a hastily organised celebratory lunch that had even drawn Mr Gardiner temporarily from his business, taken themselves upstairs to instruct the maid over the packing of her sister's belongings, and Elizabeth, recalling her failed attempt to write to Charlotte, had urged Nicholas to take possession of the desk and drawn a small side table round so that she could make use of it.

Like Nicholas, however, Elizabeth continued to make little progress with the pen, merely using it to tap idly on the table. Her relief that he had carried his point and secured Serena's hand was substantial, but conscious that her lowness of mood lingered yet, she sighed. With Jane so much more contented than of late, she could not account for this depression of her spirits. She longed to go for a walk to shake it off, but knew it was not feasible, and besides, she could not leave Serena and Nicholas alone. She glanced over at the latter and just at that moment he leapt to his feet, cast aside his pen and walked over to Serena, taking her hand as he sat beside her.

"Come with me! Come to Sutton Coker on the morrow, that we may not be parted so soon."

"How I would love to, Nicholas, but I cannot. I am but newly arrived at my sister's. I cannot turn tail and fly away without a backward glance."

"My dear girl," Mrs Gardiner's voice caused them to turn around and Elizabeth looked up to see that her aunt and Jane had returned. "Much as I love your company, this is a very special time for you." She smiled fondly at them both and walked around to face them. "Besides, Alicia deserves to share in your joy. Go with Nicholas."

"But he must leave in the morning! How can I ready myself in time?"

"I can delay until the afternoon; we can overnight at Basingstoke rather than Salisbury and do the bulk of the journey the day after."

"And we do have servants, my dear!" Mrs Gardiner frowned. "Of course, we shall need to send a maid with you in the carriage."

Nicholas shrugged. "Would Lizzy not suffice?"

"So – I am to be a servant?" Elizabeth laughed. "Pray, Aunt, do you have a cap and apron to spare that I may borrow? I fear there is not time to sew ones for myself."

Nicholas rolled his eyes at her. "No, you dunderhead. I meant, why do you not accompany Serena?"

"Tiresome boy. I knew your meaning."

"I am not a boy. I have a full two years on you!"

"Then it is a shame you did not put them to better use!"

"That will do, you two." Shaking her head at them, Mrs Gardiner smiled at Serena. "My dear, there are plenty of hands to make light work of the packing." She turned to her niece. "What say you, Lizzy?"

"Oh Lizzy, do say you will come! It would be such a comfort for me."

"Should you like to go, my dear?" her aunt prompted.

Elizabeth chewed her lip thoughtfully. Would she? She was unsurprised that her immediate thoughts were of Mr Darcy: removing herself from Town negated any continuance of the acquaintance – but had he not withdrawn from her? Any crossing of their paths henceforth would be uncomfortable, their recent rapport a thing of the past. The dissatisfaction this engendered served to reinforce her lowness of spirit, but unable to pay it the attention it warranted, she summoned a bright smile.

"Absolutely! To spend early summer in the West Country will be heavenly, and to have the chance to reacquaint myself with Sutton Coker a delight. If Mrs Harington will have me, of course!"

"Mama will welcome you with open arms, Lizzy, as well you know."

"I am certain that Mrs Harington will not object, Lizzy." Jane smiled at her, and Elizabeth could not help but feel some pleasure in the anticipation. Much as she loved her aunt and uncle, and reluctant though she was to leave Town, she would feel the loss of Jane's company less sorely in the circumstances.

"Then so be it! I do hope your mother can find spare rooms for us, Nicholas, with your bringing uninvited guests along at such short notice."

"There is always the stables. I am certain there will be plenty of dry hay in this fine spell of weather."

Elizabeth laughed, as did the others, all knowing full well that Sutton Coker boasted more chambers than could ever be warranted and that Mrs Harington's excellent housekeeper would have rooms aired and beds made up before they had finished consuming their first cup of tea.

"Well now." Mrs Gardiner clapped her hands together. "Enough merriment. Nicholas, is your letter ready for the post?"

Looking a little shame-faced, he released Serena's hand, which he had held throughout the conversation, and got reluctantly to his feet.

"I shall attend to it directly, Aunt." He gave her a mock salute and resumed his seat at the desk, but making no attempt to retrieve his pen, his attention remaining with the occupants of the room.

Seeing the fond look that Serena threw him, Elizabeth smiled. They were clearly both highly gratified that they were no longer looking upon an almost immediate separation, and she was pleased that she would be able to join them, prolonging her time in their company.

"What about you, my dear," Mrs Gardiner was addressing Serena, who held up a neatly folded piece of parchment.

"I am complete, Mary. Mama's letter could be enclosed within Nicholas' to Papa, could it not?"

"Indeed." Mrs Gardiner glanced around the room. "Now, settle down. Nicholas, attend to your duty; Lizzy, you had best pen a note for Jane to take to your father. Come, Serena, let us repair to your chamber and decide upon your packing. Lizzy can join us directly." She turned to her other niece with a smile. "Jane, my dear girl, I am afraid I leave you in charge." She nodded her head at Elizabeth and Nicholas, who were indulging in a mild squabble over who had the finer hand, and ushered Serena from the room.

✦

Elizabeth had risen early on Wednesday in order to share breakfast with Jane who was to depart by ten and, having seen her on her way, the ladies of the house had then returned to their duties. Though Nicholas had deferred their departure for Somerset until three in the afternoon, there remained a great deal to do within a short amount of time, and Mrs

Gardiner had encouraged both Elizabeth and Serena to busy themselves and assist with the preparations.

Having been in Town for such a short time, Serena's trunk was soon secured; Elizabeth, however, had possessions scattered about the house, and as her aunt anticipated her destination from Sutton Coker to be Longbourn once again, she had encouraged her to take all of her belongings, offering a spare travelling case to ensure there was ample capacity.

Thus it was that as the morning waned, Elizabeth repaired to her chamber whilst her aunt sought the additional case and Serena attempted to retrieve anything she could find of her friend's in the downstairs rooms.

Unheeding of the pile of clothes on the bed, Elizabeth walked over to the window, staring down at the busy street below, her mind yet again ensnared in the repetitious thoughts that had haunted her throughout the night.

Leaving London and all its recent associations presented a double-edged sword. On the one hand, she longed for something to distract her from her predilection for dwelling upon Mr Darcy, a change of scene where she could be secure in not anticipating his presence. Elizabeth turned her back on the window and leant against the sill, her eyes falling instantly upon the half-filled trunk. On the other, she felt unsettled by the sheer notion of removing herself from such close proximity to him, from where she might chance upon him on any day, in any place; from where she might – if fortune permitted – call at Mount Street, or that he might call in Cheapside…

It was this latter thought that brought her to her senses. Mr Darcy visiting in Gracechurch Street would never become a habit, and since the revelation of her family's latest foolishness, his absence was now a given. Hankering for his company was futile, the irony of her interest not lost upon her.

Conscious that her fate was sealed, Elizabeth sighed and walked over to the closet. Only one gown remained inside and she took it out and laid it on the bed. The fabric shimmered, and she ran a hand along the silk, her mind returning with little persuasion to the evening of the ball. How excited she had been in dressing for that evening; how high had her anticipation been. And yet… and yet perhaps it was only now that she began to understand just how much that pleasurable expectation had relied upon Mr Darcy.

An unexpected tightness gripped her throat. The memory of their dance – of his hand upon hers – assailed her for a moment, and she closed her eyes, conscious of a rising intensity behind her lids. *Can there be so much awareness in a man's touch... that it captures your heart?*

Chapter Seven

ELIZABETH'S EYES FLEW OPEN AS her aunt entered the room, a small travelling case in her hand.

"Here we are," Mrs Gardiner placed the case upon a chair and then turned to survey the room. "Lizzy!" She shook her head admonishingly at her niece. "Whatever are you about? Make haste, my dear, time is ticking away."

She scooped up some of the clothes from the bed and Elizabeth smiled apologetically.

"Forgive me, Aunt. I did not mean to be so tardy."

They both set to in an attempt to restore some order, and as Mrs Gardiner neatly folded one garment after another, Elizabeth turned her attention to placing her other possessions into the small travelling case. She only had to pick up her writing case, however, to recall the most significant letter inside and, impulsively, she turned to her aunt, the words spilling out before she could check herself.

"Is it too late to pay a call, Aunt? Can we not find the time?"

Mrs Gardiner looked over at her niece in astonishment. "Dear girl, no, we cannot! And pray, where would you be wishing to go?"

Regretting that she had spoken, Elizabeth made an attempt at nonchalance as she walked over to the dresser to retrieve her comb and hair pins.

"Oh, it is of little import. I thought that it would be polite to call upon Miss Darcy before we leave Town."

There was silence and, turning around, Elizabeth met her aunt's steady gaze. "She – she was so kind, was she not? Calling upon us on Friday?" She swallowed quickly. "We have not repaid the compliment, and there will be no further opportunity – they... she will not know that we have left..." Her voice tailed away at her aunt's smile.

"And this desire to pay a farewell call is for Miss Darcy – or her brother?"

Elizabeth could not help the blush that would steal its way into her cheeks, and she quickly placed a cooling hand against her throat. Unable to meet her aunt's eye, she gave an embarrassed laugh.

"Am I so transparent?"

"Forgive me, my dear. I should not tease you so. But sadly, there is no time. Departing so late in the day as you are, you cannot afford to delay further or you will not arrive at the inn before nightfall." Her aunt gave her a kind smile. "However, if it will make you feel more at ease, I shall endeavour to pay the call myself on the morrow and convey your farewell to Miss Darcy in person."

With that, Elizabeth had to be content; there was little she could do to alter the situation and, frustrated with herself for having given in to the urge to suggest it, she forced her mind away from such fruitless speculation. Placing her comb and the hairpins in her reticule, she turned her attention to the small pile of books on the bedside table.

"Jane will be disappointed." Elizabeth waved one of the books at her aunt. "She had but two chapters to finish in this, yet she has forgotten it!"

Mrs Gardiner laughed as she placed a pile of clothes into the trunk. "I suspect she will bear her disappointment well."

Elizabeth nodded. "Aye, true enough." She added her sewing case to the smaller bag and began opening and shutting drawers in the dresser to ensure nothing had been left behind. "I do hope Mama is a little less forward this time, Aunt. She is oft unaware of the damage she may inflict and how it may be quite contrary to her purpose."

"Do not be too hard upon your mother, my dear. Her concerns are all for your welfare, and she means well."

"Forgive me. I do not mean to be censorious, but if only she could learn to curb her tongue a little, or if that is too far a stretch, merely lower her tone when in company, that the entire neighbourhood might not hear her effusions!"

With a laugh, Mrs Gardiner added the final pile of clothing to the trunk before turning her attention to Elizabeth's ball gown.

"This is a truly striking gown, Lizzy." She looked over at her niece. "And you looked quite beautiful in it."

Assailed instantly by her earlier recollections, Elizabeth was conscious of the warmth in her cheeks. "You make me blush, Aunt! But you are very kind."

"It is not kindness, my dear, but the truth." Folding the dress carefully and wrapping it in tissue, Mrs Gardiner laid it gently on top of the other garments and lowered the lid of the trunk. "There. Now – let us see what has become of Serena and what she has found."

By noon, just as Darcy neared his destination, the Colonel and Georgiana were settling into the carriage in preparation for their own journey thither, with an overnight stop at Marlborough planned.

The carriage pulled away from the kerb, and as it turned from Mount Street into Berkeley Square, the Colonel observed Georgiana staring into the gardens before releasing a soft sigh as she turned away from the window to meet his concerned gaze.

"Do not be so downcast, Georgie."

"I am not. I merely wish that we had been able to call one last time – to say farewell."

The Colonel sighed; he had suspected the direction of her thoughts to be with Miss Elizabeth Bennet, and he was clearly not mistaken. Wishing to illustrate the futility of her observation, he shook his head at her. "And what, my dear, would you have given as the reason for our precipitous departure?"

Georgiana opened her mouth and then closed it again, before blurting out: "But we could at least have offered our congratulations. It would have been a valid enough reason for a call, would it not?"

The Colonel frowned. "No, my dear. You could not have spoken of it, for it has yet to be formally announced. Besides, how would you explain such intimate knowledge?"

Georgiana met his eye with a mournful look, as if quite lost as to what to say.

"Georgie; dear Georgie. The acquaintance was but in its infancy, and though your brother had known Miss Elizabeth Bennet, and indeed her sister, these several months, he did not anticipate continuing the acquaintance after he left Kent. There was no necessity upon you, having met them so recently and so little, to pay a farewell call when the acquaintance must end. It is not as if you might renew it upon your return to Town."

"But I liked her so *very* much."

"As did we all, dear girl. As did we all."

Georgiana looked quickly out of the window again, swallowing with visible difficulty, and conscious of her attempt to conceal her distress, he leaned forward and patted her hand where it rested upon her lap, giving it a quick squeeze before sitting back in his seat, and she turned to face him with a watery smile.

"I cannot bear to see his sadness, Richard."

"He will rally, Georgie. He is stronger than you would give him credit for. And in some ways, it is better that we heard the news of Monday night as we did."

Georgiana frowned at this. "Better? How so?"

Blowing out a huff of breath, the Colonel glanced out of the window briefly before returning his eyes to his cousin. "I will own that it puts paid to any chance of a reconciliation, but it is a blessing that it preceded your brother genuinely buying into that hope. That is something to be grateful for, despite my endeavours to persuade him to the contrary. After she rejected him, he…"

"Reconciliation?" Georgiana stared at her cousin with astonishment. "*Rejected?* What are you speaking of? How – how could – why did he not say so? She would not have him… I do not understand." A tear made its way to the surface and trickled down Georgiana's cheek.

Conscious that he had, as was often the case with Darcy, put his rather largely booted foot in it, the Colonel fell back against the seat, wincing as his tender head found leather. Then, realising the level of distress he had caused in his other cousin, he moved over to sit beside her and placed an arm comfortingly about her shoulders.

"Forgive me. I should not have spoken so unguardedly. Darcy will never trust me again, for it was not to be spoken of."

Georgiana leaned away from him, that she might better observe his face. "Then it is *true?* But when… I do not understand… when was this? Why would she not have him? He is – he is…" but Georgiana could not continue and soon silent tears were coursing down her cheeks.

Pressing his handkerchief into her hand, Colonel Fitzwilliam returned to his former seat, the better to observe and converse with her. Feeling all the discomfort of having distressed her, notwithstanding his carelessness in letting slip something of intense privacy for his other cousin, he fidgeted restlessly in his seat as Georgiana mopped her face and drew in a deep breath.

"Forgive me, Richard. I do not mean to be so mealy-mouthed, but it breaks my heart to think of his suffering."

"It is I who should seek your forgiveness, my dear. Lord knows if Darcy will ever bestow such sanction, breaking his trust as I have."

"I will not tell him. He has sufficient to contend with. But please, tell me all. I must know it."

With a heavy sigh, the Colonel leaned back in his seat and studied his companion thoughtfully for a moment. Then, coming to a decision, he sat forward again and, taking her hands in his, he began to tell her all he knew of Darcy's growing admiration for Miss Elizabeth Bennet, and the misfortune that had befallen him not ten days earlier in Kent.

⁓✦⁓

It was not unusual to arrive home at Longbourn from a stay of some duration elsewhere to find the place in uproar. Indeed, as Jane Bennet stepped from the Gardiner's carriage she surveyed the house with a mixture of pleasure and trepidation. The raised voice of her mother could be heard distinctly and, knowing that there was no Elizabeth to act as a buffer or companion, she sighed.

"Jane! Jane is here!" An excited squeal was followed by the sound of running footsteps and Kitty appeared, followed closely by Lydia, and they both ran from the now open front door to throw themselves at their elder sister, talking all at once.

Jane hugged them both, trying to accustom herself to their boisterousness once more and then turned to embrace Mary, who had followed at a more sedate pace, albeit she did skip the last few paces into her sister's arms.

"Guess what has-" began Kitty.

"Oh, hush, Kitty. How is one to ever guess such a thing, and Jane least of all."

"Lydia!" Mary's censure did little to sober Lydia, who merely stuck her tongue out at her sister and then looped her arm through Jane's, dragging her towards the door.

"There has been such a scandal, Jane, and you and Lizzy have missed it all!"

Lydia's tone was damning, and Jane threw her a questioning look, but then Kitty threaded her hand through Jane's other arm and said, "Lydia, you should not be out here. You are banned from leaving the house."

"I am still within the grounds, am I not?"

They made their way inside, Mary following behind, Kitty and Lydia bickering with each other all the way.

Chapter Eight

JANE SIGHED AS SHE ENTERED THE HALL, thankful that her sisters had detached themselves and were continuing their unfathomable argument as they headed for the drawing room. Handing her bonnet and coat to Hill with a grateful smile, Jane checked her hair for tidiness in the mirror and then turned around quickly as she heard her mother calling and the sound of footsteps on the stairs.

"Jane! There you are, my dear! Safely home at last, and not a day too soon. Mr Bingley is returned, as I said he would in my letter. Come, make haste. You must change out of that travel-worn gown."

Conscious of a sense of well-being that the gentleman had arrived safely back in Hertfordshire, Jane followed her mother up the stairs to the door of the chamber she shared with Elizabeth.

"Oh my dear," Mrs Bennet, a hand to her chest, gripped Jane's arm as she walked past her into the room. "There has been such a scandal! Thank the Lord Mr Bingley returned yesterday afternoon, for the intelligence has helped to divert the attention of others somewhat. You will never guess what has happened."

"Pray, Mama, tell me, for it is clear that something is amiss."

Mrs Bennet threw herself into an armchair near the window and Jane walked over and perched herself on the edge of the bed nearby. Flapping a small handkerchief, Mrs Bennet brushed a lock of hair off her forehead.

"Mr Wickham – he has been *arrested*, can you but believe it? And he was all set to make an offer for our Lydia."

Jane bit her lip. It was unnerving to hear it so freely spoken of; at least now there was no need for her to speak to her father in an attempt to reinforce her sister's warning. Though she could not help but feel relief for her family, she nonetheless experienced some regret for the man and the life he had chosen.

Her daughter's silent reception of her words, however, did nothing to deter Mrs Bennet in the recounting of her tale.

"I am constantly thwarted, Jane. First Lizzy turns down Mr Collins. Then Mr Bingley leaves the neighbourhood, now Mr Wickham has been taken from us just as he was about to declare himself." Mrs Bennet paused to draw breath, her voice spiralling ever higher. "And I do not know *what* is to become of us now. But I tell you this: I shall *never* speak to your father again, and I have told him so repeatedly. He says we should be glad to be rid of Mr Wickham, that we should be thankful we have protectors out there who guard our interests. Our *interests*! What does he know, shielded behind that library door day in and day out. We will all be destitute, I tell you."

"Mama!" Jane hastened to the dresser to collect a pitcher of water and a glass. "Please be calm. You will work yourself into a stupor."

Mrs Bennet sipped the water handed to her as Jane took the handkerchief from her and dipped it in the pitcher and then proceeded to dab at her mother's brow. Leaning back in the chair, the lady breathed in and out slowly a few times; then, she sat up and looked Jane firmly in the eye.

"You must make every effort to capture Mr Bingley's attentions once more, Jane. The security of this family depends upon you as never before."

Jane swallowed uncomfortably at these words. She knew that she ought to apprise her parents of the continued acquaintance; indeed, it was her duty to do so, but for once her open and honest nature recoiled against it. She could not bear to have such personal interactions talked of and assessed with an air to their matrimonial advantage.

In an attempt to distract her mother from continuing to discuss their neighbour, therefore, Jane got to her feet and walked over to the dresser to re-pin her hair and, in the meantime, returned to their original subject.

"But surely, Mama, we must be grateful that Lydia was not committed to Mr Wickham in the circumstances?"

"Grateful? She was so close to securing him, Jane. He displayed such a decided preference for her, showed her every attention, even though his time was not his own and he could never tarry at Longbourn for long, having been sent here on some important duty by his commanding officer." Mrs Bennet sighed heavily. "He would have been such a husband to be proud of, so well thought of in the regiment. And Lydia so attached to him, I am sure she could talk of nothing but Wickham from morning 'til night, and spent all manner of hours at your Aunt Philips' during his tenancy there."

Jane paled at these words, conscious as she was of Wickham's past. "How did he – do we know upon what charge he is arrested?"

Mrs Bennet sighed dramatically. "All manner of them, allegedly. I am certain 'tis all a trap. There are those that are jealous of a man such as he, with his fine countenance and pleasing manners. If only that evil Mr Darcy had not ruined him financially, this could never have happened."

"But Mama, he must have done *something*."

Releasing a disgruntled breath, Mrs Bennet hauled herself up from the chair and walked over to the window, staring out into the garden.

"'Tis alleged that he is in debt. Well – that is no surprise, left without his inheritance by that horrid man. But they say further–" Mrs Bennet threw Jane a quick look over her shoulder and then faced the window again. "There is rumour – and that is all, I am sure – that he has deserted his post." Mrs Bennet turned around and put her hands on her hips. "It hardly seems a crime, and I believe none of it, and nor does Lydia. However, your father-" Mrs Bennet's eyes flashed for a moment. "*He* says that Wickham is degenerate, a cad of the first order and that he is never to cross the threshold of Longbourn again. Well, that is for certain, is it not? The poor man is in shackles and has by now left in the prison cart for the assizes at Hertford on Tuesday week. Lydia is quite heartbroken, and now we shall all be destined to starve in the hedgerows once more."

Jane hesitated, then said, "But Mama – he has deserted his post, regardless of any other alleged misdeeds. And what do we really know of Mr Wickham and his past from so short an acquaintance? Besides, if he has no money, how was his marrying Lydia to help us from starving in the hedgerows?"

Mrs Bennet did not seem to appreciate the logic of this and frowned as she walked back to retake her seat.

"I am sure I do not know. All I do know is that Mr Bennet takes pleasure in thwarting my ambitions to settle my daughters. And you need not be so complacent, either."

Jane's eyes widened in bewilderment. "Mama?"

"Mr Bingley. Oh, he has returned – was in the neighbourhood by yesterday afternoon, as reports would have it."

"You have not – have you not seen him?"

"He has called, but only upon your father. Your *father!* He did not wait upon me. I tell you now, Mr Bennet will be the undoing of us all."

Jane had little to say to this and, having completed her ministrations to her hair, she walked over to take her mother's place at the window.

"He has come to Netherfield alone. His sister does not accompany him, nor does his friend. I only hope that he is not to be always coming and going, for it is such an inconvenience to the neighbourhood."

"It can hardly inconvenience us, Mama."

"Well – you take my meaning, I am certain. But your father tells me naught. I cannot even discover if Mr Bingley knows you were not here yesterday or that you *are* here today. I am all ignorance."

Jane, whose position at the window afforded her a fine view of the front driveway, found her eye caught by a movement near the gate, and soon her attention was quite fixed upon the figure on horseback coming towards the house. Feeling her heartbeat quicken, she put a hand to her throat and drew in a calming breath.

Then, turning away from the window she summoned a smile. "Shall we go downstairs, Mama? I believe we have a visitor."

Pleased though he was with the situation of the house Thornton had secured for them at such short notice, Darcy was less content with his present endeavour. A call upon his aunt and cousin was mandatory now that he had come to Bath, yet how he wished it could be avoided. However, knowing as he did that his aunt avidly perused the Bath Chronicle, he knew his being there would not go undetected for long, and the lecture he would have to endure, should this be the means of his aunt's learning of his presence, was not worth invoking.

He pulled the bell at the de Bourgh's usual residence in Great Pulteney Street (a level walk to the baths – a must for his cousin, according to Lady Catherine) and stepped back to look up at the imposing edifice. Within minutes he was inside and being shown into a showy first-floor drawing room. His aunt had taken the same house in Bath for as long as he could remember, and he could only assume that her predilection for the place was allied to her fondness for dark, intense murals not unlike those that adorned her drawing room at Rosings. Personally, Darcy could not abide the things.

"Darcy! How delightful. I am gratified that you followed my advice. You are right to take some time away from Town and its pollutions, and Anne will be honoured to have your company, will you not, Anne?"

Lady Catherine had risen to her feet upon perceiving her visitor and swept across the room to greet him, waving a vague hand in the direction of her daughter as she passed.

"Good morning, Aunt. Anne." Darcy bowed in his cousin's direction, noting her raised brow and rather scornful expression and wondering what caused such a reaction in her. In fact, as he followed his aunt across the heavily ornamented room to a seat at her side he reflected that he had rarely paid Anne any mind, and never in his born days could he recall considering what she might be thinking or feeling. He could only put it down to the impact of her having written to Georgiana and her having been somewhat more animated than usual on Saturday evening.

"So – Darcy. You have come to spend some time with Anne. This is most agreeable."

Darcy hesitated. On the one hand, he wished to deny this outright, yet with Anne's pointed gaze on him, he was somewhat unnerved, for her habit was to sit with her eyes averted. To deny vehemently, as he wished, to wanting to spend time with his cousin was not possible. Likewise, however, he could not tell the truth and say he had come to Bath to avoid Miss Elizabeth Bennet. Darcy's insides gave their customary lurch as her name passed through his mind. What might she be doing today? How much longer would she tarry in Town, or had she accompanied Harington to Longbourn when he travelled to speak to her father? The likelihood was strong, and a sharp pain shot through him as he drew a short breath and met his aunt's imperious eye.

"Well?" she rapped. "Has the journey addled your wits, Darcy? Speak!"

Chapter Nine

AS THE BELLS OF ST CLEMENTS STRUCK the hour of three, Elizabeth glanced at the clock on the mantel and then looked over at her friend. Serena had taken up a place on the window seat, that she might discern Nicholas' carriage the moment it turned the corner into the street. She smiled to herself; her friends' happiness was palpable, and though her own thoughts remained troubled over Wickham's presence in Hertfordshire and her present preoccupation with Mr Darcy, she could not help but be delighted over their rapprochement.

"Watching will not make him arrive any the sooner, my dear." Mrs Gardiner came into the room, a pair of slippers in her hand. "Lizzy, your dancing shoes were still by the front door. Do you have space for them?"

"In the travelling case, Aunt. Here, let me." Elizabeth got to her feet and took the slippers from Mrs Gardiner and went out into the hall, quickly placing them into the bag and sealing it again. She wished for no further reminders of Monday evening. She was about to return to the drawing room when a maid came through the door at the back of the hall and walking up to her presented her with a brief curtsey before holding out a letter.

"For me? At this hour?"

"Indeed, Miss. 'Tis from Longbourn, so I am told. 'Twas sent back with the coach that took Miss Jane home this morning – it has just this minute returned."

Taking the letter, Elizabeth studied the direction with some surprise before dismissing the maid with a nod and walking over to perch on a settle. She turned the missive over in her hand and frowned at it. A letter from her father? Convinced it came in response to hers regarding Wickham, her insides twisted in dread that it might hold ill tidings, and she hurriedly broke the seal.

The opening calmed her, it being an acknowledgement of her note about her change of plans, Mr Bennet then entering into a short summary of the family's well-being, but beyond this she was unable to progress as Serena called, "He is here!" from the drawing room and before she knew it, her aunt, her friend and a cluster of servants had gathered in the hall in preparation for their departure. In the bustle of loading the coach and donning their coats she had no choice but to stuff the letter into her reticule for later perusal.

Their farewells made, they were soon ensconced inside the carriage and set off down the street, both girls hanging out of the window to wave at Mrs Gardiner until they turned the corner and she disappeared from view.

⚜

Time had only moved on an hour before Darcy shrugged into his great coat and headed for the door of his aunt's lodgings. It had been a long, laborious meeting – hardly enlivened by Anne excusing herself part way through it – but a necessity, and now the duty was paid. As he waited for the butler to retrieve his hat and gloves, he studied his booted feet. At least on the morrow he could welcome Georgiana and Fitzwilliam and perchance they would be able to make some excursions. The weather held fair – indeed, there could not be a better month to be in this part of the world – and the distraction of new places would no doubt serve his sister as well as it would him.

Rousing himself, Darcy accepted his possessions from the servant and waved him away. He was quite capable of seeing himself out of the door, but before his hand had actually touched the handle a sound startled him: a loud '*pssst*' came from a slightly ajar door on his left, and turning with a frown in that direction, he was surprised to see a pale hand extend through the gap and beckon him. When he did nothing, an indignant huff could be heard, followed by the opening of the door to reveal his cousin, Anne.

"For heaven's sake, Darcy, come here! Do you not recognise a request for your attention when you hear it?"

Blinking rapidly to dispel the bizarre thought that a young version of his aunt had just materialised in the gloom before him, Darcy hesitated and then walked over to join Anne in the doorway of a small, dimly-lit sitting room. She waved him in and peered around the door into the hall before closing it with a decided snap.

"Sit," she said, once again waving a hand dismissively.

Darcy, who did not take kindly to being talked to as though he were a mere hound, least of all by his uncommunicative cousin, remained standing.

52

For a moment, they watched each other warily.

"You wished to speak with me?"

Anne tilted her head on one side for a moment, as if assessing him. Then, she straightened. "We have not held a conversation these many years."

Darcy blinked. "I – you – you always seem so... disinterested."

"Hmph. I imagine my reticence towards you mirrors yours towards me – we tend to the same purpose, do we not? To not raise expectations that are too ridiculous for common sense?"

Giving an indignant huff, Anne took a seat, and this time, when she waved a hand for Darcy to do likewise, he acquiesced. There was silence once more as they both eyed each other from opposite sides of a small, circular table.

"But why do you remain so silent?" Darcy frowned. "Are you like so when alone with your mother?"

She nodded. "I am. But how I behave is the one choice I am able to make for myself – it is the only thing under my control. Were I to wish it, I could argue the day away with Mother. As it is, I choose not to." Her face took on a shrew-like expression and she stared at him with dark eyes not dissimilar to Lady Catherine's. "My opportunities for amusement are slim, Darcy. I would say that I regret you being the subject of my entertainment these past weeks, but I cannot, and for you to be here now in Bath – well, suffice it to say, company other than the norm is a feast for my eyes and ears!"

Recalling the letter she had sent to his sister, Darcy felt a twinge of discomfort, and he stirred restlessly under her pointed stare. "What is it you wished to speak of?"

"I would have you marry, Darcy, and the sooner the better."

Darcy stared at his cousin in astonishment, unable to utter a word. In this self-imposed silence, he watched her as she got to her feet, waving him back into his seat as he made to rise, and began to prowl to and fro in front of the empty fireplace.

"*This* is what you would discuss with me?"

She turned on her heel and paced back across the floor.

"Consider this, Cousin. You have visited Rosings for how many years now at Eastertide?"

Darcy shrugged.

"Precisely. There are so many, you cannot, or care not to, remember. We have both listened to my mother, year in, year out, lauding the supposed intention for our connubial future." Anne turned on her heel and faced him with a fierce expression upon her face. "Yes, Darcy. I have remained as reticent as you upon the matter, despite its presence there in the room on every occasion. Had you wished for the union, you have had sufficient years to act upon it. As for myself, I have been equally reluctant, but I am no fool; though I spoke not of it, I have given it much thought, and until this year I could see no earthly solution."

Darcy threw Anne a concerned look. "You are not ailing?"

"Of course not!" Anne moved her arm impatiently. Then she took her seat again, and Darcy let out a breath of relief. Her pacing in such a small room made him feel bilious.

"I do not enjoy robust health – this has never been a secret – yet I am not close to being shuffled off this earth. But I digress. Darcy, you must marry. And soon."

Unable to tolerate such advice, least of all from a cousin with whom he had shared little dialogue and no confidence, Darcy now got to his feet. His disappointment at Rosings was yet too fresh in his mind, the outcome of Monday evening too painful to dwell upon; he would not discuss marriage.

His cousin stared up at him, a rather sullen expression upon her features. Then, she threw him a disdainful smirk.

"She is beneath you, I will not deny, but you could do far worse. Clearly, you are besotted with her. I would encourage you to overcome your scruples and take her before someone else does."

Hearing these words spoken by his cousin, despite his knowledge of the letter she had sent to Georgiana and the veiled hints therein, caused Darcy to draw in a sharp breath. He turned away from the knowing gaze upon Anne's face and walked over to the empty grate, and leant upon the mantel, one boot resting upon the fender.

"There is no future for me there, Cousin. I beg you would not speak of it."

A mocking laugh greeted these words. "Future? *Future?* And what of *mine?*" To Darcy's surprise, his cousin joined him at the fireplace, and he turned to face her, disturbed to detect anger upon her face.

"I do not advise you for altruistic reasons, Cousin. What charity have you shown me, that I should repay the compliment?"

Darcy was consumed with a wave of guilt, and he held up a hand to forestall Anne as she opened her mouth to continue.

"Forgive me. You are quite correct. I have not done my duty by you. I – we – we all should have paid you more attention, considered you more. I cannot recall the last time you were at Pemberley..."

Anne blinked as she took in these words then raised her chin. "I am not blind to your reasons for not so doing. Any attention in that quarter would have raised expectations that we neither sought nor desired." She sighed heavily, the aggression seeping from her stance as if she were being deflated. This time, she met his look with one of resignation, and when she spoke, her voice was less strident.

"I have been nowhere but Kent or Bath for longer than I can recall." Darcy winced at the wistful note of his cousin's voice as she continued. "But we both know that my visiting Pemberley would have been impossible. However, it does bring me to my point. If you marry, Darcy, *someone else*, then my future gains some prospect. If you marry elsewhere, then no longer must I conceal any interest in your visits. I would be able to make some sojourn at Pemberley – or even London. Until the prospect of our being united is beyond question, I am constrained to Rosings and unable to participate fully in the visits of cousins whom I would long have wished to make my friends."

An unexpected tightening gripped Darcy's throat at this impassioned speech. Never had he seen such animation in his cousin's face, such feeling, and her voice breaking over the word friends was more than he could bear.

He reached out awkwardly and patted her on the arm, unsure if such a gesture would be too little or indeed unwelcome, but he was rewarded by a somewhat watery smile and a nod of his cousin's head. Dashing a hand quickly across her eyes, Anne straightened her shoulders and looked about the room.

"Well. What is done is done. Now – Miss Elizabeth Bennet: she has no fortune, but she is a gentlewoman, and her character and demeanour are strongly in her favour. She will not be cowed by those that might scorn her. Did you not see the way she was with Mother?"

It was Darcy's turn to look downcast, and his gaze dropped to his feet for a second before he could meet Anne's eye. He could not quite credit this conversation at all, yet how was he to silence Anne on the subject? She would appear to be even less likely to be hood-winked than Georgiana.

"Come, Darcy. Speak. I watched you carefully on Saturday. You have not lost your inclination for the lady." Anne's voice had returned to the slightly mocking tone once more.

Darcy blew out a frustrated breath. He had absolutely no intention of revealing what had transpired between him and Elizabeth, nor the recent change in her circumstances, which for all he knew still waited to become public knowledge. His reticence did not forestall his cousin, however.

"I will own that I determined no evidence of her returning your admiration when she visited at Rosings. She was lively enough in your presence, but then she is animated by nature. She was clearly not cowed into silence by your significance – unlike some fortune-hunters I could name."

"She has no interest in my fortune."

"Really?" Anne laughed. "You must admire her very much to think her so free of guile."

Darcy remained resolutely silent. He would not be drawn upon what he could or could not vouch for, and determined that bringing an end to this interview would be the best method of silencing Anne.

He glanced at the clock on the mantel. "You will have to forgive me, Cousin. I must be on my way."

Anne frowned. "You do not fool me, Darcy. 'Tis a paltry excuse – what is there for you to hurry away for, pray? You have no company at your beck and call."

True though this statement was, it was sufficient reminder of those who would join him on the morrow. He bowed to his cousin and made for the door, pausing on the threshold to say, "I wish you good day, Anne. I shall call again with Fitzwilliam and Georgiana," and with that he took his leave, letting himself out into the street and releasing a sigh of relief as the door closed behind him.

Darcy passed the afternoon walking to Beechen Cliff and back in the hope that the exercise would tire him out. It was a steep climb up the wooded hillside, but well worth it for the view it afforded of Bath. He had spent quite some time there, walking the pathways and stopping occasionally to stare at the view, but it did little to distract his thoughts, and even less to drain his energy.

Thus it was that he returned to Brock Street in time for his solitary meal well aware that he had achieved little that day in putting Elizabeth from his thoughts and, having eaten sparsely, he took a glass of port into the drawing room where he continued in silent contemplation before the fire, determined to turn his mind to other things.

The plight of his cousin, Anne, was worthy of consideration, and as he took a sip from his glass he mulled upon it. It would provide further distraction if they included Anne in some of their activities during this stay in Bath. The only detriment would be his aunt, and he turned his mind to ways in which his cousin could be invited to participate in their ventures without the necessity for her mother to attend. Any potential rise in Lady Catherine's expectations he brushed aside. It was sufficient for him to know that Anne had as little desire as he for such a union. Besides, even should he convey this to his aunt, she would ignore it and continue blindly with her own assumptions.

Draining his glass, he got to his feet and walked over to the table housing the decanter. Conscious as he was that this focus on Anne was merely a ploy, he ruthlessly silenced the voice of his conscience which pointed out his self-interest, and he poured himself another measure of port. He would take any opportunity for distraction from his interminable thoughts of Elizabeth.

As he walked back to his seat, however, his eye was caught by an advertisement on the back of the Chronicle where it lay on the table, discarded earlier by him for having failed to retain his attention. Picking it up, his gaze narrowed as he read the detail; here perhaps was adequate diversion to aid him through the difficult weeks ahead.

Chapter Ten

By NIGHTFALL, ELIZABETH, SERENA and Nicholas were safely quartered in Basingstoke. Nicholas had elected to ride after their last watering stop, so the ladies had been left to amuse themselves for the remainder of that day's journey and, though she had struggled to prevent her thoughts from returning to Mount Street whenever silence prevailed, Elizabeth had found her friend's undemanding company sufficient to keep an unaccountable feeling of sadness in the back of her mind rather than the forefront.

Having settled into their chamber, the ladies refreshed themselves quickly before turning their attention to tidying their hair.

"Will you miss being in Town, Lizzy? I do appreciate your accompanying me." Serena was running a comb through her straight locks, and Elizabeth, who was seated before the mirror, smiled at her friend through the reflection.

"It is no hardship! I much prefer the country, as well you know, though I shall miss the company."

"Yes, Mary said you had been spending a good deal of time with some new acquaintances?"

Elizabeth sighed. "I meant Aunt and Uncle Gardiner!" Then, she added reluctantly, "But yes, it is true." She gave a final pat to her hair and got to her feet, keen to divert the conversation, but Serena forestalled her.

"So, how did you come to meet these people? Town always seems such a difficult place to make new friends, but perhaps that is just my own perception."

Taking the proffered pins from her friend, Elizabeth turned Serena about that she might fasten her hair neatly, attempting nonchalance. "Miss Darcy is but a recent acquaintance, but the introduction came through her brother, whom Jane and I met last autumn in Hertfordshire." Trying to concentrate on what she was doing, Elizabeth wished the conversation could turn on anything but this. "His friend – a Mr Bingley – took on the lease of Netherfield; you remember the property whose parkland borders the Meryton Road?" Serena nodded. "Mr Darcy is his intimate friend, and he came to make some stay in the country. There," she tapped Serena on her shoulder. "You are done."

"Darcy?" Serena wrinkled her nose as she turned to face her friend, but then her expression cleared. "I am familiar with that name. Would it be the same family that hails from Derbyshire?"

Elizabeth nodded.

"I have never met them, of course, but what is your opinion of the gentleman? And his sister? Do you find them to be good people?"

"Oh, they are the best…" The words had spilled out unbidden, and unable to stop it, the colour rushed into Elizabeth's cheeks. "I beg you would excuse me; I really would rather not talk of them."

She turned to pick up her reticule, and Serena frowned. "Forgive my selfishness, Lizzy. I have been so wrapped up in my own concerns that I have failed to consider yours. You appear… I do not wish to pry, but there are moments when you do not seem yourself. I do not like that I have unsettled you by raising the subject of these acquaintances – I had no notion your occasional air of distraction was connected with them – but I wish that you could share what burdens you."

Elizabeth could appreciate how irrational her behaviour might seem. Despite this, however, speak of them she could not. "It is all far too tedious to warrant our attention. Come, let us go down to supper."

Serena's gaze narrowed for a moment, but she seemed to comprehend that her friend desired a change of subject and bent instead to refasten the ties that held her Patten in place. Striving to push away all thought of Mr Darcy, Elizabeth opened her reticule to ensure she had all she required and came across her half-read letter.

"Oh! I had forgotten this!" she held it up. "I meant to read it in the carriage. It is from Papa."

Before Serena could respond, there was a knock upon the door and it opened to reveal Nicholas. "Shall we go down? I am famished!"

Serena walked over to him, taking the arm he offered. "Lizzy?"

"Hmm?" Elizabeth looked up and then smiled. "Forgive me. I am delaying you."

"No, indeed. Read your letter. We shall await you in the dining room."

"Do not tarry too long, though," added Nicholas as he led Serena out of the room. "I have a vast appetite this evening and cannot account for how much I may have depleted the inn's stores by the time you join us."

Elizabeth waved them both off, glad that her need for a few moments of solitude would give them likewise a short time alone together, albeit in a dining room full of other travellers. She walked over to the bed and perched on its edge, opening up the letter and beginning to read from where she had earlier been obliged to leave off. She had gone but a few lines, however, before she was on her feet, her eyes devouring every word. Having reached the signature at the end, she sank into the nearest chair, her mind a myriad of half-formed thoughts. Then, she turned the letter over and slowly began to read it once more, hardly able to credit what she saw.

Thomas Bennet stood at the window of his library and watched as the solitary horseman made his way slowly down the moonlit driveway, reflecting that, had it been a cloudy night, he might well have secured his house against visitors much earlier that evening.

He let the drapes fall into place and turned to survey his domain, his eye lighting upon that which had engrossed his attention before he had been disturbed once again by his wife to come and bid farewell to their dinner guest, and he walked over to pick up the letter he had been perusing earlier.

Mr Bennet grunted as he sat down at his desk. Mr Bingley, who had only returned to the neighbourhood these six and thirty hours, had spent what felt like most of them at Longbourn, and he could not help but wonder if he would prefer to swap houses. Mr Bennet reflected contentedly for a while upon the pleasure of being alone in the large, empty house but three miles distant, boasting a vast library that begged to be filled with reading matter – and that possessed no female inhabitants twittering and chattering like a gaggle of geese from dawn until dusk.

With a further sigh, he rubbed his chin thoughtfully. Mr Bingley, for all his absence these recent months, had certainly made up for any doubts he may have left behind him, having managed to ask his eldest daughter for her hand that very afternoon – though how he had contrived to find a moment alone with her, he could only surmise was down to the scheming of his wife – yet it had borne fruit. He had a daughter betrothed, and not only was she to wed a gentleman of means, and of good if somewhat malleable character, but she seemed happy with the situation too.

A rare smile graced Mr Bennet's face as he recalled Jane's expression of soft, beautiful peace during dinner that evening. The frequently stolen looks between her and her beau did not go unnoticed; he was confident of their being happy together, and as Bingley also had a fortune and the lease of a large property, both he and his wife were satisfied with the match.

Stirring in his seat, Mr Bennet returned his attention to the letter in his grip, one which had arrived by Jane's hand from Elizabeth. It was short and to the point, and he was well aware of its content without perusing it again, but seeing her handwriting was a comfort, for he missed her company sorely.

He did not begrudge his daughter the chance to enjoy a little adventure; his only concern was the selfish want of a companion who could converse sensibly with him. With a sigh, he dropped the letter onto the desk and got to his feet. Pouring himself a glass of port, he placed it on the mantel and picked up the poker, giving the fire a hefty stir and being rewarded for his efforts by a reviving of the flames.

Then, he settled back into his favourite leather armchair, the glass now nestled comfortably in his hand and closed his eyes. With the door shut against the noise of the house, he could finally reflect upon the most singular couple of days for some years, from the unexpected visit yesterday morning, to the arrest of Wickham, the return of Bingley and today that gentleman's application for his daughter's hand. He mused for a moment over what Elizabeth might make of the letter he had sent earlier, well aware that he had concealed some of the facts surrounding Wickham's detention out of delicacy. Opening his eyes, Mr Bennet shook his head ruefully before indulging in his drink.

If things of such diversity prevailed, he might well be obliged to put ink to paper again to his daughter, but not for the present. Jane was perfectly capable of passing on the news regarding her altered situation, and he would leave her pen to dwell upon it rather than his.

※

Elizabeth's distraction had been perceived over dinner. Nicholas and Serena were not used to their friend being inattentive or flustered when pushed into speaking. Unable to say what troubled her, Elizabeth had prevaricated, saying that her mind was at Longbourn – which was the truth –

the implication being that of missing her sister's company rather than a fascination with the thought of Mr Darcy and her father in deep discussion there.

She quickly excused herself once they had partaken, leaving Serena to Nicholas' care in the public sitting room, but instead of heading for the stairs, she made her way out into the courtyard, determined to walk off her discomposure of spirits, for she knew that sleep would evade her otherwise.

Barely paying her surroundings any mind, Elizabeth began to pace to and fro across the cobbles. The knowledge that Mr Darcy had taken the trouble to travel to Longbourn to speak to her father – that he should have been so thoughtful, so considerate – in order to protect her sisters, her family, the neighbourhood that he had disdained and had repaid him in like kind... it was almost too much to comprehend.

Further, her father's letter had implied that Mr Darcy had not returned to Town. Yet had the gentleman himself not stated quite clearly on Monday that he was fixed there for the foreseeable future? It did not take above a second for Elizabeth to deduce the probable cause of his change of plan – clearly, he wished to avoid any further likelihood of an encounter.

Disappointment that he had felt obliged to distance himself, dissatisfaction for no longer being in Town, that there would be no further opportunities to meet, brought her up sharp. What if she never laid eyes upon him again? It was more than possible – what if he chose to avoid Hertfordshire, even if Jane and Bingley came to an understanding? It would be perfectly reasonable, and even justifiable, with their past history and knowing what he now did of her family's close call with Wickham.

With a frustrated mutter, she turned on her heel and paced back across the courtyard. Reasonable it may be, yet why did acknowledging the likelihood of it hurt so very much? What answer did she seek, and what was it that had been happening between herself and Mr Darcy in recent days? That they had gradually become more at ease in one another's company, she could not deny. Yet what did it signify, other than that they had both moved on from the embarrassment and discomfort incumbent upon any party who had been through what they had? Exposure to the source of a wound surely procures one a modicum of immunity after a time.

The fact that her interest in the man had grown over the past week did not mean that he reciprocated. Indeed, why would he? He had previously declared the depth of *his* interest and had had it summarily thrown back at him. There was no progress, in theory, for him to make in that regard – indeed, it was far more likely that he would feel a retraction, the forward alteration being all hers.

Despite the sense of these reflections, no enlightenment came forth and, having covered the length of the courtyard and come up against a stone wall, Elizabeth turned around once more and retraced her steps, the same interminable thoughts tumbling around in her head.

⁂

"Lizzy is attempting to out-pace her demons." Nicholas inclined his head towards the window as he retrieved a newspaper from the side table and retook his seat by the fire. Serena got up and peered out into the inn's inner courtyard. Elizabeth could be seen intermittently as she walked, illuminated sporadically by torchlight as she passed in front of the stables.

Serena frowned, reminded of her conversation with Elizabeth earlier that day and her evasiveness over admitting what troubled her. Then, there had been the letter, and it was obvious that its content was what now caused Elizabeth such consternation and what had distracted her attention so severely during dinner. She turned away and walked over to resume her seat and, as she sat, Nicholas looked up from his newspaper.

"Do you know what ails her?"

Serena shook her head, relieved in part that she did not, for she preferred there to be no need for prevarication, and if Elizabeth had shared a confidence she would not have been at liberty to speak of it.

"I have no idea, though it seems likely it was that letter she stayed behind to read. Yet I cannot account for her being so disturbed by anything her father might report."

Nicholas shrugged and glanced at the long-case clock in the corner. "We had best retire, my love. We have a full and long day's travel ahead of us." He stood and held out his arm for her which she took gratefully before bidding the other occupants of the inn's sitting room a friendly goodnight, and Serena walked with him out into the hallway, glancing towards the door that led into the courtyard.

"Should we fetch Lizzy?"

Nicholas shook his head. "She will come in soon enough, and she looks as though she needs some privacy."

Unhappy at this, Serena nodded reluctantly and allowed Nicholas to lead her up the stairs, where they exchanged, by virtue of a shadowy corner of the landing, a warm and affectionate goodnight.

Elizabeth continued to prowl restlessly outside for a while, but the truth of the matter – that such speculation could not be answered – was eventually sufficient to rouse her, and she came to a halt under one of the torches that lit the courtyard before reaching into her pocket for her father's letter.

Not a keen correspondent, Mr Bennet had, on this occasion, deemed it both necessary and an obligation to extend his words over a second side of paper. Uncaring of reading once again of Wickham's detention, she wished to glean what she could of Mr Darcy's present whereabouts, and Elizabeth's eye travelled down the page to the paragraph she sought and read it once more:

Whither Mr Darcy tended upon his departure from Longbourn, I cannot say. Though he and his cousin arrived on my doorstep together, I quite distinctly observed the carriage bearing the former turn left out of the driveway onto the St Albans' road; the Colonel, now on horseback, headed in the opposite direction towards the London turnpike.

This departure of Mr Darcy's unsettled her deeply, and she remained confused over its purpose and mystified over whither he might have gone

Attempting to rid herself of the veil of sadness that such consciousness engendered, she glanced about. It grew late; she knew she must return to the inn, and suddenly she shivered as a chill breeze stole its way through the courtyard, bringing with it a few drops of rain. Such confused thoughts would hardly be conducive to a good night's rest, yet she realised she had little option but to return to her chamber.

Chapter Eleven

DARCY ENTERED HIS CHAMBER AS the clock struck eleven. He had passed a busy hour beforehand, considering the efficacy of acting upon the advertisement he had seen: a ship due to sail for Ireland out of Bristol docks within the week, but as the hour was so late and there was little he could do to investigate until the morrow, his thoughts returned instead to his cousin, Anne. She had given him much to consider. This recent awareness of how his behaviour had been a disservice to someone who could well use his influence caused him no little regret. The arrogance that Elizabeth had accused him of, his selfish disdain for the feelings of others, was deeper than either she or he had anticipated, for he had clearly extended it to those amongst his supposed inner circle.

Darcy walked over to the dresser and began to empty his pockets, staring at his own reflection as he did so. He looked weary. The last ten days had been a strain upon him, yet in some ways the final outcome – the devastation of Monday evening – had been what was required. He had begun to do what he had sworn he would not: he had started to believe there might be a chance for him and Elizabeth. He could only be thankful that those first tentative wisps of hope had not taken too firm a hold before all was dashed.

With a heavy sigh, Darcy dropped his money clip and hip flask onto the dresser and, conscious that Thornton awaited him in his dressing room, shrugged out of his coat and tossed it onto a nearby chair. He knew he carried an air of despondency, and something must be done to shed it before Georgiana's arrival. He must think, also, on how to redress the situation with his cousin; with a shudder, he recalled Anne's desire that he marry elsewhere. Was that his fate: to find a bride not solely to fulfil the need for an heir but also to free his cousin from her mother's oppression? If he were to fully forego his selfishness, perhaps it was.

Having made her way upstairs, Elizabeth pushed open the door to the chamber she shared with Serena and walked into the room. Her friend had settled by the remnants of the fire, a book in her hand, which she put aside to meet Elizabeth's gaze earnestly.

"Dear Lizzy! Please let me help you; tell me what ails you."

Elizabeth removed her shawl, throwing it onto a nearby chair and dropping the letter onto the bedside cabinet, unsurprised that Serena had perceived her distraction, yet she remained fearful of putting into words what caused such a disturbance of mind.

Reluctantly, she walked over to join her friend near the hearth. "I do not know what you would wish me to say, for I cannot guarantee that I can contribute anything of sense."

Serena gave a small smile, but then she reached out and took Elizabeth's hand.

"I – *we* – are concerned for you. I do not wish to pry or ask of its content, but it is blatant that something in your father's letter has caused you some disturbance of spirits." She waved a hand towards where the letter now rested.

"It would be foolish to attempt a denial. But it is impossible to explain the severity of my… distraction, for I little comprehend it myself."

"But something has deepened your discontent, Lizzy. I am no fool; your manner has changed dramatically since reading it."

Releasing a frustrated breath, Elizabeth turned and walked over to the dresser, but Serena got up and followed her, and they both stared into the looking glass for a moment. Then, Serena reached out and took the hand nearest to her and squeezed it, before saying tentatively to Elizabeth's reflection, "I know that I am not Jane, Lizzy, but I would not have you without a confidante in her absence."

Touched by Serena's affection, Elizabeth returned the squeeze of her hand and likewise addressed her through the mirror.

"It is not Jane's return to Longbourn that lowers my spirits, though your support is much appreciated." Elizabeth attempted a smile and then turned around to face her friend. "I find myself affected by something that Mr Darcy has done." At Serena's look of surprise, she sighed and turned away. "Not negatively; indeed, quite the contrary."

Serena frowned and followed her friend over to the bed where they both perched themselves on its edge. As succinctly as possible, Elizabeth related the history of Wickham's acquaintance with her family, of some of his dealings with the Darcys and of the happenings of recent days, from her revelations to Mr Darcy at the ball to Wickham's arrest not four and twenty hours ago.

"But why should his actions affect you so?"

Elizabeth chewed her lip for a moment. "Because it is above and beyond the call of duty. Even if he... if we..." she stopped abruptly and made a movement with her hand, unable to continue the thought. "I cannot believe that he would take such steps – that he would put himself out so to travel to Longbourn to speak with Papa, all in aid of protecting the family."

"He must be a very good man, Lizzy.

Elizabeth sighed. "Of that I have no doubt. Every encounter of late has shown me how far from the truth my original perception of the man was." She glanced quickly at Serena. "My opinion of him was once not so high. I cannot deny that he has his failings." A glimmer of a smile appeared but faded quickly. "But even the faults that I suspect were ingrained from his upbringing he seems determined to attempt to alter. And now this," she gestured at the letter where it lay. "His taking the trouble to visit Papa and reinforce my words – even in the aftermath of his blatant displeasure when I revealed the truth to him – it is incomprehensible. Why would he do such a thing when he holds our family in such low esteem?"

"He cannot, Lizzy, or he would not have acted so. Besides, why do you care so much? I have never seen you so discomposed."

Getting to her feet, Elizabeth began to pace to and fro. "After my disclosure to him on Monday of how my family had behaved, I came to the realisation that I could not bear for him to think ill of me; I was saddened that I no longer held his good opinion." She looked over at her friend as she turned on her heel. "He once told me that his approbation, once lost, is irreversible. Yet when we first met, it was all I sought – I took delight in courting his disapproval." She sat down heavily on a chair beside the bed.

Serena spoke softly. "You are in love with this Mr Darcy, I think."

"Impossible!" Elizabeth shook her head, but her heart lurched in her chest and with a sickening clarity, she knew it to be the truth. Her friend had expressed the very words that Elizabeth had been unable to find: she was indeed in love with him. It must have been coming on so gradually, she had not been aware of it happening, but enamoured of him she most decidedly was, just when all hope of his returning her affection was over.

Her face must have expressed her disquiet, for Serena leaned forward and took her hand. "Lizzy, are you well? You are dreadfully pale."

Elizabeth opened her mouth, but no words were forthcoming, and she closed it again, conscious of the ache in her throat. How could this have come to pass? How could she not have seen him for the man he was, that she might not have lost her opportunity to be with him? Had she been in love all along she could not have been more blind.

Moving closer, Serena patted her on the arm. "And he, Lizzy? What is his opinion of you? Do you know it?"

Her mind was instantly filled with all manner of memories from the past ten days: Mr Darcy's avowal of his admiration for her when he proposed, the pain of rejection upon his features as she refused him, being held in his close embrace when she fell, the conversations they had shared of late and the closing of his expression when she talked to him at the ball.

"Lizzy?"

Lowering her head to stare at her hands, Elizabeth absent-mindedly smoothed her fingers across the back of her hand; then, she returned her gaze to her friend.

"I do – or at least, I did. Now, I have no notion of what he thinks of me, nor am I ever likely to discover the truth of it."

"What did you know?"

"He – he did hold me in affection once, but sadly, I held him in very low esteem at the time."

"Oh my poor Lizzy." Serena leaned over and hugged her tightly, and Elizabeth felt tears well but shook them fiercely aside as her friend released her. "And you have been given no indication that his interest continues?"

Casting her mind back over her few days in Town, Elizabeth had to concede that he likely still harboured some feelings for her then. But now?

She shook her head and summoned a weak smile. "'Tis discovered too late, Serena. The moment for us has passed. Whatever admiration Mr Darcy held me in has long been quashed by recent events. Suffice it to say, he is well rid of me."

Unable to bear the thought of what she had lost, Elizabeth got to her feet, keen to seek the oblivion of sleep but doubtful she would be blessed with its comfort.

"Is there no likelihood of a continuance of the acquaintance?" Serena walked over to the nightstand and poured some water from the pitcher into the bowl before picking up a towel. "Though I am not fully conversant with the circumstances, I find it hard to believe that someone who had the good sense to once value you so highly would be prepared to give you up, dear Lizzy."

Letting out a humourless laugh, Elizabeth picked up her shift and began to prepare for bed.

"It was blatantly obvious from his manner on the last occasion I saw him that Mr Darcy could not quit my company soon enough. Further, Papa's letter confirmed that he has taken himself off; I can only suppose his intent is to ensure he is no longer subjected to my company. I think there is as much likelihood of him seeking me out as there is of Aunt Gardiner running off with the coal man."

Serena choked back a laugh but quickly sobered. "It pains me to see you thus, Lizzy. I would do anything to not see you so unhappy."

Elizabeth smiled somewhat forlornly. "I would not see me so sad either, if I had a choice. But it is all my own doing, Serena. I deserve little sympathy, though I will accept it willingly if it is on offer."

Walking over, Serena gave her a consoling hug before clambering in between the covers, and Elizabeth took her turn at the basin before coming to perch on the edge of the bed to plait her hair. It all made such perfect sense now that she understood her condition; all the interminable thoughts, the confusion over why she could not curtail her interest in Mr Darcy, the contrary desire to see him again and again… with a sigh, she leaned forward and blew out the candle before swinging her legs into the bed and lying down. Was this to be her fate, to love a man she had thought she hated?

She closed her eyes, willing herself not to think of him and what might have been, and eventually sheer exhaustion from their journey combined with her many sleepless nights of late led to her falling asleep, a solitary tear escaping as she did so and running down her cheek onto the pillow.

Chapter Twelve

AS THE CARRIAGE PULLED UP OUTSIDE Darcy's lodgings in Bath, Colonel Fitzwilliam detected a rise in his young cousin's spirits, despite the onset of some inclement weather during the latter part of their journey. Though Georgiana clearly felt deeply for her brother in his disappointment, more so now that she knew its full import, he could not help but believe that this change of scene would be of aid to them all.

They stepped down onto the wet pavement and Georgiana looked about quickly before he ushered her into the shelter of the house. The building was at the end of a row of similar imposing edifices on Brock Street and had the benefit of being adjacent to some fields of grass with views over the open country that filled the area immediately below the imposing Royal Crescent, and the Colonel nodded his head in approval as he turned to follow his cousin into the house.

Darcy greeted the travellers at the door to the first-floor drawing room, a light and airy space, with windows overlooking both the front aspect and also the long walled garden at the rear.

"You have a diligent man in your valet," the Colonel mused as he stood at one of the long windows and looked down into the street. "This is an excellent location to be secured at such short notice." He turned away from his contemplation of the view outside and observed both of his cousins who were seated on a couch near to the fireplace.

"It is almost the end of the Season. I think Thornton was spoilt for choice, but knew that we would appreciate the proximity to open spaces."

The Colonel grunted as he took a seat opposite his cousins. This self-imposed exile must be made to benefit them both, but Darcy in particular. He needed distraction and little opportunity to become withdrawn into himself. Thankfully, the fact that he had suggested having company so willingly hinted at his own desire to do likewise.

"And what of Aunt Catherine. You have seen her?"

"Indeed." A frown crossed Darcy's brow, but before the Colonel could question it, Georgiana spoke.

"Is there a problem, Brother?"

"No – no there is not. I paid a call of duty. She was much as we saw her last. They both travelled comfortably and are well situated in their usual lodgings."

"And shall we visit with them on the morrow?" Georgiana spoke quickly, and the Colonel studied her for a moment, though it was Darcy who expressed the thought that had come instantly to mind.

"Though we are obliged, you do not normally express a desire to visit your aunt."

Georgiana looked somewhat abashed for a moment; then, she met her brother's eye firmly. "It is Anne that I would wish to see. I think she enjoyed our time at the pianoforte the other day; I wish to discuss music with her."

Darcy narrowed his gaze as he studied his sister, and the Colonel observed him thoughtfully. Further discussion of Miss Elizabeth Bennet was futile, thus there was little danger in the meeting of the two cousins.

Then, Darcy nodded. "Very well. But it will have to be late morning for I have an appointment first thing at the booksellers in Stall Street." He turned to the Colonel. "A rare first edition. Would you care to accompany me? I believe they have a substantial selection of military titles that might interest you."

"Of course. We can return to collect you, Georgiana."

"Mrs Annesley is due to arrive early, and we may wish to go out. Would it not be better to all meet at Aunt Catherine's?"

The Colonel exchanged glances quickly with Darcy. This was a step forward for Georgiana and an indication of increased confidence. That she felt secure enough to arrive on a call, albeit upon relatives, with only her companion at her side was a good sign. It was therefore agreed that they would all meet at Great Pulteney Street by the hour of noon, and Georgiana then excused herself to go in search of her maid, that she might refresh herself from the journey.

No sooner had the door closed upon her, than Darcy turned to look at him, and knowing what it was he most wished to learn, the Colonel motioned that they walk over to the windows furthest from the door. For a moment, they both stared out into Brock Street. Though the rain had lessened, the pavements remained full wet and a stiff breeze continued to blow, thus no one could be seen out walking.

Throwing Darcy a quick glance, the Colonel flexed his sore right hand, still encased in a glove. "You may put your mind at rest. He is under lock and key and, last I heard from Whitehall, on his way to the Assizes in Hertford."

A heavy sigh emanated from his cousin. "It gives me little pleasure, though there is comfort in knowing the general populace is safe from him." Darcy frowned. "I trust there was little trouble in Meryton? I would not wish for there to be any scandal reflected upon the Bennets or their relations."

Shaking his head, the Colonel slowly eased the glove from his hand and waved the discoloured knuckles under his cousin's nose. "You may rest quite assured, Darce. All there was to observe was a fallen man being manhandled with little ceremony into the village lock up, and as Mr Bennet and I were able to secure the matter soon after the sun had risen, there were few witnesses to his ungainly arrival."

A look of concern crossed Darcy's face. "What the devil happened? And what of Bennet – all he was charged with was to forewarn his Brother Philips and keep watch on his daughters…"

The Colonel held up a hand. "Be not alarmed. I encountered the scoundrel quite by chance; there was a struggle, he was overcome. It pains me to own that Bennet struck the telling blow, but his presence eased my passage in getting Wickham locked up, so I can forego my pride in this instance."

"And your injuries?"

"The aforementioned blow to my pride was the severest. A few bruised knuckles – which I am, of course, endeavouring to keep concealed from Georgiana – and a sore head are easily mended."

Darcy shook his head. "You were fortunate. He would have killed you, given the opportunity."

The Colonel nodded. "Avoiding capture was essential to him; I think he would have done for me if he could, but his aim has not improved since he was younger."

"Was he not armed?"

Reflecting upon Wickham's activity when he came across him, the Colonel grunted. "He had been dallying with a milkmaid, and I think he was intent upon wielding a weapon of an entirely different nature, if you take my meaning."

A look of distaste crossed Darcy's face. "I am relieved that you are well, and I am thankful that he is under lock and key." He held his hand out and the Colonel shook it. "Thank you, Cousin. I am in your debt."

Fitzwilliam laughed. "On the contrary. It gave me immeasurable satisfaction to be so actively involved in his defeat! I assure you, it is I who thanks you for the opportunity!"

Darcy smiled faintly, and turned once more to stare out of the window, and the Colonel glanced over at the clock on the mantel.

"Come – let us talk no more of the scum. His future – what is left of it – is sealed by his own hand and deed. What say you to planning our stay in Bath, that Georgiana feels the benefit of the change of scene?"

"Of course. Though I beg of you, no visits to the Upper Rooms."

The Colonel stooped to pick up the Bath Chronicle from the table as they walked over to the chairs by the hearth and settled himself opposite his cousin.

"Honestly, Darce. With your aversion to dancing and Georgiana not yet out, do you think I would be such a simpleton as to suggest it?"

Darcy raised a brow. "I put nothing past you, Cousin."

"Wise man. Now – what had you in mind?" The Colonel tapped the paper that rested across his knees. "There will doubtless be plenty of amusements still to partake of, despite the lateness of the Season."

"I have a mind to take Georgiana out into the countryside. It is very pretty hereabouts, with ample fine walks to be had. What say you to a carriage ride on Saturday, should the weather bid fair?"

The Colonel turned his attention to the paper. "A good plan. We could make a day of it, if you wish. Tell me," he raised his eyes to meet Darcy's. "How long do you intend to tarry here? Had you given it any thought?"

Darcy nodded. "I am considering taking Georgiana on a trip further afield – perhaps Ireland."

The Colonel frowned. "Might I enquire why?"

Running a hand through his hair, Darcy sighed. "Bingley. His intention is to secure Miss Bennet. If I am in Town, few excuses will hold sway with him over not visiting in Hertfordshire or even attending his nuptials. A valid absence will save me the pain of offending his good nature."

"Ah. I see."

"Precisely. I appreciate that once the connection with the Bennets is secured, I cannot guarantee that I will never cross paths with... any of the family again; yet, at this particular time..."

His thoughts had clearly meandered down another path, and the Colonel was fairly certain he could discern where they had gone – to the implications of Elizabeth's engagement to Harington, and how soon that marriage might take place.

"But you cannot constantly be on the move, Darce."

Darcy met the Colonel's eye. "No – no, I understand that. But just now – in the interim – I would rather be active, doing something, going somewhere. You do comprehend?"

The Colonel nodded. "Most indubitably. I will support you in whatever decision you come to, though I will not always be at liberty to accompany you."

"Thank you. I have set Thornton the task of investigating a sailing that I saw in the paper. It departs for Dublin on Thursday next, and I thought that we might pass the interim here."

"It sounds a fair plan, Cousin. Let us see what intelligence he finds."

With that, they changed the subject, and turning their attention to the Chronicle, soon identified several suitable diversions, including a recital in St Swithens at Walcot and a play at the newly restored Theatre Royal, either of which would provide entertainment and distraction enough. A concert in Sydney Gardens on Sunday, weather permitting, was also considered a possibility, and putting the paper aside, the Colonel settled into his chair and listened as his cousin outlined his intentions with regard to including Anne – and if need be, their aunt – in some of their excursions during their residence in the city.

Elizabeth had passed a disturbed night at the coaching inn. Her acceptance of her condition as she owned what it was she had been fighting these past few days had drawn her spirits low. Yet she knew she must endeavour to overcome her depression of mood. It was sufficient that Serena comprehended the situation, and without Jane to confide in she had to own that her friend's ear would be invaluable over the coming days.

They had risen to a dull morning, and as their carriage made its way further westwards, the heavy clouds had broken and a downpour had ensued.

Nicholas had sensibly opted to travel inside with the ladies and thus was adequate distraction at first for Elizabeth's wayward attention. She was conscious of Serena's concerned gaze, but beyond a gentle hug from her that morning, she had not alluded again to their conversation of the night before, and Elizabeth's throat had remained too tight for words. Now, as the steady stream of water spilled down the windows, obscuring all from view, she found the weariness borne of a disturbed night overcome her; soon her eyes closed to the rhythmic sensation of the carriage and she slept.

The two friends studied the sleeping Elizabeth for a few moments before Nicholas turned to whisper to Serena.

"Is all well? Did she reveal what ailed her last evening?"

Serena bit her lip and shook her head.

"I am not at liberty to talk of it." She spoke softly, keeping an eye upon Elizabeth's slumbering form. "She is troubled; yet, it is not something that any of us can resolve for her."

Nicholas frowned. "I do not like to think of Lizzy suffering. Has someone upset her? What was in that letter?"

With a sigh, Serena turned to face him, and he took her hand in his.

"It merely brought word from her father." She glanced over at Elizabeth once more. "She will be well. You know Lizzy; she will not countenance being troubled for long."

Nicholas grunted at this, but let the matter drop, turning the subject instead to their imminent arrival in Somerset and how to break their news to his parents, and Serena, leaning her head upon his shoulder, closed her own eyes, relishing the opportunity to be so close to him, and listened to him talking. She could only hope that she spoke the truth and that her dear friend would be able to soon overcome her disappointment. She had been shocked to see how affected she was; Elizabeth had always been so resilient, the one everyone turned to in times of strain. Who would be strong enough to aid her in her own hour of need?

Chapter Thirteen

THE COLONEL HAVING REPAIRED TO his chamber to wash and change from his travel-worn clothes and Georgiana still doing likewise, Darcy took himself up to his own room to secure his writing case. He had yet to apprise Bingley of his direction and had determined that it would be an opportune moment to rectify the matter.

He was forestalled, however, upon entering, by the sight of his valet brushing down a dark blue coat which rested on a stand in the corner of the room.

Having heard the door open, Thornton turned around, the brush held aloft and, discerning his master's expression, he stood up straighter. "Is there a problem, Sir?"

Darcy walked over to stand beside him, eyeing the garment intently; then, he shook his head.

"No – no, not at all. For a moment, I thought…"

His valet frowned and turned to study the coat. Then, he said, "This is not the one that was damaged in Kent, Sir."

"Of course. I see that now." A question hovered on his lips, and with a sigh he gave into the temptation. "What has happened to it – that coat?"

Thornton hesitated. "Err – it remains in Town, Sir. I did not see the need to bring it, as you no longer wished to retain its use."

Darcy nodded. "Quite. And – and its condition?"

"Almost as new, Sir. They were able to replace the silk lining and the wool was of sufficient quality to survive the soaking it received. I had yet to pass it on, as you requested."

For a moment, Darcy said nothing. He knew the futility of what he wished to do; yet, he could do nothing but succumb to it. With a sigh, he turned towards the travelling case that carried his personal effects, saying over his shoulder as if it mattered little, "Do not concern yourself, Thornton. If the coat is as restored as you say, I may retract. I will examine it upon my return to Town and perchance we shall return it to the closet instead."

Letting out a breath of relief at this, though uncertain why the coat had now taken on such significance that he wished to retain it, Darcy flipped the catches on the case and raised the lid, reaching for his writing case, but as he did so, his eye caught the centre compartment.

Slowly, he reached for the ring of keys that Thornton had laid beside the case and placing one in the centre lock, released the drawer. The compartment was empty. Feeling a tightness across his chest, Darcy cursed under his breath at his own frailty, drawing once more the attention of his devoted servant.

"Sir?"

Conscious that Thornton had come to his side, Darcy quickly locked the drawer again, dropping the keys onto the dresser.

"It is safely restored to the safe in Mount Street, Sir. There is no need for alarm."

Darcy nodded, but unwilling to remain under the kindly but speculative look of his old servant, he grabbed his writing case and hurriedly left the room.

As the day waned, so did the inclement weather, and as the Harington carriage made its way through Sherborne and out onto the Yeovil turnpike, the rain ceased and the cloud began to break up.

Having fallen asleep again after their final stop to water the horses, Elizabeth woke suddenly and took a moment to realise her surroundings, but then quickly cast an anxious glance at her travelling companions. She was relieved to see that they both slumbered likewise, unaware that they had both deliberately assumed such a position the moment they had detected her rousing from her sleep.

Thankful to have a moment to gather her thoughts, Elizabeth stared out of the window. The clouds were being hurried on their way by a strong breeze and the sun even now appeared between them, casting a refreshing glow over the countryside. She shook aside the remnants of her heavy sleep, pleased to have awoken, that she could shed the recurring images of her angry confrontation with Mr Darcy in Kent, no doubt influenced by the inclement weather.

Seeing the landscape become so familiar, confirmed by the next milestone they passed which indicated they were but a mile from the village of East Coker, Elizabeth felt her spirits lift slightly in anticipation of their arrival, and as the carriage turned off the main turnpike onto Sutton Hill, she looked back over at Nicholas and Serena, surprised to find them both now wide awake.

"We have made good time," Nicholas returned his watch to his waistcoat. "Mama will be delighted to see that I do not return alone." He smiled at Serena. "Do you have any objection to my speaking to Papa as soon as we arrive?"

Serena's cheeks coloured, but she shook her head without hesitation, and Elizabeth looked away as she saw the trust upon her friend's face, noting that they were holding hands under cover of Nicholas's folded great coat between them. She was more than pleased for them both, but their blatant happiness only served to reinforce the loss of Mr Darcy's regard.

Tuning out the murmur of voices, she saw that they had reached Sutton Coker, and as they turned into the long, tree-lined avenue that led to the East Front, she sank back into her seat, taking herself to task. She was a long way from London now, and distant from the man himself, wherever he had gone. She would focus on her friends, be happy for them, and relish the opportunity to become reacquainted with the beautiful Somerset countryside.

Within minutes, they had drawn up before the entrance and were being helped down by a footman. They had barely turned to survey the house, however, before Mrs Harington came hurrying out of the front door, and Elizabeth watched in amusement as she almost threw herself at Serena, hugging her so tightly she was surprised her friend did not squeak.

"Dear Lizzy! Come here!" Upon releasing Serena, Mrs Harington swept Elizabeth into a similar, if somewhat less intense embrace, then stood back to observe them both. "What an unexpected pleasure! How is it that you are here? Come, you will be tired. Let us take some refreshment and you shall tell me all about it."

They entered the vast wood-panelled hall with its ornate plasterwork ceiling, and divesting themselves of their outdoor things into the hands of a waiting servant, Elizabeth smiled as she watched Mrs Harington fussing over Serena, helping her to remove her Patten. Nicholas quickly excused himself, saying that he would seek out his father, and Mrs Harington nodded, unseeing of the look exchanged between her son and the young lady before her.

"There," she exclaimed, sitting back upon her heels and taking Serena's hands in hers. "My dear, you cannot be surprised to hear me say how delighted I am at your return, your having left us so precipitously last month."

Serena looked a little conscious at this allusion to her earlier flight, but allowed herself to be hugged once more before Mrs Harington got to her feet and ushered them both out of the hallway and down a long corridor, its tall latticed windows filled with the late afternoon light, before leading them into the familiar drawing room of Sutton Coker.

It was a beautiful space, very much lived in and filled with warmth. They had barely crossed the threshold, however, before Mrs Harington turned to Elizabeth and gave her an affectionate smile.

"There now. Come, Lizzy, sit down and tell me how you are. I do not think I have seen you these two years at least! You are quite the young lady now. My dear friend never fails to lay praise upon you in her letters, and I can see for myself that she does not exaggerate. You have grown quite beautiful."

Elizabeth blushed as she seated herself next to Serena on a comfortable sofa, thanking the lady for her compliment, but denying it.

"I think that you and my aunt are being extremely kind, Mrs Harington. I pale in comparison to Jane, who is a true beauty."

Serena made as if to protest, but she was over-ridden by Mrs Harington, who walked over to pull the bell for a servant, remarking over her shoulder as she did so, "Jane was born such, and I can only imagine how lovely she must be now."

Returning to take a seat opposite them, she smiled. "And much as I would wish to promote my dear friend's talent, I do not set too much store by her collection of likenesses!" The girls laughed at this. "But Lizzy, do not disparage your own appearance by comparing it to Jane's. You may not have the colouring of a traditional English rose as your sister does, but there is great beauty in your eyes and you have a light and pleasing figure. Tell me – you must have many suitors! I have lacked female company so much raising three sons – you must indulge me," she leaned forward and patted Serena's knee before turning back to Elizabeth. "*Both* of you! I insist on hearing all the matters of your hearts whilst you sojourn with us that I may feel as though I have daughters of my own!"

Elizabeth smiled weakly, exchanging a quick look with her friend. There was so much she had to conceal, and with relief she saw the door open and the tea urn being wheeled in on a trolley, an adequate distraction for the moment from the intimacy of a conversation she was ill-equipped to withstand.

∼❦∽

The announcement of Nicholas and Serena's engagement had gone down much as Elizabeth had anticipated. Mr Harington, who had known of the challenge Nicholas faced following his earlier visit, had been both welcoming of the news and openly supportive of his son's choice; Mrs Harington's happiness had been beyond words at first. Nevertheless, she had soon made her delight in the news apparent, her only regret being that James and Patrick were away from home at present and thus unable to share in their joy, both having taken themselves off to enjoy the remainder of the Season in Bath. This aside, however, once the initial effusions of pleasure had been expressed, the ladies were left to their own devices over a tray of tea and cakes whilst the gentlemen repaired to the study to discuss the settlements that might be put before Mr Seavington.

Mrs Harington had then been true to her word from earlier, and no little amount of talk about suitors, real or imagined, would quiet her. Though she named no names, Elizabeth had consented to relate the tale of her unwanted offer of marriage from her cousin Collins, causing much merriment in her audience as she recounted the incident. Beyond that she refused to be drawn, and as Mrs Harington was understandably more interested in Serena's news and how the engagement had come about, Elizabeth did not have to deflect her enquiries for too long.

"Nicholas is typically reticent on the details that a mother wishes to hear. *'We are engaged, Mama. We are both very happy. What else is there to say?'* is the whole of it from him! Boys!"

Serena herself made no mention of Nicholas's first proposal at Sutton Coker at Easter. She merely spoke of their coming to an understanding in London, and gave out as much as she felt comfortable sharing. It was clear that her natural reticence combined with her genuine love for the woman seated opposite vied with each other in determining what she could or should reveal. However, as it was evidently much more than Mrs Harington had managed to extort from her son on the subject, she was content for the moment.

"You know that you have long been as a daughter to me, and now that you are to be that in law, I feel truly blessed."

A wash of colour stole across Serena's cheeks, and she bit her lip. "You do me great honour, Aunt Alicia. I hope that I will not let everyone down."

"Let us down? Good heavens, girl, why on earth should you think that?" Mrs Harington got to her feet with the grace and ease of a woman half her age and took a seat on the other side of Serena to Elizabeth, taking hold of her hands.

"Listen to me, my dear. I desire nothing more in life than to see my children happy – you have made Nicholas so by agreeing to be wed. There-" she paused and reached for a small pocket handkerchief and patted Serena's cheek as a stray tear slid down it. "Do not distress yourself so. You are the perfect wife for him; you will both be very happy at Crossways Court."

"Forgive me." Serena straightened in her seat, glancing quickly at Elizabeth before looking back at Mrs Harington, who still held her hand in hers. "I promise that I shall endeavour henceforth to be accepting of my good fortune, to make Nicholas proud of me." She paused as Mrs Harington leaned forward and gave her a hug. "Though you must excuse me if I occasionally feel a little daunted by what is in store for me. Crossways is such a large property."

"I will support you and guide you for as long as you have need, my dear." Mrs Harington got to her feet. "Now – I shall leave you both to entertain yourselves for a while. I must send word to James and Patrick this instant. It is only right that they share in their brother's good news." She turned towards the door, saying over her shoulder, "I have had a notion, and I wish to put it into play, but first I must speak with my husband."

Serena's face was troubled. "I do not want a fuss – Papa, he has yet to give formal consent."

"My dear girl, I am sure you doubt his blessing as much as I do. He and your Mama will be delighted for you. But though I agree we cannot make any formal announcements, we can celebrate within the family, can we not?"

Throwing Elizabeth a beseeching look, Serena nodded reluctantly, and Mrs Harington bade them take some amusement from the pianoforte or the periodicals on the table before making her escape.

Determined to keep her thoughts occupied, Elizabeth quickly took up a position at the instrument, selecting a piece of music that was beyond her capability so that she was obliged to concentrate fiercely. Serena had taken up a book from the nearby selection on a side table, and they continued thus together for a half hour, only to be interrupted as Mrs Harington came sweeping back into the room, a wide smile on her pleasant features.

"There, my dears! 'Tis all arranged."

Sitting back on her stool, Elizabeth rested her hands in her lap, smiling. Mrs Harington's enthusiasm was infectious, and glancing at Serena, she was pleased to note that she strove to hide her trepidation and affect some interest in whatever it was Mrs Harington had agreed with her husband.

"What is, Aunt? What is happening?"

Resuming her earlier seat beside Serena, Mrs Harington took her hand and looked over at Elizabeth, beckoning her to join them, which she did with alacrity.

"An *Express* has been despatched forthwith to James and Patrick in Bath. Though we are unable to share the occasion with your parents as yet, my dear, both my husband and I feel a celebratory family evening within the privacy of our own walls will answer both my wish for an engagement dinner and the need for circumspection in the absence of formal consent."

Elizabeth smiled. The addition of further company could only aid her in her desire to keep herself occupied, and she was pleased to see Serena giving a genuine smile to the lady at her side.

"Do you anticipate that they will return directly, Aunt? 'Tis fortunate that it is but a short journey."

"Oh no, my dears!" Mrs Harington's smile widened even further as she looked from one to the other of the young ladies before her, and Elizabeth could not help but laugh at her palpable excitement. "The letter does not summon them home! It announces our imminent arrival!"

Serena threw Elizabeth a quick look, clearly startled by this pronouncement, but she said nothing, and taking the silence as a need for clarification, Mrs Harington clapped her hands together in apparent joy.

"In the morning, we are for Bath!"

Chapter Fourteen

THURSDAY EVENING HAD PASSED pleasantly for those in residence at Sutton Coker, and the sun rose into a pale blue sky the following morning, its warmth soon dispersing the wisps of mist that clung to the fields and lanes around the estate. After partaking of an early breakfast, Elizabeth, Serena and Mrs Harington had been installed into one of the carriages and, with a flurry of goodbyes, were seen on their way to Bath.

Serena had, on first comprehending the detail of the scheme, expressed the wish that they remain at Sutton Coker until Saturday, as that was when both Mr Harington and Nicholas would be free to join them, but Mrs Harington had persuaded her to enjoy four and twenty hours of purely female company, that the ladies might indulge themselves as was their wont without either interruption or complaint from the men of the family and, seeing the sense of this and accepting that it was but a short separation, she had in the end agreed quite happily to the plan.

Thus it was that the three ladies travelled together; yet, they were barely five miles distant from Sutton Coker before Mrs Harington was lulled into a slumber by the carriage's steady gait, and not long after, Serena succumbed likewise.

Elizabeth studied her friend affectionately for a moment. Serena had spent many hours on the road in the past seven days, and her fatigue was understandable, but she could not help but appreciate the time it afforded her to gather her own thoughts.

Disinclined towards low spirits by nature, Elizabeth felt certain she would rally from the oppression of her current state of mind. There was, however, a part of her that almost relished in her present pain; in some small way, it made her feel more in accord with Mr Darcy and what he must have suffered of late.

Such had been her reflections as the carriage made its way north through Shepton Mallet and Radstock, yet before long the hedgerows and fields were replaced by farmsteads and small holdings, and Elizabeth felt some relief in discerning that they were soon approaching Bath, where extended company, variety and distraction would no doubt suffice to ease her way through a difficult few days. With good fortune, by the time they returned to Somerset on Monday, she would have herself under better regulation and would be able to enjoy a few more days with her friends before petitioning for a return to Longbourn and the solace of family ritual and her dear sister's companionship.

Restless, and wishing to dispel the sense of sadness that would persist in lingering, Elizabeth moved to the edge of her seat to peer out of the window as they approached the descent towards the river that flowed around the city. In general, an appreciation for the countryside would have far outweighed any interest in architecture and townscapes, but her eyes were keen to capture anything that might provide distraction.

"Where are we?"

Serena, who sat diagonally across from her friend and next to Mrs Harington, had awoken and peered out of the window to her left.

"Nearing our destination. I can see the bridge just ahead." Elizabeth spoke softly.

Serena glanced at the lady slumbering by her side before throwing an apologetic look at Elizabeth.

"Forgive me, Lizzy. I did not mean to leave you alone with only your thoughts for company."

Elizabeth shook her head. "Do not concern yourself. I was adequately diverted by the passing countryside – it is but a short journey, after all."

Conscious that Serena studied her thoughtfully, clearly not convinced of the veracity of this statement, she turned to look out of the window once more, refusing to permit any further indulgence in melancholy. The sooner they were installed in the Harington residence and able to go out into the city and seek diversion the better.

❧

Friday morning had passed uneventfully for Georgiana Darcy, her brother and cousin having set off for their prearranged appointment with the bookseller in the lower part of the town soon after breakfast. Thus it was that once Mrs Annesley had safely arrived and taken a moment to refresh herself, Georgiana was keen to go out, and she had made haste to repair to her chamber to collect her outdoor garments.

Saddened though she had been over the cause of their departure from Town, she found she could not miss it or repine – her only regret was the loss of her burgeoning acquaintance with Elizabeth Bennet, and likewise her sorrow on behalf of her brother. How he bore his recent disappointments, she knew not. On the surface, he appeared to be in reasonable spirits, but he was a master at concealing his emotions and even her more recent study of him had not taught her how to read the inscrutability that had settled upon his features of late.

With a sigh, Georgiana fastened the ribbons of her bonnet, picked up her gloves and, wrinkling her nose at her appearance in the mirror, she made her way out onto the landing and down the stairs to the hallway.

"There you are, Miss Georgiana. Come now, let us take some air and refresh your knowledge of Bath." Mrs Annesley greeted her kindly, and shaking off her concerns for a moment, Georgiana smiled warmly at her companion before preceding her out of the open door.

The inclement weather of the previous afternoon had passed over, and a fine day was evident. Georgiana inhaled deeply with pleasure as she paused on the pavement, glancing to her left to look out over the expanse of green that stretched from the end of Brock Street to Marlborough Buildings, forming a swathe of open land in front of the elegant sweep of the Royal Crescent. The morning sun bathed the stonework in a warm glow, and she could feel her spirits rise in anticipation of a pleasant stay.

"Shall we stroll across the fields?" Mrs Annesley waved a gloved hand in the direction of her charge's gaze.

"No," Georgiana shook her head decisively and turned her back upon the temptation of greenery. "Let us walk down into town, Mrs Annesley. I would very much like to explore the shops."

They set off along Brock Street, pausing as they reached The Circus to admire the uniformity and grace of the smart houses that comprised its three sections, before making their way downhill and turning along George Street, where they paused once more to enjoy the vista down Milsom Street as it sloped towards the distant river, beyond which rose the steep, wooded rise of Beechen Cliff.

It took a while to cross the busy thoroughfare, but soon the two ladies were safely on the other side and made their way down the wide pavement, turning into Union Street to visit a well-known haberdashery and thus begin their purchases.

As they emerged into the sunlight from a shop near the abbey some time later, Mrs Annesley said quietly, "Look, Miss Georgiana. I do believe that is your cousin."

Turning around, Georgiana, who had instinctively expected to see the Colonel coming towards them, took a moment to recognise the slight figure of her cousin Anne as she made her way down the steps from the Pump Room, shadowed by Mrs Jenkinson. Waving a dismissive hand at the servant holding open the door of a sedan chair, Anne began to walk hurriedly in their direction. So intent did she appear upon some steady purpose, they were almost level with Georgiana and Mrs Annesley when Anne happened to raise her eyes and realise who was before her.

"Georgiana!" she exclaimed, but though it was clear she was pleased to have encountered her cousin, her voice was rather breathless. She swayed slightly as she came to a halt, and Mrs Jenkinson stepped forward quickly to support her elbow.

"Miss Anne," she chided gently, "You must not exert yourself so. You should take a chair – let me summon one."

Anne rolled her eyes at her companion.

"Here, Cousin. Walk with me." Looping her arm through Georgiana's, Anne turned them back towards whence she had come, saying over her shoulder, "Come, Jenkinson."

Anne did not speak as she led the small party across the cobbles and up the steps to the Pump Room, pausing whilst the footman swung the door aside, whereupon she preceded her companions into the cool interior.

At this hour of the day, the place was pleasantly full but not over-crowded. The fair weather meant that perambulations could be successfully completed out of doors and the early visitors to take the waters had long returned to their lodgings. Though there was little seating, the ladies found themselves a place along the far side of the room, near the fountain spouting forth the famed spa water. Anne sank onto a bench and pulled Georgiana down beside her, and the latter, conscious that Mrs Annesley, who stood to one side with Anne's companion, eyed her charge thoughtfully, felt obliged to open the conversation.

"I trust you received my card yesterday, Anne? I was rather weary from the journey after my arrival, or I would surely have called upon you and Aunt Catherine. Indeed, we are due to meet Fitzwilliam and Richard in Great Pulteney Street soon as it is."

"It is of little consequence; such trifling formalities are of no interest to me." Anne's breathing had returned to normal yet her complexion, always somewhat sallow, had retained some of the colour brought about by her exertions. "Darcy had apprised us of your joining him, and I must own that I was on my way to pay a call in Brock Street when we happened across you."

"You were to walk all the way? 'Tis a steep incline up Gay Street."

Anne tutted. "I am not of strong constitution, I will grant you, but I am no invalid. I am perfectly capable of walking, even if it does rob me of my breath at times." She frowned. "Perchance, should I make the habit more frequent, it would be less of a trial, but so it is."

Georgiana swallowed uncomfortably, worried that she had somehow offended her much older cousin by implying criticism, but Anne, who seemed to repent the bluntness of her reply, patted her cousin on her hand and half smiled.

"I have been taking the waters – for my health, of course." She leaned a little closer to Georgiana. "Do not tell my mother, but we sit for a while. I take much enjoyment from watching the people." She paused and threw a sharp glance at Mrs Jenkinson, who looked harassed and shook her head at her charge as if to stall her words.

With a disdainful raising of one brow, which forced Georgiana to quickly put a hand to her mouth in an attempt to hide her smile, so like her mother was she at that moment, Anne returned her attention to her cousin.

Leaning forward again, she glanced quickly about, then said quietly, "We peruse the entries in the arrivals book every time we come! It is such fun! Since our last visit we even found that announcing Darcy's arrival, and yours!"

Georgiana blinked in astonishment, and she looked quickly at Mrs Annesley before returning her gaze to her cousin.

"But what if it was noted, what you were doing? It is not fitting for someone of your status."

Anne made a noise somewhat reminiscent of the Colonel's familiar snort. "What if it was? The book is there for people's perusal."

"But Richard said that it is frequently those who do not have the standing to be announced in the book who study it – not those of the society whose names are listed."

Anne's dark eyes flashed. "Well, if I am in the wrong, so be it, for on this occasion I have realised a certain benefit that I believe far outweighs any error on my part. Imagine, Cousin, what I discerned from bending the rules of society this morning?"

"I confess I have no idea."

"Then come."

Getting to her feet, Anne pulled Georgiana up behind her.

"Save my seat, Jenkinson." Anne pointed to her recently vacated place and Mrs Jenkinson, head bowed, scurried to do her mistress's bidding. Georgiana sent Mrs Annesley an apologetic look as the latter stepped forward to sit next to the hapless companion of her cousin.

Before she could regret further the way Anne spoke to Mrs Jenkinson, Georgiana found herself being dragged to the far end of the room where the book lay upon its stand, open to the current day's date. There was a servant in full livery making an entry, and they waited for him to finish his task and depart before Anne stepped forward to take his place. Georgiana, feeling dreadfully conspicuous, cast a glance over her shoulder to see if anyone would remark their behaviour, but was relieved to see that no one seemed to pay them any mind. Feeling rather guilty, she moved forward to join her cousin. It was but eleven in the morning, and there were only a couple of entries listed on the current page yet Georgiana, casting her eyes swiftly over the lettering, could see nothing of interest.

"What are we seeking?" she whispered anxiously to her cousin. "What did you see?"

Anne let out a small laugh. "I shall show you. It is news indeed."

With a quick movement, she flipped back a page and placed her closed fan across the bottom of it as a reading mark, where she then pointed to the entry immediately above it, and Georgiana read the words written there:

Mrs Alicia Harington of Sutton Coker returns to her house in Marlborough Buildings on Friday.

Georgiana frowned. "Harington? I have recently become acquainted with a *Mr* Harington. Is she a relative?"

"Perhaps she is. But no matter – that is not what caught my eye. See." Anne moved the fan down the page to reveal a further entry on the line below, the last of the previous day.

Mrs Harington is to be accompanied by Miss Serena Seavington of Lambton, Derbys. and Miss Elizabeth Bennet of Longbourn, Herts.

Chapter Fifteen

GEORGIANA LET OUT A SMALL GASP. Then she looked quickly at her cousin, her eyes wide with confusion. "It cannot be... not here, not now!"

Anne nodded and a small smile graced her pale face. "Indeed. Mrs Harington and her guests seem due to arrive here in Bath this very day. I am not familiar with this other lady, though. Are you?"

"No, I am not. But – oh, Anne, how wonderful. My only regret in removing from Town had been the loss of Miss Elizabeth Bennet's society. Now I am able to... oh!"

Biting her lip, conscious of a warmth in her cheeks, Georgiana looked down at the book once more, censuring herself for her rash words. How could she be so foolish as to think that a continued acquaintance would be conceivable? Fitzwilliam, in his pain, could not be expected to suffer, that she might build upon the friendship so recently begun.

Conscious of Anne tugging at her arm, Georgiana raised her eyes to meet those of her cousin. Taking in the narrowed gaze and thoughtful expression, Georgiana suspected that Anne recalled her suspicions, outlined so blatantly in her recent letter.

She said nothing, however, merely turning on her heel and setting off back across the room to where their two companions awaited them, and perforce Georgiana went with her. No sooner were they spotted, their seats were once more vacant as the ladies stood to accommodate them and, conscious as she was of the truth of her cousin's surmising now, Georgiana was anxious that Anne be distracted from saying anything in front of others that might betray that partiality.

"What is it, my dear?" Mrs Annesley eyed her with concern.

Thinking quickly, and in need of further private discourse with her cousin, Georgiana smiled weakly at her companion.

"Pray excuse me, Mrs Annesley." She hesitated, hating to be duplicitous. "Would you be so good as to fetch me some water? Perhaps Mrs Jenkinson would be so kind as to pay my cousin the same service? Not spa water!"

The latter remained where she was, blinking and looking bemused, but Mrs Annesley, who had far more wits about her, smiled and turned away. "Come, Mrs Jenkinson," she urged, guiding that lady away. "Let us see if we can procure some fresh water for the young ladies."

"Nicely manoeuvred, Cousin," said Anne dryly. "You show a good sense of discretion in one so young!"

Georgiana did not pause to acknowledge the compliment but spoke hurriedly.

"Anne, this is a disaster. What shall I do? Fitzwilliam – he cannot – he must not – oh, I do not know what to *do*!"

"Calm yourself, Georgiana! One moment you are affecting composure, then you turn into a quivering puddle!"

"But you do not understand. Fitzwilliam – when he learns of Miss Elizabeth Bennet's being in Bath…"

Anne's gaze narrowed, and she peered intently at her cousin.

"I spoke with him yesterday. As you know from my letter, I have had my suspicions over your brother and his interest or otherwise in the lady." She paused and threw a quick glance in the direction of their companions. "They seemed in accord with each other well enough last Saturday, yet he informed me that there was no hope for him in that quarter and would not give his reason for such an outlandish supposition." She threw her cousin a sharp glance. "Is this why you are anxious that he does not see her?"

Georgiana fretted for a moment. She was aware of Mrs Annesley across the room watching her, relieved to see that her guard appeared to be more about allowing the two cousins time to talk rather than a desire to come and interrupt them prematurely. How much could she say to her cousin? She could not tell Anne about her brother's failed proposal, nor was she at liberty to speak of the lady's recent engagement. It was essential, however, she impress upon her cousin the need for Fitzwilliam to not come across her if at all possible.

"He has suffered some disappointment over the lady, it is true, Anne. Their re-acquaintance in Town was but a coincidence. I believe his coming to Bath was an attempt to remove any and *all* chance of encounter during the remainder of her stay. Now that she is to arrive here, what can be done?"

With a sigh, Georgiana stared ahead, unseeing of the elegantly dressed people promenading before her. What *was* to be done? Bath was so much smaller than London, and yet even there they had been thrown into each other's company. How could they not meet?

Anne was silent too for a moment. Then, she said, "I do not profess to comprehend what the impediment is, and I am not blind to the implication of some concealment in the matter. I cannot conceive why he must avoid her when he seemed quite content in his attentions to her but days ago in his own home." She stared at her cousin, and Georgiana sent her a beseeching look. "But I see that you are not going to enlighten me either." She sighed. "So be it. Thus, it would seem that it is essential he be told without delay; then he can make his own decision. There is nothing to prevent him returning immediately to Town if that is his desire."

Georgiana nodded, relieved that Anne had not pressed her for further explanation.

"Then I will tell him as soon as we are home, though I must find a way to break it to him gently. Enlisting Richard's help will be futile. He has all the subtlety of a wayward cannon ball."

Anne laughed and reluctantly Georgiana joined in. Her amusement was short-lived however. Her concern for her brother over-rode all, and conscious that their spurt of amusement had drawn their two companions back to their side, they determined to make their way to Great Pulteney Street directly.

Their appointment with the bookseller concluded, Darcy and the Colonel had begun to walk towards their aunt's lodgings. Their stroll along Stall Street was halted, however, by the congestion often to be found at the turning circle near the baths. Two of the principal coaching inns, the White Hart and the Bear, were located nearby, and a confusion of carriages, carts and horses was a daily occurrence.

Restrained as they were on the pavement for a few moments as a tangle of conveyances rattled to and fro, and a confrontation developed between the recently arrived Post and a cart carrying sacks of coal, a large and elegant carriage drew to a halt nearby, the coachman waiting for the obstruction to clear before continuing its journey towards the upper levels of the city.

Darcy idly studied the livery of the servants and then the coat of arms upon the carriage door as they waited, his cousin chuckling away at some of the antics taking place in the jumble of conveyances ahead. Something caught his eye, however, and glancing up he found himself meeting the gaze of a young woman who had been peering through the window, no doubt in an attempt to see what delayed them.

Looking away, he failed to see that same lady suddenly turn her head in response to someone else within the conveyance, and soon after the street cleared and the traffic began to move along. Darcy and the Colonel made their way under the colonnade and walking across the abbey forecourt, both oblivious to the elegant carriage as it lumbered on its way, and heedless of the two pairs of eyes that followed them, one with curiosity, the other with despair.

⤜✿⤛

Thankful that Mrs Harington continued in her repose, Elizabeth put a hand to her face, conscious of the heat upon her cheeks.

"He is a very handsome man, Lizzy. How came you not to mention his fine features?" Serena's voice was soft-spoken but also teasing, and Elizabeth, whose heart had been pounding fit to burst upon perceiving Mr Darcy stood just outside their carriage window, eyed her friend with mock sternness for a second before giving a grudging smile.

"How indeed. Oh Serena," Elizabeth whispered. "What am I to do when the poor man has clearly hastened here to avoid me? I can only thank heaven that I was concealed from view. Lord knows what his reaction might have been had I sat on the same side as you!"

Serena smiled sympathetically, but as Mrs Harington chose that moment to stir and finally rouse herself, expressing her pleasure that they were in Bath so soon and indeed, at that very moment, approaching Queen Square, nothing further was said on the subject. Yet Elizabeth stared out of the window, unseeing of the familiar streets and buildings. What fate was this, to so conspire against them? How was she to proceed, knowing that Mr Darcy appeared to be in residence there, doubtless thinking himself freed from her presence once and for all?

⤜✿⤛

Darcy and the Colonel had negotiated a busy crossing and were approaching Pulteney Bridge when they found their path obstructed by a small party of young gentlemen deep in conversation. The fair-haired man with his back to Darcy and the Colonel turned to face them when prompted by one of the group and begged their pardon, making as if to move aside, but as he went to do so he peered more closely at Darcy's visage and put out a restraining hand, a smile forming as he did so.

"Mr Darcy? Sir – you may not recall me, we met-"

"In Bruges. Yes, of course I remember." Darcy smiled and shook hands with the gentleman, racking his brains for a name and then feeling all the shock of realising his identity. The flash of his smile, despite his taller stature, was unmistakable. This was James Harington, the elder brother, and now he understood why he had found the name vaguely familiar.

The surprise of this realisation caused Darcy's mind to blank for a moment, but then his inherent breeding took over.

"Forgive me. Harington," he cleared his throat to cover his hesitation. "This is my cousin, Colonel Fitzwilliam. Richard, this is James Harington. We met as he set out on his Tour a few years back, as I returned from my visit to the Netherlands."

The Colonel exchanged a quick glance with Darcy, but he then made little hesitation in putting himself about to be pleasant.

"And how did you find the Continent, Sir? Was it to your liking?"

"It was. I have been back since on more than one occasion. I found Belgium particularly favourable. And you, Mr Darcy? Did your companion successfully manage to utilise the methods you observed for reclaiming land?"

"Indeed, he did. Well remembered!" Darcy could not help but smile as he recalled a pleasant few days spent in Bruges as he returned home with an old friend who had an estate in Norfolk and sought knowledge from the Dutch of how to reclaim low lying land from the sea to extend his farming capabilities.

Harington smiled in return, and Darcy was once again reminded of his younger brother and perforce Elizabeth. His silence however went un-remarked, for the Colonel spoke.

"Have you been enjoying the Season, Sir? We are arrived but recently and have yet to partake of the city's amusements."

"I have been here these seven days. My youngest brother came with me, and we anticipate more of the family over the forthcoming days."

"You prefer the quieter end of the Season, then?"

Harington nodded. "My parents keep a house here, and it makes a convenient base for us whenever we feel the need of a change of scene from the country. Yet the family do not come to partake of the amusements." He turned to Darcy. "One of my brothers has recently become engaged, though it is yet to be formally announced; according to a note from my father last evening, my mother made such haste to come to Bath to shop for the new bride that he swears he merely saw her skirts as she flew out the door the moment the news landed!"

The men laughed, as they knew they must, but Darcy was conscious of a searing pain within his chest. He knew from his cousin's expression that his sympathies were with him as the conversation took such a difficult turn.

"It is not a golden match," James Harington lowered his voice. "She has no dowry to speak of and has been raised in the country, but she is a good girl, who has long been close to the hearts of the family, and I am convinced that my brother shall be more than content."

Darcy swallowed hard, unable to utter a word. Thus it was that the Colonel spoke the words that must be said on these occasions. "Then we offer you our congratulations."

"I take them gladly, Sir. He is forwarder than me, I will own. When one is learning to manage an estate, one has no time for wife-hunting!"

"Darcy would attest to that, would you not, Cousin?" The Colonel nudged Darcy in the arm. "He has spent the best part of his twenties doing such and raising a younger sister."

Harington, who clearly had much respect for Darcy, seemed to be even more impressed by this statement.

"Then it is I who congratulate you, Sir. That must have been no easy task."

Darcy forced a smile. "It is one I share with my Cousin. He is only feeding me the line so that he may be praised likewise."

Harington laughed, and then, seeing that his party was about to disperse, they made their farewells before continuing on their way.

Chapter Sixteen

NOTING THAT HIS COUSIN STARED AHEAD but suspecting he saw little of the street before them, Colonel Fitzwilliam sighed. Here was a conundrum, and he wondered if Darcy had realised its implications. Somehow, judging by the preoccupation upon his features and the fact that he had said nothing, he suspected that he did not recognise the imminent danger. If Harington's inference was what it seemed, his mother was on her way to Bath, and might that not lead to her other son and the future Mrs Nicholas Harington arriving there too?

The Colonel threw his cousin a further glance as they strode into Laura Place. They were but moments from their aunt's lodgings. There was no opportunity now for putting forward such a supposition. He would wait until they were safely ensconced back in Brock Street and trust to an opportunity to reveal his suspicions. It would not surprise him if they were in the carriage and on their way to Bristol docks by nightfall to await the first possible sailing.

Having been persuaded by her cousin to take a chair back to her lodgings, that she might not alarm her mother by any breathlessness – an attention she admitted she would prefer to avoid – Anne de Bourgh arrived in Great Pulteney Street a little ahead of the others.

Thus, she was in the hall, divested of her outdoor garments when Georgiana, Mrs Annesley and Mrs Jenkinson were admitted by the butler, and as her cousin removed her Spencer and bonnet she sent the two ladies to the small sitting room to partake of their tea together. Then, taking Georgiana firmly by the arm, she led her upstairs, only to be greeted by Lady Catherine thus:

"Ah, there you are, Anne. Darcy has called upon you, as you see. Come, greet your cousin."

Throwing Georgiana a lightning glance, Anne bowed her head and walked slowly across the room, offering a cursory curtsey to both her cousins, who had got to their feet upon the ladies entering the room, before taking a seat as far from her mother as possible.

Georgiana, who knew she would have to bear examination from her aunt, glanced at her brother who gave her a somewhat strained smile that she put down to the company before turning to face Lady Catherine, who looked her up and down critically for a moment.

"You are somewhat dishevelled, girl. You must learn to take a chair rather than walk everywhere. It is not good for your attire to be so – so –" she waved a dismissive hand. "So disturbed."

Georgiana cast a quick glance down at her clothing. Seeing little amiss other than a button of her sleeve being undone, a situation she quickly remedied, and the bow below her bodice had come loose, she threw her brother a beseeching look, but before he could come to her aid, the Colonel spoke.

"I think fresh air and exercise are more beneficial than such fastidiousness of dress, Aunt. Georgiana, you look very well."

Giving him a grateful smile, Georgiana hurried to join Anne on the couch, hoping that attention would be diverted from her.

"You were out far too long, Anne." Lady Catherine turned her eye upon her daughter, who bore her scrutiny with little expression upon her face. "You should not wait to take the waters. Your rank alone should secure you immediate attendance."

Anne said nothing to this, merely returning her mother's stare with one of her own.

The Colonel cleared his throat. "Well, Aunt, you were about to inform us of some piece of intelligence, I believe, before the ladies joined us."

Lady Catherine's beady eye roamed over Georgiana to Darcy and then to the Colonel before she spoke. "Indeed, I was! It is not a pleasing report, as such, but news is sparse as the Season draws to a close, and one must make do with what one can."

She gestured towards the side table against the far wall that held various books and papers.

"I happened upon last week's Chronicle and came across a name that intrigued me – Harington."

With a start, Georgiana looked quickly over at her brother, but he displayed little surprise, merely exchanging a glance with the Colonel.

"I was curious, the name having been raised so recently in my company. Then, I was called upon this very morning by Lady Gwendolyn Giles," she broke off to fix Darcy with a beady eye. "You will recall the Sellwoods, of course. Terribly well to do, a connection worth courting, as I have cautioned you often, Darcy." She gave a flick of her head as her gaze swept the room and Georgiana pressed herself back into the seat as she came under her aunt's scrutiny. "She knows everybody who is anybody, so I asked her about these Haringtons. It appears they are old acquaintances of hers, and she had only this morning received word from the matriarch that she descends upon Bath herself this very day!"

It took Georgiana a few moments to realise what it was that her aunt might be about to disclose, and when she did, she threw Anne a frantic look. Her cousin frowned at her but before Georgiana could whisper her concern, the Colonel spoke.

"Let us not indulge in idle gossip, Aunt. Let us talk of the pleasures of Bath. Have you had the opportunity to attend any events since your arrival? Anne is looking particularly well – I am certain she could well avail herself of all sorts of amusements here."

"We have only been to the gallery thus far. Anne was tired by the travelling, for we were on the road three days in all. She has taken the waters, but yesterday we were confined to the house by the inclement weather."

"Well, we must ensure that we find opportunity for Anne to enjoy some entertainment before the Season finally draws to a close, must we not? Indeed, there will be fewer people here now that May is progressing, and that will mean less crush, which I am sure you will agree is beneficial, Aunt."

Lady Catherine nodded, and then she sat up straight. "Precisely, Fitzwilliam. And on that note, it reminds me of what I wished to speak. We are, as you know, here at a time when most fashionable people will be returning to Town. Which leads me neatly to my point…"

"Brother!" Georgiana's interruption was unexpected, and all faces turned to look at her, something she wished to avoid at all costs, but conscious as she was of the danger of her aunt revealing something she might have learned before she herself had chance to acquaint her brother was unthinkable.

"Georgie?" Darcy's concern was apparent as he came across the room to where his sister sat. "Are you unwell?"

"Yes – yes, I am. I feel – somewhat light-headed. Could we, do you think, return home directly?"

Darcy frowned as he studied her flushed complexion. It was apparent that he did not think she looked in danger of fainting away. He patted her hand and walked over to a long table between the windows, pouring a glass of water from the pitcher there and bringing it over to her.

"Here, drink this and take a few deep breaths. When you are feeling more yourself we will head back so that you may rest. You are possibly fatigued from the journey."

Georgiana sipped at the unwanted water, exchanging a quick look with Anne.

"My *point*," Lady Catherine continued, throwing Georgiana a withering look, "being that no people of fashion would be arriving for any duration at this time of year."

It seemed to have failed her notice that she was, to all intents, including not only herself in that category, but also her two nephews, but no one chose to enlighten her.

"Lady Gwendolyn informed me that her friend, Mrs Harington, would bring two guests with her to Bath. I would not recall either name, such detail being so trivial, had it not been revealed that one of them is *Miss Elizabeth Bennet!* She is to arrive in Bath today. Did you know of this, Darcy? I do not recall it being mentioned at your home the other night, even when there was talk of our intended sojourn here. It is very underhand of her to keep this information quiet when the subject is being canvassed, but then, I always did think her breeding in question."

Silence followed this statement, and Georgiana turned pale as she observed the shock and subsequent sadness that overcame her brother's countenance, comforted only somewhat by the squeeze of her hand by Anne.

She looked beseechingly at the Colonel, and he gave her an understanding smile before turning his attention to Lady Catherine. "It may well be, Aunt, that Miss Elizabeth Bennet was unaware of her trip to Bath at that time. Plans can alter unexpectedly."

"Indeed. And that girl is always flitting here and there at the shortest notice. Did she not quit Kent all of a sudden? An inconvenience to her hosts and to me."

The Colonel snorted. "To you, Aunt? How so?"

Lady Catherine chose not to answer this. "It is all to do with not having a governess. Those girls – brought up at home under a mother clearly unable to tame the spirit in that one. I dread to think what the others are like."

"You met one of them last Saturday, Aunt. Do you not recall Miss Bennet being of the party?"

Lady Catherine waved her hand dismissively and continued as if the Colonel's interruptions had never taken place.

"I am only pleased that we shall not have to entertain her presence here in Great Pulteney Street. I am not aware of her Bath abode, but it is unlikely she will reside anywhere but the lower parts of the town where people of her rank tend to be quartered."

"It is untrue."

Georgiana's words fell into a proud silence. She had watched her brother's glazed expression as Lady Catherine had continued; her heart ached for him, and her aunt's derogatory words were more than she could bear, drawing from her a defence of the lady who held her brother's heart.

Lady Catherine's look of astonishment, not only at being interrupted by her young niece, but at the contradiction, was prolonged. Darcy blinked and looked about as if coming to from a sleep. The Colonel, clearly conscious of his cousin's distress and Darcy's lack of attention, smiled reassuringly at Georgiana and walked over to sit beside her.

"What is untrue, Georgie?"

Taking courage from his presence and another encouraging squeeze of her hand from Anne, Georgiana raised her head and looked to her brother who bore an air of bewilderment.

"Miss Elizabeth Bennet. She is not staying anywhere unfitting."

"And how do you know this?" Lady Catherine had found her voice at last.

Georgiana exchanged a quick look with Anne, who nodded, before turning back to look at her brother.

"Her arrival was noted in the Book. We – I – I happened to see it this morning, in the Pump Room. She is due to arrive today and is staying in Marlborough Buildings."

The Colonel stood up.

"There we are, Aunt. Marlborough Buildings. Merely spitting distance from our own abode in Brock Street. Not too shabby at all, I would say. Right, Darcy – the day presses on. Let us make a move."

The Colonel helped Georgiana to her feet.

"Aunt." He bowed once, turned to his cousin and repeated the gesture.

"Come, Darcy." And without a backward glance, Georgiana found herself and her brother removed from the room before their aunt could draw breath to protest.

Chapter Seventeen

THE CARRIAGE BEARING THE PARTY from Sutton Coker soon reached Marlborough Buildings and, within minutes of entering the house, Mrs Harington became engaged with the housekeeper in her room, intent upon her plans for the celebratory meal on the following day. James and Patrick, they had been advised, were out at present, and having settled into their chamber on the second floor, Serena and Elizabeth soon made their way down the stairs to the drawing room.

It was a beautiful, light space, with high ceilings, delicate plaster cornices and three full-length windows, bounded on the outside by a small wrought iron balcony, facing over the Crescent Fields towards the city, all of which had been thrown open to allow the sunshine and fresh air to invade the room.

Serena made her way over to the small instrument in the corner and began to rifle through the music that lay upon it, and Elizabeth walked over to one of the windows to admire the view. It was a beautiful day and, after the confinement of the carriage, a walk would have been a pleasing diversion, yet the knowledge that Mr Darcy was himself out in the city caused her to shy away from making the suggestion.

The shock of discovering the gentleman to be in Bath had receded somewhat, though Elizabeth's concern over its implications lingered yet. Then, releasing a soft sigh, she turned her back on the pleasant vista. There was little she could do about the situation but bear it, but if only it was not so...

"Lizzy?"

Serena's voice caused her to start, and she looked over at her friend who now sat on the piano stool. "Forgive me, my mind was off a-wandering."

"You are concerned over the likelihood of an encounter." It was a statement of fact rather than a question, but Elizabeth nodded.

"Yes – there is no denying it, for I know full well that I cannot hide away." She gave her friend a rueful smile. "Though 'tis not the first time I have been surprised at his presence somewhere, how different are my feelings to what they were on discovering him to be at Rosings this Easter."

Serena gave her a sympathetic look. "We are to be here but a few days, Lizzy. Come Monday, we will be on our way back to Sutton Coker; there is a chance your paths may not cross."

"It would trouble me less, I am certain, had I not become aware of my – condition. The thought of meeting him fills me with dread, for I can predict neither his manner towards me, nor how I will act in the circumstances."

"I have little I can offer by way of counsel, Lizzy, other than to wait and to let his behaviour be your guide."

Elizabeth stared thoughtfully at her friend. "Advice is far easier to give than receive, is it not? As for acting upon it-," she turned back to stare out of the open window. "That may well be impossible."

Serena began to play a melody, and as the tune filled the air, Elizabeth considered her words. Upon reflection, she had to own that there was some merit in her friend's suggestion. If their paths did cross, she would be able to determine the truth of the matter soon enough by ascertaining whether his withdrawn manner from Monday evening persisted or not. She held little hope that the pleasure of their more recent interactions could be recaptured. For a moment, her sadness overcame her, and Elizabeth released a forlorn sigh. How would it feel to face him now?

At that moment, the door opened, and she turned to see the tea things being brought in by a young serving girl, who deposited the laden tray on a side table and took her leave. With a last glance over her shoulder at the beautiful day outside, Elizabeth walked over to join Serena, who had risen from the stool to set cups onto saucers in readiness. There was little she could do at present to relieve her situation, and with determination, she fastened a smile upon her face and turned her attention to the distraction of company and a welcome cup of tea.

There had been little opportunity for conversation on the walk back to Brock Street, yet Darcy relished the fact for it gave him time to consider the news that had so recently been broken to him.

Elizabeth's coming to Bath had taken him by surprise, there was no question, yet this had soon been replaced by the intensification of his sadness. His recent interactions with her in London had given him more pleasure than he had dared acknowledge at the time; to know that she was near again, yet so blatantly out of his reach, was a crushing blow to his battered spirits.

As the four of them made their way through the city, Darcy found his eye seeking Elizabeth in every direction, and though he chided himself for the indulgence, his will was not strong enough to resist the temptation. Was she here now, or was she yet on her way? Had she travelled from Town directly, or had she come from Longbourn? To be certain, she would have had to go home, either when Harington went to speak to her father or soon after... the memory of his meeting with Mr Bennet flashed through his mind for a moment, but Darcy forced it ruthlessly aside, having no desire to picture that gentleman welcoming Harington into the family with his blessing.

The Colonel, who had been a few paces ahead of Darcy for a while, motioned them all to a halt as they reached Queen Square, where they had need to wait on a chance to cross the busy street. Darcy glanced over his shoulder to where Georgiana stood with Mrs Annesley and gave her a reassuring smile, for she looked quite anxious. Turning back, he was conscious of his cousin throwing him a questioning glance, but he shook his head at him. They would talk when they were safely indoors.

He knew that he needed to make some decisions, and just now he could not conclude what those might be. That he should quit Bath immediately was the first thought that had sprung to mind, and he was hard put to think of any other solution to his present dilemma. Only a regard for his sister prevented him from considering this his only option and saddling a horse the moment he reached the house.

Once across the road, they made their way over the Square to its far corner, Darcy's thoughts immediately resuming the interminable ramble through a raft of questions for which he had no answer. Why was Elizabeth even coming to Bath? And where was Harington? His aunt had made no mention of any of the family, other than the mother... a sudden desire to turn about and head directly to the Pump Room gripped him which he instantly quashed. Desperate for answers he may be, but taking the ignominious step of perusing the Book to identify Harington's date of arrival was not a consideration.

With the others following in his wake now, Darcy finally climbed the steps to a gravelled walk, waiting at the top until they joined him before setting off once more. He was nearly home, yet in his distraction he had discovered no solution to his present trouble other than to remove himself once again. Yet fleeing did not sit well with him. He had felt all the indignity of leaving London so precipitously, despite it seeming a welcome relief at the time. Yet, there was no denying that he would cross paths with Elizabeth in Bath. The city was not only small, it was also compact and at this end of the Season, the entertainments were less varied and therefore the same people were more likely than ever to frequent the same places.

Having reached the corner where the walk ended, adjacent to the path that bounded their own garden wall, Darcy paused, his gaze drawn across the fields to Marlborough Buildings. Was she there even now, and if so, in which of the elegant town houses was she residing? Blowing out a frustrated breath at such futile speculation, Darcy turned on his heel and strode up the path to the side door.

The others followed him inside, and, Mrs Annesley having excused herself to place an order with the housekeeper for tea things to be brought, they handed over their outdoor clothes to the waiting servant and repaired upstairs to the drawing room. It was only as the doors closed behind them that anyone spoke.

"Have you formed a plan?" The Colonel asked the question that Darcy had anticipated, and to defer responding he walked over to the tray of spirits and uncorked some wine. "It is wretched bad luck, Darce. I cannot conceive of the coincidence."

Darcy said nothing in response to these words but poured three glasses of wine, turning to offer one to his cousin before walking over to where Georgiana sat with an uneasy countenance.

"Here, my dear. It is but a small measure, and I think that it will aid you." Acknowledging her grateful smile, Darcy handed her the glass and then walked over to one of the long windows fronting on to the street. With determination, he refused to cast his eyes to the left towards the Crescent Fields and the row of houses beyond that climbed the hill.

The Colonel came to stand beside him and took a hefty drink from his glass before saying, "Well? What is to be done?"

Shaking his head, Darcy spoke quietly, that Georgiana might not hear them. "I have no plan, other than that of Dublin. I am at a loss as to what can be done in the interim other than remain here. My removal from Town seems foolish in hindsight. If I had but waited four and twenty hours, then perhaps this scheme would have come to light, and we would all be content in Mount Street."

"Content?"

"Fair comment. But we are here now, and we must make the best of it. "

"Brother." Darcy turned to look over at his sister. "I am so sorry that I perused the Book. I did not mean to do anything untoward."

"Do not concern yourself so, Georgie. It is not a sin, my dear." Darcy's smile intended to reassure her. "And, indeed, perhaps it is as well that you did, for at least you managed to silence our aunt. I believe congratulations are in order!"

The Colonel inclined his head. "Well done, Darce. You can still jest – this is promising."

Darcy threw him a look, but the Colonel merely raised his glass in a mock salute and downed the contents. He indicated to Darcy to do the same and then took the empty glasses to the table to refill them before returning to stand at his cousin's side once more.

"You do realise the likelihood of an encounter?"

Darcy nodded as he accepted his refilled glass. "Absolutely. But at least I am forewarned."

"Fitz?" Georgiana's voice drew his attention once more, and they turned to face her. "If you wish to return to Mount Street, I am quite able to travel. With an overnight stop, the journey is no strain at all. I am only sorry that your strategy for distraction has failed."

Darcy shook his head. "That is very sweet of you, Georgie. Bear with me, and I will let you know directly what decision we come to." She nodded and resumed her study of the book upon her lap, and he turned back to face the window, speaking in a low voice to his cousin.

"Though I am determined that removing to Ireland is a good solution in the short term, I am, as we have previously discussed, full aware that I am unlikely to avoid Miss Elizabeth Bennet entirely."

The Colonel frowned. "Yet with Bingley in Hertfordshire and, one would assume, Miss Elizabeth residing in whatever county Harington hails from, I cannot see that you would be likely to meet above once a year if that."

Darcy had, throughout the course of the past few weeks, often thought he had looked his last upon Elizabeth. The thought of seeing her but once a year as another man's wife caused his insides to twist with discomfort, and he took a hasty swig from his glass to ease a sudden constriction in his throat.

"Thus, I think my decision makes sense. If I cannot hide, and more fool me for the attempt, then I should face the situation head on like a man. I am ashamed of having left Town so hastily."

Darcy lowered his head, but his cousin patted his arm consolingly and said, "Really, old man, you are too hard upon yourself. You did not flee per se. You took positive steps to alleviate not only your distress but to ensure that Miss Elizabeth could be comfortable in her new situation without the constant reminder of you and your – well – you know."

Darcy gave a rueful laugh before finishing his drink. "Yes, Cousin. Quite."

The Colonel retrieved the glass from his hand and headed back towards the tray of drinks, and Darcy walked over to join his sister.

"Are we to stay, then, Brother?" Georgiana looked up as he took a seat near her.

"I think we will remain for a few days at least. I do have a plan to remove elsewhere later in the week, Georgie, but do not concern yourself with that at present. Let us strive to do as we planned, and attend a few entertainments and perhaps drive out to the country on the morrow."

"And – and what of Miss Elizabeth? In normal circumstances, would we not call upon her?" Georgiana's voice was somewhat hesitant, as if she were unsure whether or not to make the suggestion.

Darcy blinked. For some reason, such a routine gesture had yet to cross his mind, but before he had need of words, the Colonel spoke.

"Were she staying anywhere but with her betrothed's family, it could be considered, my dear. But I fear it should not be attempted in the circumstances."

Georgiana let out a soft sigh, but nodded her head, and the Colonel took the seat next to her and patted her consolingly on the hand. As Mrs Annesley chose that moment to join them, followed soon after by a maid with a serving tray, nothing further was said on the matter, and the conversation turned to where they might make their excursion on the following day.

Chapter Eighteen

SERENA AND ELIZABETH ENJOYED THEIR tea before settling in with their embroidery whilst they awaited the return of Mrs Harington from her discussions with the housekeeper. A comfortable silence endured for a while, though Elizabeth was conscious of making little progress with her sampler. It would not be in Serena's nature to pry, and she had made little comment beyond their earlier exchange over Mr Darcy, yet Elizabeth eventually became aware that her friend eyed her every now and then, and was therefore unsurprised when she addressed her.

"He will discover that you are arrived at Bath, Lizzy."

Not wishing to dwell upon that gentleman and what he may or may not comprehend, Elizabeth made no response, keeping her attention on her needle and thread.

She heard a sigh emanate from Serena. "The Haringtons are a renowned and respected presence here: all their visits are reported, as are those of their guests. It will have been noted in the Book, and it will be in the Chronicle when next it is published."

Elizabeth refused to be drawn. She had discovered that talking of Mr Darcy, thinking of him – impossible though it was not to do so – hurt. She lowered her head and attempted to continue her stitching, only succeeding in stabbing herself with the needle. Letting out a yelp of pain, she inspected the injured finger and then reluctantly put her work aside, throwing her friend a resigned look.

"It is of little consequence, Serena, whether he learns of my presence or not." She paused, then let out a disbelieving laugh. "And perusing the Book would be somewhat below his dignity!"

"But he must read the papers."

"The society pages of the Bath Chronicle? I trust not."

Serena shrugged. "Then he will be most surprised when your paths do cross."

"When?" Elizabeth gave a reluctant laugh. "No longer even 'if?'" Her friend met her look with a guileless one of her own, and she acceded to her point. "No, I see you have the right of it. It is quite unavoidable in a place such as this. Heaven knows what he will think when he..." She stopped suddenly as a further uncomfortable notion took hold. "Oh dear heaven, Serena. What if he believes I purposefully came here, that I am intent upon throwing myself in his way?"

"Why would he think so? You are being irrational, Lizzy."

With a sigh, Elizabeth acknowledged the hit. "I fear all reason has fled. I cannot seem to think clearly or sensibly."

"Dear Lizzy. Do not torment yourself so. You could little have known his destination. 'Tis all innocence."

Before Elizabeth had the opportunity to respond to this, however, the door opened and Mrs Harington entered the room, a satisfied expression upon her kindly features.

"Well, my dears, it is all settled, and a fine repast we shall enjoy!" She walked over to where Serena sat and leaned down to pat her affectionately on the arm. "It is only fitting we should mark the occasion in some small way."

Serena seemed to be becoming inured to the lady's enthusiasm somewhat, as she merely smiled at this, but before anything further could be spoken of, a commotion was detected outside the door which was soon thrown back to reveal James and Patrick Harington. They both entered the room smiling widely, the former greeting his mother warmly, then turning to acknowledge both Serena and Elizabeth.

"I offer my congratulations, Serena. Nicholas is a dark horse; he gave me no inkling!"

She got awkwardly to her feet, and James stepped forward to embrace her quickly before he was elbowed out of the way by Patrick.

"So we are to have a sister! It seems odd to *welcome* you into the family after all these years, Serena, but I declare it *is* welcome that you are!" Patrick swept her into an enthusiastic embrace, only releasing her when admonished by his mother. "So – shall you like to have two such handsome brothers?" He waggled his eyebrows at her in much the same way that Nicholas had an inclination for, and Serena laughed, though her cheeks were very pink, and she seemed somewhat embarrassed by the attention.

"I am, indeed, most fortunate in my new kin."

"Come, boys," Mrs Harington urged them to take a nearby sofa, and once everyone was comfortably seated, she continued, "Now – tell me what you have been about since we last saw you at home."

James merely smiled, but Patrick, who favoured Nicholas in both stature and demeanour, taking more after their mother as they both did, grasped the conversational reins with relish.

"We have indulged in every possible entertainment, Mama. We have even attended the Upper Rooms on more than one occasion," he paused and threw the young man at his side a quick glance, "and James-"

"The fishing has been particularly fine sport." James' interruption of his brother did not go unremarked, nor did the colour that had crept into his face. Patrick smirked, and Mrs Harington looked from one to the other of her sons with an expectant expression.

"James… *what?*"

Seeing the colour deepening in that young man's cheeks and watching him get up and pace over to the window, Elizabeth felt for him amidst her amusement at a familiar scene. Having been raised with all the responsibility of being heir to the estate, James was, in general, inclined to a little more seriousness than his two younger brothers, though lively enough in the main. His good fortune in being part of such a warm and loving family circle was at times countered by the fact that both his younger siblings took much pleasure in the art of teasing, with James often being the person they practised their talent on.

It seemed this occasion was no exception, for Patrick's eyes lit up as he continued, "He danced, Mama, not once – but *twice* – and with a rather fetching young woman, it has to be owned."

James turned from his self-imposed exile by the window and glared at his brother. "And what of it?" He turned to address his mother. "Partners were sparse; there are so few couples to be made at this end of the Season, Mama."

Mrs Harington eyed her eldest son for a moment. "Aye, Son, you are quite correct."

James seemed relieved at this reprieve, but to Elizabeth's amusement, his peace was short lived, for Patrick let out a derogatory snort. "It was no lack of partners that had you offering her your arm with all the speed of a bullet from a rifle in Sydney Gardens the other day."

"So," Mrs Harington fixed James with a mother's keen eye, and Elizabeth could not help but smile. Only the day before, the lady had been bemoaning the fact that James displayed a blatant lack of interest in finding himself a partner in life, and clearly now her interest was roused. "Does she have a name, this lady who needed rescuing – twice – with a gentleman's arm?"

James opened his mouth, then closed it with a snap, throwing his brother a speaking glance. Patrick, however, as the youngest, had spent most of his life being the one who had to constantly scurry to keep up in all manner of things as he grew up and was not about to relinquish the reins yet.

"She is a Miss Wallace from Dorset. She is in Bath with her aunt and uncle who have a house on the Paragon." He laughed as James walked over to resume his seat, shaking his head at his brother.

"Yes, and she has a sister, does she not, Patrick?" His equanimity somewhat restored, a triumphant smile graced James' features as his brother took his turn at becoming pink in the face.

"Truly?" Mrs Harington turned on her youngest with a wide smile. "And is she well looking, too? Did you partner her?"

"Mama!"

Fortunately for Patrick, his brother seemed to feel sufficient had been said on the subject, particularly in front of the ladies, and James smiled apologetically at Serena and Elizabeth. "Let us speak no more of assemblies."

Patrick nodded quickly, clearly thankful for the suggestion, though one glance at Mrs Harington convinced Elizabeth that she would be returning to the subject again whenever the opportunity should present.

James, however, was able to offer a topic of adequate distraction for his mother. "We had plans for this evening, Mama, before we learned of your impending arrival. Shall you join us?"

The afternoon progressed without incident in Brock Street, other than a request from Mrs Annesley to be given a few days' leave from her position as companion. It transpired that she had several acquaintances in the environs of Bath and had just received an invitation to spend some time visiting with one of them. As Georgiana had the company of the gentlemen in the house, and her cousin Anne at not too far a distance, both the Colonel and Darcy could see no fault with the scheme, provided Georgiana was happy with the arrangement. Her approbation was soon secured, and by mid-afternoon the lady had been removed by her friends to the village of Swainswick with the intention of re-joining them on Monday morning, when they would have a clearer understanding of their movements.

Darcy sat at the desk in-between the long windows, engrossed in some correspondence that had arrived that morning, with Georgiana curled up in one of the window seats reading, but just then the Colonel came breezing into the room, having walked down to speak to their aunt about Anne joining them on the following day for their drive into the country.

"Well, Cousins, we have something to occupy ourselves with this evening. There is, unfortunately, a condition attached, but one that is likely worth the bearing."

Darcy, who had turned in his seat, raised a brow at this and Georgiana put aside her book and swung her feet down to the floor.

"Are we to go out?"

"Indeed, if your brother can be so persuaded." He looked to Darcy who shrugged his shoulders.

"It depends, Cousin. You know my preference and there is a limit to what social gatherings Georgiana can yet attend."

The Colonel shook his head. "No, no. I fully comprehend the boundaries, I assure you, and I certainly have your interests at heart."

He walked across the room to join them both.

"There is a performance of *The Taming of the Shrew* at the Theatre Royal this evening – fully booked, as I am sure you can imagine. However, Aunt Catherine had secured a box for herself and Anne some days ago in which she claims there is ample seating for the addition of three more. Therefore, shall we go? It would do you both good to get out of the house, and the protection of a private box precludes you from any obligation to socialise."

Darcy looked to his sister. "Georgiana? What do you think?"

She glanced from her brother to her cousin, who gave the ghost of a wink, and then smiled. "I would dearly love to go. I have heard that the new theatre is delightful inside, and it will be nice for Anne, I am certain, to have the addition of company."

Darcy studied her thoughtfully. There was no denying the convenience and protection of a private box was the added attraction. Not only would it secure him from any encounter should Elizabeth happen to be present, but it would also shield them from any passing acquaintance, something Darcy was particularly mindful of with his young sister in tow.

"Then let us go." He turned to look at the Colonel. "And the morrow? Did Aunt Catherine consent to Anne accompanying us?"

With a snort, the Colonel turned and walked over to the drinks tray, saying over his shoulder as he went, "Her *consent* was hard-won and begrudgingly bestowed, and you will not be surprised to learn that attending her this evening was part of the bargain I had to wager."

He poured out a small measure of brandy and knocked it back before turning to look at Darcy and indicating the decanter, but his cousin shook his head. If they were to spend the evening under his aunt's eagle eye, he would need his wits about him.

Chapter Nineteen

THE NEW THEATRE ROYAL WAS certainly as elegant within as its exterior implied, and as James saw to his mother's comfort and Patrick settled Serena into her seat, Elizabeth cast her eyes over the people assembling in the auditorium. She could detect no sign of Mr Darcy, and she released a soft sigh as she turned to Patrick who offered the end chair to her before taking his own in the row behind.

The theatre was well-designed in many aspects, with there being hardly a bad seat in the house. The same could not be said, however, for the private boxes, which were not, despite Lady Catherine's opinion, particularly spacious. Any party larger than four, therefore, struggled for adequate space, sacrificing their toes for the satisfaction of privacy. Thus it was that Elizabeth, with the three ladies seated to the fore and the two gentleman behind, found herself sitting close up against the partition wall of their box, with her knees almost pressing against the half-height balustrade in front of them.

James' revelation earlier that they had long had seats secured at the theatre for a performance that evening had been greeted by Mrs Harington with evident pleasure. Serena had thrown Elizabeth an anxious look as the invitation was accepted on all their behalves and had later confessed that she had been tempted to affect tiredness from recent travelling and beg for her friend to remain at home with her, that they might both be excused from attending.

Elizabeth had thanked her for the consideration, but acknowledged that distraction and company would aid her far better than the quiet of an evening at home, and thus had willingly prepared for the outing.

Conscious of the murmur of voices around her, Elizabeth made an attempt to push aside any distracting thoughts, and leaning forward, she turned her attention to admiring the sparkle of gowns, feathers and jewels that filled the stalls below. She did not fool herself, however, for she was conscious that she was in truth scouring the rows of seats for a sign of Mr Darcy's familiar form once more.

Annoyed with herself for so doing, but unable to cease, her eyes rested upon each new arrival, her insides churning with unease. Yet as the auditorium filled, including the boxes aligned opposite their own, she recognised no one, and with disgust at her own frailty, she sighed heavily. The sense of disappointment that overwhelmed her made it perfectly clear that she wished he had come more than hoped he had not, and that though she dreaded speaking with him, she longed to lay eyes upon him.

"*Lizzy!*" Serena's low-voiced hiss called her attention and she turned to her friend who sat by her side with a questioning look.

Serena said nothing, only inclined her head towards the neighbouring box, which had, from the sounds of movement and the murmur of low voices, just become occupied.

Once seated it was not possible for the residents of one box to see those within an adjacent one, by the nature of their alignment towards the stage; yet when arriving and departing and thus standing and moving about to arrange the seating, it was impossible not to discern voices and occasionally gain a partial glimpse of a person.

Swallowing hard on the tightness that gripped her throat, Elizabeth heard quite suddenly the Colonel's jovial tone and, as if that were not confirmation enough, her eyes were drawn to a hand that had come to rest on the balcony rail. Someone stood at the edge of the neighbouring box and, if she were not mistaken, Serena had detected that it was Mr Darcy, a suspicion confirmed within seconds as the owner of the hand leaned forward slightly and then drew back again. It was he.

Sitting back in her seat, Elizabeth blew out a breath and then turned to look again at Serena.

"Thwarted in one's best endeavours," she said quietly, that Mrs Harington, who sat the other side of her friend, might not hear.

Serena nodded, a sympathetic expression upon her features and she gave Elizabeth's nearest hand a comforting squeeze. "It is no matter," she whispered as the orchestra began to tune their instruments and the lamps were progressively dimmed. "We need not quit the box in the intermission, and they will not discern us."

And so the performance began.

Colonel Fitzwilliam had been quite in favour of Darcy's decision to arrive as late as possible at the theatre, the intention being that if they entered the building after the bell had called people to their seats, they would pass relatively unnoticed up the stairs and to the sanctuary of their private box. Lady Catherine had aided them somewhat in this endeavour, by refusing to enter the carriage when they called to collect her and Anne until she had completed reeling off a list of instructions to her footman and butler, all of which necessitated being done in her absence.

Thus it was that they reached their destination without obstruction, the only dilemma being the seating arrangements. Lady Catherine had insisted upon Anne and Georgiana taking two of the three chairs in the front row, and her daughter had quickly secured a seat against the far wall, leaving Georgiana to sit in the middle. Darcy had seemed distracted, stood at the balustrade and staring down into the crowd, but a panicked look from Georgiana alerted the Colonel, and before his aunt could take the remaining chair, and thus be seated next to his young cousin throughout the entire performance, he urged Darcy to sit where he was stationed and swept Lady Catherine into the chair next to his in the back row. His timing was impeccable, for the lamps dimmed and the curtain rose, stalling any attempt by his aunt to petition for a change of places, and thus they sat as the play began.

Darcy's intention to not quit the de Bourgh box during the intermission would normally have frustrated the Colonel, but in the circumstances, he was all understanding and consideration. However, Lady Catherine's pre-ordered supply of refreshments was inadequate for their enlarged party, and with Darcy unable to get out with ease, the Colonel took it upon himself to seek reinforcements.

"I shall return directly," he said as he made to stand up, only to be brought to a halt by a hand upon his arm.

"I wish to accompany you, Cousin."

The Colonel stared at Anne who had turned in her seat and then got to her feet. "I feel the need for some exercise; it is so cramped in here."

"Do not be ridiculous, Anne, you will over exert yourself." Lady Catherine rapped her closed fan on the back of her daughter's chair. "Sit!"

The Colonel looked to his cousin who had also got to his feet, and Darcy nodded at him before turning to address Lady Catherine.

"Aunt, let Anne take a walk with Fitzwilliam. It is no distance, and a servant shall be carrying the tray."

Before any further argument could ensue, the Colonel assisted Anne in extricating herself from the closely ranked chairs and escorted her from the box, ignoring her mother's indignant, "Well, really!"

Having descended the main stairs to the foyer, Colonel Fitzwilliam set about ordering some drinks and a large platter of fruit and cheese, but when he turned back to his cousin, she was nowhere to be seen.

"Anne?" he called her, but there was no response, and he turned slowly on his heel, his eyes narrowed as he scanned the milling crowd. He began to feel the first stirrings of concern when the doors to the main auditorium swung open to admit some more theatre-goers, and he glimpsed her before they once more fell shut, the dark silk of her dress and her unadorned hair striking against the array of bright colours surrounding her.

He bounded over and pulled the doors open and stepped inside, finding himself now in the stalls. His cousin had her back to him and appeared to be staring at their own box, and looking up, he could discern that Darcy's attention was with Georgiana. All that was visible of his aunt, being sat further back, was the feathers atop her head, and he stepped forward to stand beside Anne, bending down to hiss in her ear: "Do you wish to be seen by your mother? 'Tis a little fool-hardy, to be certain, to…"

"Look," she interrupted, without turning her eyes from whatever she saw, and the Colonel straightened, following the line of her vision beyond the de Bourgh box to that on its right. "I believed I caught a glimpse of something when the doors swung open and came to see if my mind deceived me."

With a start, he recognised Elizabeth; her head was turned away as she listened to one of her party, an older lady with an animated face, but her profile was unmistakable. Of the remainder of her party, he could detect little, the light being so poor at this distance. With a sigh, the Colonel realised that – did he but know it – Darcy was sitting side by side with her, but for the partition wall of the boxes.

"Come, Anne, let us return. It is as well if we forewarn him; he may well be able to depart before the end to prevent a meeting."

"My mother will not permit it."

"She would not permit you to leave the box, yet you are here."

Anne turned and preceded him out of the auditorium. "I still do not see why he wishes to avoid her so assiduously, when only days ago he entertained the lady and her family at his own table. It is unfathomable."

Her tone was petulant, and the Colonel motioned the waiting servant to follow them before responding quietly. "This is neither the time nor the place, Anne, and if Darcy has chosen not to enlighten you, then I certainly shall not."

"Hah!" Anne flashed him a fierce look of triumph. "So there is *something* to tell; at least that has been confirmed."

The Colonel glared at her, but as they now approached the box he said nothing further, swinging open the door for his cousin to enter, followed by the servant with his heavily laden tray, and whilst the refreshments were passed around, the Colonel remained outside in the hallway to allow the man space to work.

Thus it was that he detected a gentleman making his way along the landing, and he was but three paces from him before the Colonel made the connection.

"Harington. Good evening."

Nicholas looked up and smiled at the Colonel before shaking his hand.

"Well met, Sir. I am somewhat tardy, having just arrived in Bath to find the entire household bent upon pleasure in my absence." He laughed. "To be fair, they do not anticipate my arrival until the morrow, so they shall be forgiven."

The Colonel nodded thoughtfully, certain that it was not the performance that had drawn the gentleman from home so precipitously after a late arrival. "The play is well enough. I will wager it will be worth your efforts."

Nicholas smiled widely. "That is good to hear. Well, excuse me, Colonel. Enjoy the remainder of your evening." With that, they exchanged a bow and the gentleman soon disappeared into the neighbouring box, a welcome cry of "Nicholas" floating from the doorway before it closed.

Forewarned as he had been, Darcy made no attempt to leave the theatre ahead of the neighbouring party. It would be untruthful to say that the temptation was not there, or that the possibility did not cross his mind, but he had his sister's comfort to consider, and he could not abandon her to her cousins. It did mean, however, that he heard or saw little of what remained of the final acts of the play.

Once it had ended, though, and the lamps were once more lit and those thronging the stalls had risen to their feet in preparation for departure, he found himself roused from his stupor by his sister, who tugged at his arm to attract his attention.

"Fitz? What do we do now? Do we leave?"

Darcy glanced over at the Colonel, who shrugged.

"I think we will wait a short while, Georgie, for the crush to lessen in the foyer."

"A wise decision, Darcy," Lady Catherine smoothed her satin skirts where she sat in regal elegance on her chair. "It would not do for either Anne or Georgiana to become hemmed in. Crowds are so tiresome. But there is a decided lack of space in here with so many. Fitzwilliam!"

The Colonel turned from his contemplation of the theatre-goers below and looked at his aunt.

"Open the door, Nephew. Let some air circulate before we all expire."

The Colonel made for the door and swung it open, bringing in not only a rush of air but the sound of voices as a gentleman passed by, a lady secured upon each arm.

"Colonel."

Coming face to face with Elizabeth was, whilst not entirely unanticipated, a surprise at that moment and the Colonel stepped quickly outside into the corridor before making a hasty bow in response to the lady's curtsey.

"Miss Bennet. What a pleasure to see you again. You have been enjoying the performance?"

Looking somewhat conscious, she detached herself from Nicholas Harington who bowed and walked on with the other lady, and threw a quick glance over the Colonel's shoulder. It was sufficient, combined with the lack of surprise upon her own features, to convince him that she had been aware of who her neighbours were.

"Who is it, Fitzwilliam? With whom are you speaking?" Lady Catherine's imperious tone forestalled Elizabeth from responding, and she smiled as the Colonel rolled his eyes.

"It is Miss Elizabeth Bennet, Ma'am."

Within seconds, Lady Catherine appeared in the door frame behind her nephew.

"You appear with disturbing frequency, Miss Bennet."

"A common trait, I find, Lady Catherine, amongst my own acquaintance of late."

The lady frowned, her eyes scanning the party beyond Elizabeth, and finding nothing of interest she gave a brisk nod of her head by way of dismissal and turned away.

"Excuse me, Sir. I must move on; my friends await me."

The Colonel bowed and watched Elizabeth take up the offer of James Harington's arm as she joined the remainder of her party where they lingered a few paces away. He acknowledged the gentleman with a smile and an inclination of his head, and watched as they made their way to the staircase and eventually disappeared from view.

Returning to the box, Colonel Fitzwilliam looked over at Darcy; from the pained look in his eye, he clearly wished himself anywhere but here – the sooner they removed to Bristol docks the better.

Chapter Twenty

SITTING BY THE HEARTH IN HER CHAMBER, Elizabeth released a soft sigh as she stared into the dying embers of the fire. Serena had claimed weariness not long after they had returned from the theatre, and Elizabeth had been more than happy to accompany her friend upstairs, for she had no desire to sit around drinking tea whilst endeavouring to discuss a performance that she had barely paid any mind to.

She glanced over at the bed and smiled faintly. Her friend had been reading whilst Elizabeth prepared for the night, but Serena had not feigned her tiredness. Having been on the road every day but one in the past seven, she now slept, curled up in a ball, her open book still beside her. That her dreams were pleasant Elizabeth did not doubt.

Nicholas' unexpected arrival in the box at the theatre had been greeted with muted profusions of affection at the time, bearing in mind their location, but once inside their own walls, everyone had been keen to understand how he came to be there a day ahead of time. It transpired that his father had released him earlier than anticipated that afternoon and, rather than wait until the following morning to travel in the carriage with his parent, he had asked Mr Harington for his sanction and had saddled a horse directly, intent upon reaching Bath – here he had cast a quick glance at Serena – without further delay.

After a few congratulatory slaps on the back from his brothers, Nicholas had turned to greet the lady in question, his gaze lingering on her before his eye had moved to Elizabeth. She smiled at the memory, recalling how the tension that had gripped her during the evening had begun to fade a little, soothed to have her friend restored to their company and confident that there would now be adequate distraction all round.

Staring once more into the embers, however, thoughts of the evening would intrude, and conscious that sleep remained as evasive as ever, Elizabeth got up and grabbed the poker, giving the remains of the fire a hefty poke in the hope of stirring some life from it. She was pleased to observe a few flames take hold, and dropping another log onto them, she settled back into her chair, hugging her knees against her chest and wrapping her shawl about her toes.

Had Mr Darcy known she sat in the neighbouring box that evening? Did he realise that it was she at the door when his cousin and aunt spoke to her? To be certain, Lady Catherine's voice could carry a fair distance, and the confines of one of the theatre's boxes was hardly likely to conceal it. Yet the gentleman had, if he perceived her presence at all, made no effort to come out and speak to her.

A wave of sadness swept over her, and she dropped her chin onto her knees. The familiar ache was in her throat once more, and closing her eyes, she tried to will her thoughts away from Mr Darcy and all that might have been.

In Great Pulteney Street, Anne de Bourgh studied her reflection in the mirror as a maid plaited her hair. Ruminating upon the evening that had just passed, her curiosity was at its peak. Having rarely been out in the world beyond the boundaries imposed by her mother, every day brought delight to her senses, and she knew that extended time in the company of her cousins was a sizeable contributor to this enjoyment.

With a dismissive nod, she excused the maid and got to her feet. Of all her cousins, Darcy intrigued her the most. His unfathomable behaviour towards Miss Elizabeth Bennet required considerable thought, and with the lack of any other distraction, Anne had bent her mind to the matter with much frequency over the past few days. The alteration from Saturday's dinner party, when the lady had appeared to be welcome, both in his house and to his company, was inexplicable. As for the lady's tendency to appear wherever Darcy was – first in Kent, then in Town, now Bath – there was no denying it begged an obvious question.

Anne walked over to her bed and clambered between the covers, leaning over to extinguish the candles on the bedside table before flopping back onto her mound of soft pillows. She was quite determined to find out more; it was merely a question of how to set about it. Her participation in the excursion into the countryside on the morrow, without either her companion's irritating presence or her mother's beady eye, could prove most enlightening. Further, she began to have a taste for company, for being active and *doing* things.

She rolled onto her side and hugged her pillow. If she was to be her cousins' new mission – and she had no objection to it in general – then so be it. She deserved to be amused and entertained by them in turn, and on this thought and with a smile upon her lips, she drifted off into a contented sleep.

The weather remained fair as Saturday dawned and, waking early to sunlight filtering through a crack in the shutters, Elizabeth stretched as she attempted to shake off the remnants of a dream before glancing at Serena, who continued to sleep peacefully beside her.

Attempting to push aside the solemnity of her mood, Elizabeth eased herself from the bed so as not to disturb her friend. She padded over to the window and pulled aside one of the wooden shutters to peer out over the fields. It was a beautiful morning and, determining that a short walk would be just the thing to improve her spirits, she made a hasty toilet, dressed herself in a simple gown and grabbed her shawl before making her way down the stairs, where she encountered the housekeeper coming out of the dining room.

"Good morning, Miss Bennet." The lady had long been in the employ of the Haringtons at Sutton Coker but, on the passing of her husband and her children having grown, she had petitioned for a removal to the Bath townhouse and had been the resident housekeeper ever since.

"Good morning, Mrs Foden." Elizabeth gave her a friendly smile. She was a short lady, with very curly hair and a motherly manner that had made her a firm favourite with the young people of the family. "Should the ladies come downstairs in my absence, would you please be so kind as to let them know I have gone for a walk?"

"Of course, Miss. Enjoy the fresh air." She dropped a brief curtsey to Elizabeth and turned towards the back of the hall where a door led to the service areas of the house, and Elizabeth let herself out into the bright morning, standing on the steps for a moment as she settled her shawl about her shoulders. She glanced left in the direction of the Royal Crescent, then to the right where the open fields of grass sloped down towards the distant river, the opposite bank heavily wooded and climbing steeply. It was an attractive prospect, and she turned her feet in the direction of the fields, setting a keen pace in her determination to leave melancholy reflection behind her.

Some time later, having meandered along the riverbank for a considerable distance, Elizabeth paused to get her bearings. Though she had taken little notice of the passage of time, the position of the sun alerted her to the fact that her walk had lasted far longer than she had anticipated, and she reluctantly turned towards the rise of land that would bring her back to the fields in front of the Royal Crescent.

Elizabeth focused upon her feet as she walked, the ground being somewhat uneven and the land rising steadily in places, and her exertions were sufficient distraction, not only for her thoughts but also to her direction. Thus it was that when she paused for breath, her hands upon her hips, to confirm her position, she found she had strayed further to the right than she had intended and instead of approaching Marlborough Buildings she neared instead the rear of Brock Street.

Letting out a huff of laughter at her poor directional skills, she continued along the rough track she had been following and soon had reached the more secure footing of a metalled path.

Her eye was caught immediately by a fine carriage drawn up to the side of the end house in Brock Street, a bustle of servants going to and fro from the nearby door as they loaded the rear box of the conveyance with what appeared to be rugs and a large picnic basket. She was about to turn her steps across the field towards the Harington house when a figure crossed the threshold, and with a start she realised that it was Georgiana Darcy, closely followed by her cousin, the Colonel.

Her heart leapt into her throat, and she looked frantically to and fro before hurrying to step behind a nearby tree, thankful that this part of the field was amply supplied with them and that this particular specimen was blessed with a trunk of considerable girth and extensive low-hanging foliage.

Leaning back against the tree, she brushed a hand across her forehead and sighed. So this must be their Bath lodgings. Could the Fates be any more unkind in their determination to thrust them into each other's company? If this pattern continued, she would arrive home to Hertfordshire to find her father intent upon moving his family to Derbyshire...

The sound of voices intruded upon this nonsensical rumination, and Elizabeth realised that Mr Darcy had joined his sister and cousin outside. It appeared they were to be gone for the best part of the day and, unable to resist the temptation of a sight of him, Elizabeth peered cautiously around the tree.

Mr Darcy had his back to her, but the sight of his broad shoulders and the sound of his voice were sufficient to cause her heart to intensify its ache and the familiar constriction to grip her throat. Conscious that the Colonel had also now entered the conveyance and that Mr Darcy was about to follow him, some instinct alerted Elizabeth to quickly conceal herself once more behind the trunk, thankful for its solidity and size as she sank back against it. If she was not mistaken, something had caused Mr Darcy to turn his head at that moment in her very direction.

Chapter Twenty One

NOW THAT ELIZABETH'S ARRIVAL AT Bath was no longer speculation, Darcy had been astounded at how intensely he longed to set eyes upon her. Discovering that she sat in the box next to theirs on the previous evening had been a sore trial, compounded by the knowledge of Harington's joining her, but at least he finally had answers to some of the questions that had haunted him.

The Colonel had speculated, upon their return to the house on the previous evening, that Harington's delayed arrival had been down to his detour to Hertfordshire. Darcy was not so certain. Elizabeth was, he understood, close to her father. If a gentleman were approaching Mr Bennet for his blessing, he was certain she would wish to be at home.

Yet whatever the truth of the matter, they had both determined that the betrothal, so many days after the event, must now surely be approved, and had acknowledged that it would be incumbent upon them to extend their congratulations should they encounter either Harington, Elizabeth or both during the time they were in Bath.

Such ponderings as these did not give rise to a restful night, and Darcy woke the following morning frustrated that he could not shake thoughts of Elizabeth, despite the futility of the indulgence. Thus it was that he quickly prepared for the day ahead, thankful that company and distraction were afoot.

Even so, throughout an early breakfast he had fought with the urge to take a quick stroll, just along the Royal Crescent. He did not fool himself; he knew that his intention would be to study every house on Marlborough Buildings as he walked, desperate to know which one belonged to the Haringtons.

The temptation had never been stronger than when he was about to step into the carriage, when he suddenly felt as though he were being watched – a foolish notion, as proved when he turned to look. There was no one about in the stillness of the fine morning but themselves.

He hurriedly joined his companions, closing the door with a decisive snap, but as they set off along Brock Street, he remained unable to shake the sensation that he had not been alone back there.

The carriage entered the Circus and then began to make its way slowly down the steep incline of Gay Street, and the Colonel turned to his cousin.

"Have you given any further thought to travelling to Ireland?"

"Thornton has confirmed that there is passage yet available on the vessel I saw advertised." He looked over to his sister, whose interest had been caught. "Georgie, I thought you might like to accompany me?"

"Truly, Fitz?" Her eyes had brightened, and she looked eagerly from her brother to her cousin. "How soon could we go?"

Georgiana's enthusiasm was infectious. The Colonel laughed, and Darcy could not help but smile at her reaction.

"There is a sailing on Thursday next from Bristol." He threw his cousin a questioning glance. "Shall you be able to join us?"

"My duties will probably prevent it, though I may be able to come over and join you for a short while in the future."

Georgiana looked from one to the other. "How long would we be gone? Is it for a lengthy duration?"

"I had thought a few months, at least. There is much to see and history a-plenty. I am certain you will gain enjoyment from it, my dear, as well as education." He turned to his cousin. "I had wondered – Anne…"

The Colonel ruefully shook his head. "Not yet, Darce, old chap. A good thought, a kind one, but let us take small steps. You know what Aunt Catherine is like and her grip upon her daughter is vice-like. We need to pry it loose a little further before we can free the captive more. These outings in Bath should provide a sound beginning."

"Then let us aim to bring her to Pemberley in the autumn."

Colonel Fitzwilliam rolled his eyes. "Well, we know we shall get approval for *that*. It will give her notions."

"Then let us make sure she knows they are nothing *but* notions. We shall cross that particular bridge when we reach it." He turned to his sister. "You are happy to make the journey?"

Georgiana smiled widely at him, clapping her hands together. "I am more than content, Brother! To be able to venture to places I have but read about will be so rewarding, but to have the chance to do so in your company makes it all the more pleasurable." Her eyes sparkled in anticipation. "I have yet to set foot upon a ship!"

Warmed by her approbation, Darcy smiled. The novelty of their travels together would aid him greatly in his attempts to recover from his recent disappointment, and content that he had prescribed a solution that would avoid causing Bingley any offence by allowing him a valid reason for not visiting Hertfordshire for the foreseeable future and would also please his sister, he felt his spirits rise.

Glancing out of the window, he perceived that they were pulling up at their aunt's lodgings, and the Colonel had soon jumped out of the carriage, advising Darcy and Georgiana to remain within whilst he fetched their cousin. He returned in no time with Anne upon his arm, and soon the conveyance was on its way, heading for the turnpike which would take them south of the city.

⁂

Elizabeth returned to the house out of breath in her haste to remove herself from the proximity of Brock Street. She hurried up the stairs, thankful to meet no one, but it was only as she entered the chamber, shut the door and leant against it that she realised her heart pounded fiercely in her breast and the traitorous constriction had yet to lessen its hold upon her throat.

Seeing Mr Darcy again – hearing his voice – even though she had known he was in Bath and that they had endured a shielded proximity the night before, had brought a sadness far deeper than she could have imagined. It began to take hold that this was to be her destiny: forever estranged from the man she loved.

She pushed away from the door and walked over to the open window, which afforded her a complete view of the side of the end house in Brock Street. The imposing presence of the Royal Crescent paled into insignificance, and the panorama across the fields towards the river held little interest now; all she was conscious of was that house, and for a moment she simply stared at it.

"*Lizzy!*"

The sound of her name being called drew her attention, and she turned around as the door was opened by Mrs Harington.

"There you are, my dear! How was your walk? It has certainly given you some colour!" The lady turned and walked off along the landing, beckoning Elizabeth to follow. "Come, we are about to breakfast and plan our day!"

The company at table was invaluable in directing her mind. Nicholas made a lively enough addition to their party, and as the three brothers were close, the banter and teasing was non-stop, and Elizabeth found herself smiling and indeed laughing a vast deal, something which did much towards restoring her equanimity.

Thus it was that the breakfast hour passed pleasantly enough, and though the recollection of Mr Darcy's being lodged just across the field from them would encroach upon occasion, Elizabeth was able to deflect the intrusion with more ease than she would have anticipated.

To add further to her desire for occupation, they had barely finished their repast when a commotion in the hallway drew the attention of everyone in the room, and soon after, Mr Harington entered, newly arrived from Sutton Coker. He received a warm greeting from those present and, as his most pressing need was for a cup of hot tea, they were all more than happy to remain together at the table to bear him company.

⁂

The reunited Harington family passed a pleasant few hours together, culminating in the partaking of some further refreshment, and it was as the remnants of this were cleared away that plans for the remainder of the day were finalised.

Mrs Harington was fixed upon taking Serena and Elizabeth out into the town to visit some of the shops; Mr Harington was equally focused upon doing nothing of the kind. As it happened, both James and Patrick had been anticipating a further turn upon the riverbank with their fishing rods, and soon it was agreed that the men would indulge their love of angling.

Serena and Elizabeth had gone out into the hallway, intent upon heading for the stairs and their chamber, and Nicholas soon followed them, *his* intent being to remain in Serena's company in what little time he had, but they had barely gone three paces when Mr Harington appeared.

"Forgive me, Lizzy, dear. I forgot to give you these earlier," he dug into his pocket and produced two letters. "They arrived at home for you yesterday after you had set off."

"Thank you, Sir." Elizabeth took them with a smile which the gentleman returned before leaving them once more, and quickly studying the hand on each, she looked up at Serena and Nicholas.

"One from Jane and one from Aunt Gardiner."

"Come, come girls," Mrs Harington came out into the hallway, followed by James and Patrick. "Fetch your outdoor things and let us be on our way."

Serena cast a regretful glance in Nicholas' direction, but he was hauled away by his brothers, intent upon retrieving their angling equipment from the cellar.

Shaking her head at their antics, which were accompanied by a certain amount of noise, Elizabeth smiled and turned to follow Serena up the stairs, breaking the seal on Jane's letter as she went.

It was very short but contained such news as made Elizabeth stumble on the staircase and grasp the rail.

"Oh my!" she exclaimed, and Serena, who had reached the landing turned around.

"What is it? What has happened?"

Elizabeth climbed the remaining steps two at a time, a habit of her youth that she had attempted to curb in recent years but that instinctively took over in moments of excitement.

"See. Read for yourself!" She thrust the letter into Serena's hands and waited as her friend scanned it quickly, then looked up at Elizabeth with a wide smile.

"How wonderful! Such happy news!"

Elizabeth smiled and took the letter back. "It was the only fitting end for them both: engaged to be married. Oh, Serena, I am so happy for her."

"You must wish you were there to see your family's pleasure." The girls walked along the landing towards their room but as they paused outside the door, Elizabeth shook her head.

"Indeed, I do not. Much as I love my sister, I do not think I could bear being witness to my mother at such a time."

Serena pulled a face, and Elizabeth understood her thoughts, her friend having been the victim of Mrs Bennet's unfettered and thoughtless tongue before now.

They began to gather their outdoor things and Serena, realising that her Patten remained in the downstairs hallway, where she had discarded it the night before, hurried from the room in search of it.

Closing the door behind her friend, Elizabeth leaned against it for a moment before picking up the letter and reading it once more. Dear Jane. She promised a longer message would follow, but had been so eager to share the knowledge with her beloved sister she could not wait to send news directly.

Elizabeth walked slowly over to the window, gazing out over the greenery below. It was indeed fortunate that she was not at Longbourn. However, she acknowledged her own failing: though, she did not miss the effusions of her mother over such news, being privy to her sister's state of happiness would, whilst bringing pleasure to her, only reinforce her own loss.

Turning around, she walked over to the bed where she sat for a moment, Jane's letter still in her grasp. Though she wished Mr Darcy had never interfered in the first instance in her sister and Bingley's affairs, she could not help but feel gratitude towards him for his attempt at making things right, and even some pride in his behaviour in doing so, a realisation that brought a glimmer of a smile to her lips, though it soon faded.

Dropping the letter onto the counterpane, Elizabeth picked up the one from her aunt. It took only a moment to discern its purpose: Mrs Gardiner had paid the promised call upon the Darcys on Thursday morning, and her letter was merely to advise Elizabeth of that which she knew full well – the family had gone away. It appeared that she had met Miss Darcy's companion as she was herself preparing to follow them, having remained in Town a day longer to rearrange some of Miss Darcy's lessons. She had not revealed her destination, and Mrs Gardiner had not liked to appear too inquisitive by asking the question, but she did express to her niece her surprise at the trip, bearing in mind there being nothing said of one during their encounters with the Darcys.

Mrs Gardiner's curiosity was clearly roused, and her hints that Elizabeth might have gleaned more, *"having been not only so much in Mr and Miss Darcy's company of late, but also deep in conversation with the former on more than one occasion,"* merely reinforced the sense of despondency she experienced in recalling a happier time.

Elizabeth got to her feet and dropped both letters onto the desk in the corner that held her writing case. No amount of speculation by her aunt could be answered positively, and thankful that their going out prevented her from having to pen an immediate response, Elizabeth picked up her shawl and made towards the door.

Chapter Twenty Two

HAVING ENJOYED A PLEASANT TRIP into the pretty, undulating countryside outside Bath, culminating in a gentle walk and a generous picnic, the party from Brock Street returned to the city in reasonable spirits late on Saturday afternoon.

Darcy breathed a sigh of relief as the carriage drew to a halt once more by the side door to the house. He felt some considerable benefit in removing himself from Bath for the day, for he had been tormented by dreams throughout the previous night, and Elizabeth had remained elusively out of his reach in them – near, almost visible, yet never tangible.

As he stepped down onto the pavement and turned to offer a hand to Georgiana he quashed any urge to walk beyond the carriage and stare across the field at Marlborough Buildings. His sister was followed by Anne, who had been persuaded to join them for afternoon tea before she was returned to her lodgings. Lady Catherine had refused to allow her daughter to accompany the Brock Street party on their evening excursion, for they planned to attend a recital at St Swithens; indeed, she had only relented in allowing Anne to accompany them for the drive into the country after much persuasion.

Anne had seemed content with the concession granted her, however, and as he assisted her from the carriage and saw her link arms with Georgiana before entering the house, Darcy could not help but reflect on the satisfaction he had drawn this day from seeing his cousin take enjoyment from their activities.

"Darce?"

He turned about to face the Colonel.

"Are you planning on joining us, or do you intend to play footman for the remainder of the day?"

Shaking his head, Darcy followed his cousin into the house and up the stairs to join the ladies and partake of the tea that had been laid out for them.

⁂

Whilst the Harington men enjoyed an afternoon of sport on the banks of the River Avon, Mrs Harington and her two charges had indulged in the things that ladies better enjoy when left to their own devices.

Following a few hours of browsing the many wares on offer in the multitude of shops that Bath heralded, they had called in at a patisserie to sample the delicacies, along with welcome cups of tea, and once refreshed had stopped to listen to a street entertainer who had located himself outside the Pump Room in the shadow of the abbey and had garnered quite the number of spectators, being possessed of a melodious voice and moreover a rather fine face and figure. It could for this reason, perhaps, be excused that there were so many more ladies in his impromptu audience than men.

On leaving the amusement behind, however, they had started to make their way back to the house, only for Mrs Harington to become diverted by a haberdashery in a side street that professed from its window card to having just received a supply of very fine lace from Wales. Serena was persuaded to join her in inspecting it, but the warmth of the day was sufficient for Elizabeth to beg to be excused, that she might walk on, her professed intention being the penning of letters to both Jane and her aunt, and with Mrs Harington's willing acquiescence, Elizabeth turned her steps towards the upper part of the city.

⁂

Their afternoon tea had soon been completed, and Darcy walked over to one of the windows overlooking Brock Street, his teacup in his hand. Georgiana and Anne were seated near to the fireplace whilst the Colonel re-read some post that he had brought from Town, and Darcy idly watched a barrow boy in his attempts to persuade some passing walkers to purchase his wares.

"Brother." His sister's voice drew his attention back into the room, and he glanced over to where she sat. "What time must Anne return to Great Pulteney Street?"

He looked over at the clock on the mantel and then to the Colonel, who had put aside his letter when Georgiana spoke.

"Perhaps the question should be asked of Anne." He looked at his other cousin. "Do you wish to go directly?"

For a moment, Anne did not speak, her gaze moving from Darcy to the Colonel, and finally to the young girl at her side. "No. If I must forego the evening's pleasures, at least let me enjoy those of the day for as long as possible."

Darcy nodded. "Of course. You are welcome without question to stay as long as you wish. Perhaps the sensible thing would be for you to dine early with us, and then we could drop you back at your lodgings on our way to the recital."

"A capital notion, Darce." The Colonel got to his feet and walked over to where the ladies sat, folding the letter in his hand as he walked. "What say you, Anne? Can you tolerate our company for a few more hours?"

Anne stared up at him, her face expressionless, and Darcy could perceive Georgiana fidgeting in agitation at her side. Then, his cousin smiled and nodded at the Colonel, before looking over at Darcy once more.

"I would like that very much; I thank you for the invitation."

"Should we send word to that effect to your mother?"

She shook her head. "I think not. What she is unaware of cannot ail her. For all she knows, we were away from Bath for the entirety of the day and you will drop me on our return."

Darcy frowned, and the Colonel laughed.

"Now, Darce, let us have no noble intent here. Anne will secure a better and more peaceful evening at home if her mother has little to complain of."

Accepting the wisdom of this, even if he was not entirely happy with the method, Darcy conceded the point and walked over to deposit his cup on the tray, just as the Colonel turned for the door.

"Well, I must leave you for a moment." He waved the letter in his hand. "A matter of business that I have postponed long enough. I shall join you directly."

"I was about to walk down into town and collect the book that we secured yesterday." Darcy turned to his sister and cousin. "You are welcome to accompany me if you wish."

Georgiana threw Anne a quick look. "Fitz, I think we would prefer to remain here. We could go and sit in the garden once we have finished our cups of tea; it is still so very warm."

"Of course. I will return shortly."

Darcy left the room with the Colonel, parting from him on the landing as he headed up to his chamber to do his duty. Checking his pocket watch and realising that the booksellers would be closing within a half hour, Darcy headed down the stairs and out into the street without delay. Coming out of the side door, he deliberately turned quickly to the left. The carriage had long been returned to the mews on the opposite side of Brock Street and should he have wished to indulge it, his eye would have had a clear view of Marlborough Buildings. As it was, he kept his gaze on his feet and within a matter of paces had reached the end of the garden wall and turned left onto the gravelled walk.

With a sigh of relief, he raised his eyes as he walked along the path, only for his step to falter within minutes. Coming towards him along the path was Miss Elizabeth Bennet – alone.

Heart pounding frantically, Elizabeth looked around, seeking somewhere – *anywhere* – that she might conceal herself from view, but there was nothing for it. Mr Darcy was headed straight towards her, and the encounter she had feared was upon her. He was sufficiently close for her to see his features, the closed expression that had come over his face at the ball soon in place, reminiscent of the early days of their acquaintance, and though the racing of her heart had calmed somewhat, her insides appeared to be turning somersaults.

"Ohhhh," she muttered under her breath, for want of words that could express her tumultuous feelings. Conscious that the gentleman had now reached her, she performed a perfunctory curtsey in response to his bow and waited for him to speak.

"Miss Bennet."

It seemed that was all she going to receive, her own response of 'Mr Darcy' falling into a silence of profound proportions.

Typically, they both then spoke at once:

"I did not know-"

"Is your sister-"

They both hesitated for a second before he spoke again. "Forgive me. Pray continue."

Striving for a modicum of composure, Elizabeth essayed a smile, before attempting her sentence once more. "Does your sister accompany you?"

He nodded but did not smile in return. "Yes – yes, she is here. She arrived on Thursday. And yourself? I had not understood that you were for Bath. When we last met…"

"An alteration of plan placed me in Somerset with the Haringtons, and Mrs Harington wished to come here for a few days. I had no choice in the matter, as I am at her disposal."

He nodded at this, but said nothing, and Elizabeth, her discomfort increasing by the second, knew that she must end the encounter swiftly. She struggled to overcome the tightness of her throat which had returned in full measure, but before she could say anything further, he made a gesture with his hand.

"I – I must offer you congratulations, I understand." The words seemed torn from him, and there was no concealing the bitterness of his tone or the solemnity of his expression that seemed to give lie to his words.

Conscious that Mr Bingley would have apprised his friend of his success in securing Jane's hand, Elizabeth was nonetheless surprised at his appearing so dissatisfied with the outcome and was left with the uncomfortable conjecture that perhaps he had not meant what he said in London of wishing to atone or that, since this latest example of her family's folly, he had changed his mind, that the belief he had long held of her family's inferiority and lack of suitability was too deeply ingrained to fully forego.

This thought was sufficient aid to Elizabeth in restoring her equilibrium, and she raised her chin and met the gentleman's eye squarely.

"Indeed, Sir. I thank you. I am, of course, delighted."

She felt a sting of regret as she saw him wince, but he did not look away.

"Your family must be well pleased."

Elizabeth's eyes flashed. "I can assure you, Sir, that the hand was not accepted for my family's sake or for their pleasure. It was accepted for nothing but the deepest of affection."

The satisfaction Elizabeth felt at delivering these words was brief. The look of pain in Mr Darcy's eyes surprised her, and feeling somewhat guilty, she knew her only option was to remove herself and ensure that neither of them discussed the matter again.

Yet before she could speak, he freed her by return. "Please excuse me, Madam." He bowed quite formally. "I am on an errand and cannot delay."

"I trust that you will enjoy your stay in Bath, Sir." She curtsied and with no further words they parted company. It was only once she reached the safe haven of Marlborough Buildings that Elizabeth detected the wetness upon her cheeks.

Chapter Twenty Three

HAVING FINISHED THEIR CUPS OF TEA, Georgiana led her cousin outside and down the path towards the rear of the garden where, next to the wall, was a wide swing amply supplied with soft cushions and a canvas canopy that shielded them from the sun. Settled upon it, they kicked in unison to set it in motion and, for a while, they drifted to and fro in a gentle silence.

Georgiana, however, was desperate for someone to talk to, and she turned slightly in her seat that she might study her cousin's face better.

"Anne – have you happened across Miss Elizabeth Bennet at all?"

Anne threw her a sharp look before facing forward again. "Other than a glimpse of her last night at the theatre, no, I have not. I cannot imagine why you would think that I might."

Georgiana sighed. "I wondered – well, I just thought, perhaps, you may have crossed paths with her in the Pump Room this morning."

They continued to swing in silence for a while; Georgiana's mind was distant, embroiled in all sorts of hopes and dreams, all of which she knew were quite impractical, but then Anne shifted in her corner so that she faced her cousin.

"Why do you ask? What particular interest do you have in Miss Bennet?"

Georgiana hesitated for a moment. "I found that I liked her very well. Very well indeed. I had hoped to further the acquaintance."

Anne let out a delicate but not particularly ladylike snort. "I am certain Darcy would not agree with *that* sentiment!"

"You should not mock him, Anne." Georgiana stopped, shocked at her own audacity in berating her much older cousin, colour flooding into her cheeks.

Anne raised a brow at this and smirked. "You are growing in confidence, child. But you will never carry your point if you are to be so blatantly embarrassed by speaking your mind!"

Lowering her gaze, Georgiana mumbled an apology, but raised her eyes again when she felt the touch of Anne's hand upon her arm. The look she bestowed upon her was not censorious but almost kindly.

"Do not distress yourself, Cousin. I am paying you a compliment of sorts. It will do you good to speak out more often."

Georgiana sighed. "I know that you are aware of my brother's – former interest in Miss Elizabeth Bennet. How could I not be? It was you who opened my own eyes to the possibility. He was distressed by the news of her being in Bath."

"Ah, yes. His *former* interest, and his being so extraordinarily discomposed by her coming here." Anne eyed Georgiana narrowly for a moment. "What has caused him to profess the loss of this interest? I do not believe it for one second."

Staring at her cousin, Georgiana's silence was clearly sufficient for Anne to continue.

"And do you not suspect her of some attempt to ensnare your brother? She appeared in Kent, and now she seems to be following him, first from Hunsford to London and now to Bath."

"Oh, indeed, no! Not at all. I am certain she would never do anything of the kind, she is not – her nature is not grasping – I have it on the highest authority that she is not mercenary."

Anne gave a light, mocking laugh. "The highest authority? This would be Darcy, no doubt. Yes – he said as much to me. I do wonder at the veracity of it, how he can be so certain."

Georgiana threw her cousin a frantic look. Everything she knew of her brother's feelings for Miss Elizabeth and her rejection of his offer of marriage, were not to be talked of, yet she had a natural urge to defend the lady's character against any potential slur.

Anne was silent for a moment, staring at her cousin. Then, she said, "As I mentioned to you yesterday, I am conscious of their being some form of impediment. I fail to see what it could be, but so it is."

Fidgeting in her seat, Georgiana bit her lip. She wished so desperately to talk to someone, a confidante. She had no close friends, and Mrs Annesley, much as she liked her, was not someone she could speak of her brother to. Anne was family, however; she would not breathe a word to another. She sent her cousin a beseeching look, and Anne leaned forward and took her hand and gave it a gentle squeeze.

"You are troubled, that much is clear. You can trust me, Georgiana. I have no desire to bring harm upon any of my cousins, least of all you."

Drawing in a quick breath, Georgiana then said in a rush, "He has discovered that Miss Elizabeth Bennet is engaged to be married."

Anne frowned. "It must have been sudden, for no mention was made of it in Kent, nor on Saturday evening." She stared at her cousin intently. "Is it certain?"

Georgiana looked down at her hands clasped in her lap. "Oh yes, it is most definite." She faltered; she did not wish to reveal that Darcy himself had been privy to the proposal. "I believe the commitment only stems from earlier this week. She is to marry a Mr Nicholas Harington." She raised her head and met her cousin's eye. "He seems a very nice man. I made his acquaintance briefly in London."

Anne shrugged her shoulders dismissively. "That does explain a vast deal, if she is promised to another." She turned in her seat and pushed her feet against the chippings to send the swing into motion once more. "Come, this is clearly disturbing you. Let us speak of it no more. I promise that I shall not breathe a word to anyone. "

Feeling both a little guilty for having said so much and quite relieved at having silenced her cousin's curiosity at last, Georgiana turned in her seat, and they swung to and fro for a moment in silence.

Then, Anne threw her another glance before saying, "Finally, I appreciate his desire for distance and distraction. So – tell me more of this plan of Darcy's to take you to Dublin. Is it true that you sail on Thursday?"

Georgiana grasped the opportunity to talk of the proposed journey as they awaited the return of the gentlemen and, enjoying the breeze created by the swing in the somewhat oppressive afternoon heat, the two cousins indulged in a long conversation about Ireland and travelling abroad, all the more remarkable for two ladies who had yet to set foot beyond the shores of their own small island.

❧

Elizabeth's intention of responding to her letters had fled from her mind following her encounter with Mr Darcy, and she had turned away from the house at first to lose herself in the paths that skirted the field whilst she gave herself a severe talking to.

Suitably calmed, she had then returned to the house, washed her face in her chamber and returned to the drawing room to await the ladies. However, with Mrs Harington and Serena yet to appear, she struggled to find a diversion, first attempting to read a book, but not getting beyond the first page, then persevering with her needlework, but before long it was all a tangle and she had not the patience to unravel it.

Stuffing it haphazardly into the work basket, she then walked over to the windows to enjoy the view and breathe deeply of the warm summer air, only to find herself staring across the fields to the end house in Brock Street, bringing inevitable thoughts of its occupants to mind. Frustrated, she turned her back on the scene and repaired to her chamber to collect writing materials. She had been back in the drawing room, sat at a small circular table and attempting to do as originally intended and respond to Jane's letter, when the door burst open and Serena came into the room.

As the door crashed back against the wooden panelling, Elizabeth's head shot up, and on perceiving the expression upon her friend's face, she leapt to her feet in concern.

"Good heavens, what is it? What has happened?" She hurried towards Serena who had stopped to unfasten the Patten, flinging it away with impatient fingers. She was breathless and pink in the face as she stared at Elizabeth with wide eyes.

"I just found out-" she gasped, then drew in a breath. "You will never believe what I have heard!" She struggled to regain her breathing once more, and Elizabeth, concerned for her well-being, ushered her into a seat and fetched a glass of water from the dresser, pressing it upon her friend and urging her to drink from it before taking a place by her side.

Serena did as she was bid, taking a long drink from the glass, and as her colour returned to normal she sank back against the cushions and then, to her friend's astonishment, began to laugh. Becoming seriously troubled, so out of nature was this present behaviour, Elizabeth reached forward and took her by both hands.

"Serena – please. Do tell me what it is. Is it Mrs Harington? What has happened?"

Serena sobered somewhat but could not prevent a smile from overspreading her features.

"I believe I have discovered why your Mr Darcy has withdrawn his attentions. It is astonishing – indeed, it is quite ridiculous, and I can scarce believe it myself, but you must trust me in this."

If there was one thing she had not anticipated, it was that Serena's strange behaviour might have anything to do with Mr Darcy. Elizabeth got to her feet and walked swiftly across the room to the window, but confronted immediately as she was by the sight of the Darcys' lodgings again, she turned her back.

"I have told you why he seems to have decided against continuing our friendship. It is no secret – leastways, not to me."

Serena, who appeared to have become more herself, got to her feet and limped over to join her friend. "Dear Lizzy. How you do yourself an injustice, and me into the bargain. You must begin to have some faith! Do you not wish to learn of the fanciful notion Mr Darcy is labouring under?"

Conscious that, despite her best endeavour to prevent it, a small sliver of hope had begun to steal through her, Elizabeth nodded, aware of her insides clenching in anticipation.

"I have quite unintentionally overheard a private and most peculiar conversation!"

"Serena! How could -"

"Be patient, Lizzy. Let me tell my tale before Aunt Alicia returns." She glanced out of the window behind Elizabeth, as if to ascertain that their moment of privacy was secure, then met her friend's eye once more.

"I left my aunt in Milsom Street – we met with some of her acquaintance there – so I excused myself and began to make my way home alone, taking the short cut as usual along the walk that runs behind Brock Street. Yet before I reached its end, I realised I had gained a small stone inside my Patten which stabbed me sorely in the instep, so I took advantage of the only bench in the vicinity that was not occupied and seated myself to repair my foot. I had just redone the fastenings when I became aware of voices – female voices – drifting through the wrought-iron gate in the wall beside my seat. Anyone walking past on the path would no doubt have been unable to decipher the words, but positioned as I was against the very wall behind which the owners of these voices were most likely seated, I heard them well, and what caught my attention was the mention of your name!"

With a growing sense of trepidation, Elizabeth cleared her throat. "Do you know who the ladies were?"

Serena nodded. "One of them, for certain." She paused. "I cannot recollect the given name, but she sounded young and was, from what she said, Mr Darcy's sister."

Elizabeth paled. "Miss Darcy?! Is that whose garden wall you sat beside?"

"It would appear so. And you will thank the stone for paining me when you allow me to finish my tale!" Serena dragged Elizabeth over to sit beside her on the couch opposite the empty hearth. "Listen. For 'tis not who they are that is significant, 'tis what was said!" She paused for breath, then said in a rush: "Mr Darcy believes you are engaged, Lizzy!"

Chapter Twenty Four

ELIZABETH SAT FORWARD IN HER SEAT, staring at Serena as if she had run mad. "Engaged? To be married?"

"Yes, of course, Lizzy. What other sort of engaged is there?" Serena tutted and continued, "But this absurdity goes beyond even that for strangeness. You must essay a guess as to whom it is they would have you promised to!"

Serena's countenance was animated, but Elizabeth slumped back into her seat, her mind all confusion.

"I cannot conceive how anyone could suppose such a thing, let alone to whom!"

Serena nodded. "Well, then. You leave me no choice but to reveal it: *Nicholas*."

Elizabeth stared speechlessly at her friend for a moment. Nicholas? How on earth could it have got about that she was betrothed to her friend? To have the rumour at large that she was engaged at all was beyond belief, but to have her coupled with a man who was so lately promised himself...

"Is it not astonishing news? How do you think such a report came about? And how is it that Mr Darcy should have such knowledge, clearly shared amongst his family, when none of us is aware of it? Do you not love this mystery and does it not finally account for his altered behaviour towards you of late?"

Elizabeth got slowly to her feet, uncertain as to her purpose but knowing that she could sit no longer. She walked back towards the windows again and this time allowed herself the indulgence of staring at the Darcys' lodgings, trying in vain to assimilate the intelligence that her friend had brought.

"Lizzy?"

Turning about, she met Serena's gaze across the room. "I cannot comprehend how Mr Darcy may have supposed such a thing, or indeed why he would do so, and-" With a gasp, her hand flew to her mouth "Oh no!"

She hurried back across the room to her friend who got to her feet as she reached her.

"Oh, Serena!" grabbing her friend's hands, she squeezed them. "Was that his meaning when I saw him earlier? He offered me his congratulations, and I thought – I assumed he meant in relation to *Jane* and her recent understanding with Mr Bingley. What if he referred to my supposed engagement to Nicholas?"

It was Serena's turn to fetch a glass of water, which she pressed into her friend's hand as they both resumed their positions on the couch once more.

Conscious that Serena watched her carefully, Elizabeth gave a tremulous smile. "I thank you for the intelligence you have brought. I am grateful, truly I am, but I am still at a loss as to how such a notion could be taken."

"When Mr Darcy last spoke to you in London, did he seem to be labouring under the same belief?"

Elizabeth cast her mind back to the evening of the ball with great ease. Though she had found Mr Darcy to be a little quiet at first, they had soon been conversing with ease, or so it had seemed to her.

"I can recall nothing that marked a change in him other than my disclosure over Lydia's letter. He became – reserved, more as I was used to seeing him in the earliest days of our acquaintance. It was as if he withdrew before my very eyes. He remained perfectly civil, of course, and we completed the set in a cordial enough manner, but his distraction was evident."

"Does it not occur to you that his preoccupation was concerned with the knowledge you had given him? Did you not say that he travelled the following morning – very early – to Longbourn to warn your father against that man?"

Elizabeth sighed. "It was a very noble gesture, in the circumstances. I thought well enough of him for doing it, but if he did so believing I was engaged to another..." Raising her head, she gave Serena a watery smile and let out a small laugh. "No matter how much I learn of the man, I never seem to do him justice!"

"Yet we are none the wiser as to why he might think what he does." Serena frowned. "From what I can recall, they seemed to think the commitment stemmed from earlier this week."

"But it makes no sense. By the time you and Nicholas had come to an understanding, Mr Darcy was gone from Town."

Serena chewed her lip. "Then we are missing something... oh, Lizzy! Do you not see? *This* must be why he removed himself to Bath! You said he had made no intimation of leaving Town; thus, he must have left because he thought he had lost you!"

Feeling all the seriousness of the distress that this false rumour must have caused Mr Darcy, whether he continued to hold her in high regard or not, Elizabeth felt terribly upset. Unfortunately, before she could make any further attempt to question Serena or consider the inference of her supposition, the door opened to reveal Mrs Harington, putting an end for the time being to their private discourse.

Colonel Fitzwilliam had dealt satisfactorily with his correspondence before joining his cousins in the garden, but as a distant church clock chimed the hour, he frowned. Darcy had been gone a good while, considering the brief nature of his mission, and excusing himself from the ladies, who were enjoying some refreshing lemon barley under the shade of a tree, he headed out through the gate onto the path.

There was no sign of his cousin coming from town, and he pulled his pocket watch out to confirm that he had not miscounted the bells. It was definitely the hour of six, and they were due to be at St Swithens by seven thirty, with supper yet to be consumed and Anne to return to Great Pulteney Street beforehand.

Some instinct caused him to glance to his right, and he walked a few paces to the end of the path and looked out across the fields. There were still people out enjoying the lingering warmth of the day and the last rays of sunshine before dusk began to fall, yet he saw no sign of Darcy. He turned back, but as he did so, he realised that his cousin sat on a fallen tree trunk not half a dozen paces away, his gaze distant and his shoulders slumped.

With a sigh, he retraced his steps and joined him, conscious from his start as he sat beside him that Darcy had been unaware of his presence until that moment.

The Colonel threw him a quick all-embracing glance.

"No book, I perceive."

This garnered no response.

"Well, either you failed to reach there before they closed – understandable, of course. At your age, a steady pace is a bit of a challenge, especially after a long day. Or," the Colonel glanced at Darcy again. "You never went in the first place, and you have been sitting here for the best part of an hour instead."

Darcy stirred slightly, but said nothing, and thus he continued. "I suspect the latter; which means one of two things. Would you care to enquire what those are, or shall I just inform you?"

Determined as he was to gain a rise out of his cousin, the Colonel shifted his position and fixed Darcy with a stare. "You do not fool me, Darce, and you never will, so get used to the notion."

For a moment, there was no reaction. Then, Darcy stretched his legs out in front of him and sat up, straightening his shoulders before glancing over at his cousin.

"Go on, enlighten me."

The Colonel inclined his head. "Either you merely wished for an excuse to escape the company for a while, having been stuck with us for the whole day, or something has happened to discompose you, and you felt it best to remain here until you were in sufficient control of yourself to return to the house."

Darcy got to his feet and stared out across the fields. "As you have probably decided which of these is correct, you may as well continue with your deductions."

Standing up, the Colonel studied his cousin thoughtfully for a moment. Though he made light of it, he could not deny that his cousin's eyes betrayed him, and though he might jest at the best of times, he felt deeply for him at that moment.

"You have seen Miss Elizabeth Bennet."

Blowing out a breath, Darcy turned back towards the house, and the Colonel fell into step beside him.

"We met just there," he waved a hand towards the gravelled walk, but continued up the side of the house rather than going in through the garden gate, and perforce the Colonel went with him.

"And?"

As they reached the side door, Darcy stopped and turned to face his cousin.

"And what? What is there to say? She was alone; it was awkward. It was obvious that she had no desire to cross my path. I offered my congratulations, and she expressed no surprise at my doing so, thus we must assume our speculations were correct and that the formal approval has been given."

The Colonel let out a slow whistle, and then he patted Darcy consolingly on the shoulder. "I am sorry, Darce. That cannot have been easy – for either of you, given the circumstances of a fortnight ago."

"Precisely. She made it plain…" he stopped as if unable to continue.

The Colonel eyed him carefully. "Well, it is over now, that first meeting. Come," he waved a hand towards the door. "We must make haste with supper if we are not to be late for the recital."

Darcy nodded, though he did not move. "You do not think-" he paused again and cleared his throat. "The Haringtons may well be in attendance."

The Colonel shook his head. "I understand your concerns, old man, but I truly do not think so. When I secured the seats they were the last ones available."

"Oh." Darcy's response was flat, and he turned and entered the house. The Colonel stood for a moment deep in thought; if he was not mistaken, that disappointed 'oh' was more about the lady not being in attendance, despite her altered situation, than the contrary. With a sigh of regret, he glanced about him once more at the beautiful day before entering the house and closing the door behind him.

Soon after Mrs Harington's return, the gentlemen of the family came back from their sojourn on the banks of the River Avon, full of tales of fish they had caught and fish they had lost, and in an attempt to continue their private discourse, Elizabeth and Serena managed to extricate themselves soon after on the pretext of needing to prepare for the evening ahead.

Thus it was that as soon as their chamber door closed behind them, Elizabeth threw herself into a chair by the writing desk and Serena took up a perch on the bed, and for a few moments they simply stared at each other in silence.

Then, Elizabeth closed her eyes, thinking, straining, trying to recall what could have happened to cause such a conflicting report to be abroad.

"Something had to have been said before he left Town, Lizzy. Some word of this supposed commitment must have reached his ears at the ball; it must have. Did anything untoward happen that you can recall?"

"*Oooh!*" Serena's words brought clarity, and Elizabeth's eyes flew open as she realised in an instant what may have occurred. "Oh no!" Getting to her feet, she stood in indecision for a second, then began to walk quickly to and fro across the hearthrug.

"What is it? Truly, Lizzy, you are alarming me!" Serena turned in her position on the bed and eyed her friend in concern.

"Oh I cannot believe that he saw – or that he heard… Oh, Serena! What a tangle!"

Chapter Twenty Five

ELIZABETH TURNED TO FACE HER FRIEND. "I am quite certain I understand why he is so convinced, Serena. He must have somehow either overhead part of my conversation with Nicholas on the terrace at Lady Bellingham's..." she closed her eyes again, remembering, then opened them to stare at her friend in dismay. "Or he saw something that he misinterpreted! Oh dear Lord."

Elizabeth began to pace again. "Nicholas told me that evening how he had asked you to marry him. I was so delighted I did not give him chance to explain the full story, but threw myself at him." Elizabeth put a hand to her head. "There were people outside, of course there were, but we were out of sight in the main, and only someone who leant over the parapet could have observed us. Indeed, they would have had to overhear the tiniest portion of our conversation to still deduce such a thing, for of course, the subject of our discourse was entirely *you* and Nicholas, not me."

"There is something further, Lizzy."

Elizabeth stopped her pacing and walked over to where her friend sat on the bed.

"What?" She watched as her friend bit her lip, her expression anxious. "What further do you know?"

"He is leaving the country. They are to depart on Thursday next from Bristol. I know not for how long or any further details, for I did not linger beyond that point. You were right – he has quite given you up, but not because of what you feared – because he believes there is nothing to hope for, that you are taken."

Sinking onto the bed beside Serena, Elizabeth put a hand to her face, conscious of how cold her skin suddenly felt. Might she never see him again?

"Lizzy," Serena took one of her friend's hands in her own. "You do not look at all well. Let me get you some wine."

"No!" Getting quickly to her feet, Elizabeth shook her head. "I am quite well, I assure you. I know not what I can do or say, but I must see him before we quit here. He must be made aware of the truth."

Walking over to the window as if in a daze, Elizabeth stared across the field to the end house in Brock Street. Was this the way of it? Would she depart for Somerset, and he be gone from the country and henceforth from her life?

Just then, a servant knocked upon the door and as the hot water for bathing was ferried in, both girls turned their attention to getting ready for the evening and, in the presence of the maid, there was little else that could be said. Once she had finished her ministrations to their hair, however, and left the room, Serena turned to her friend.

"You are right; you must reveal the truth to him. I am sure it is what drives him to behave as he is."

Elizabeth shook her head and walked over to the dresser. "I have had time now to reflect upon it, and I do not see that it alters anything. He distanced himself before Nicholas and I went out onto the terrace; I have told you so."

"And I believe you misinterpret his reasons for that detachment, that it was not distance per se, merely distraction."

Letting out a pent up breath, Elizabeth shook her head. "Fine. Let us not debate the finer points, for we shall never agree."

"But you must tell him, Lizzy." Serena walked over to her friend and turned her back to her so that she might fasten the buttons of her gown. "He has a right to know at least that you are not betrothed."

Elizabeth feigned concentration on the tiny fastenings of Serena's dress. Of course he must be told. It was a falsehood and needed correction. So why did she not wish it to be her that delivered the intelligence? *Because you are afraid*, whispered a voice in her head. *You have been given reason to hope, and you do not wish to see that it means little or nothing to him, that hope is futile.*

"There," she patted Serena on the shoulder and turned her about to look in the full length mirror. "You look lovely, and Nicholas will be very proud."

Serena sent her a grateful smile and limped over to the bed to put on her slippers. Then, she stood up and looked over to where Elizabeth was fastening a necklace before stepping over to inspect her own appearance in the mirror.

"Lizzy?"

Elizabeth glanced over her shoulder.

"When you told me about Mr Darcy – about what he had done for your family and of his troubled past in relation to Mr Wickham – you said, if I recall correctly, that there was a time when you believed he held you in high esteem."

Saying nothing, Elizabeth turned to stare into the full-length mirror once more, certain that Serena could not fail to note the rising colour in her cheeks.

"Was it a long time ago? Both ladies today alluded to Mr Darcy's former interest in you."

Unable to prevent it, Elizabeth winced at this confirmation of his having put his regard for her into the past.

"How long has your acquaintance been in existence, that you can claim an earlier affection from him that you now profess to have lost?" Serena paused. "The older lady did not seem to believe it – that he had lost his inclination."

Elizabeth realised how deeply she wished it to be so. Then, she turned to face Serena.

"There is something I have not told you; something that I have kept from you." With a frustrated gesture of her hand, Elizabeth walked over to the bed and dropped down heavily onto it, her head down-bent. Concerned, Serena hurried to her side, perching herself beside her and taking one of her hands in her own. She leaned down, trying to see Elizabeth's visage.

"What is it? Dear Lizzy, please talk to me."

Elizabeth raised her head and smiled ruefully at Serena. "You ask how long ago was it, that I last understood Mr Darcy's feelings for me. What if I told you that it was but two weeks back?"

Serena stared at her incredulously. "A fortnight? Only fourteen days ago, this man had feelings for you, yet now you claim he has none?"

"You do not understand. You have no notion of what has transpired…"

Serena got to her feet and stood in front of her friend, forcing her to look up at her. "No, I do not. But I will, if you choose to let me. Tell me, Lizzy. Tell me what could possibly have happened in the past two weeks to alter things so radically."

With a reluctant smile, Elizabeth nodded. "I will. But be warned, you are likely to be amazed. You may wish to be seated whilst I relate this tale."

Despite his cousin's assertion that the Harington party was too lately arrived at Bath to secure such a number of seats to the recital, Darcy could not help but search every group of people within the hall at St Swithens for a sight of either Elizabeth or Harington.

Even when it became clear that his cousin had the truth of it and they had been spared the ignominy of a strained evening in company with each other, he could not stop looking for her, and the sense of disappointment that gripped him when in every case he was unsuccessful only served to reinforce how much he wished to lay eyes upon her.

Fortunately, the music was of an excellent standard, and for a time, Darcy allowed it to take over, and he was able to reflect upon how much pleasanter it was to be in Bath as opposed to London. Admittedly, it was the end of the Season, and thus there were fewer people about in general, and those in attendance certainly were not the more aggressive of the social climbers one encountered in Town – his aunt certainly had the right of it when she had said people of fashion would not be in Bath at this time of year. For this very reason, however, Darcy realised that it made life much easier for him, and more feasible for his sister to attend some smaller engagements, bearing in mind she had yet to come out.

This reminder of Georgiana's welfare was timely, for it aided Darcy in his attempts to push thoughts of Elizabeth and what she might be doing that evening with the Haringtons to one side and focus upon his sister instead.

Thus it was that as soon as the interval arrived, he left the Colonel to seek refreshments and made a concerted effort to discuss the performance with his sister and to study the remainder of the programme for the evening. Upon Fitzwilliam's return, he accepted a glass of wine from him with a smile that was briefly delivered but genuine and gave the second movement almost all the attention it deserved.

⁂

Nicholas had been concerned about Elizabeth for some days now, and he eyed his friend thoughtfully as the family dinner drew to a close. The gentlemen had eschewed separating from the ladies, the occasion being what it was and they being such a close-knit party, and he poured himself a port from the decanter before passing it to Patrick, his eye still upon the lady who had now risen from her seat and walked over to the small pianoforte against the far wall.

Both she and Serena, despite having excused themselves earlier that they might prepare for the evening, had been so tardy at arriving downstairs that his mother had gone up to find out what was delaying them. Serena had thrown him an apologetic look when they had entered the room, but Elizabeth, despite her attempts to prove otherwise, had looked quite out of sorts.

That her spirits were troubled he could tell. They had not been close friends all these years without him noticing such a detail, and as Elizabeth had by nature such a sunny disposition, any lowering of her mood was most apparent to those who knew and loved her best.

Suddenly conscious of a dig at his side, he turned quickly to look at Serena, who inclined her head towards Elizabeth and whispered, "I must speak with you in private. Can we find a way?"

Nicholas narrowed his gaze as he looked at her, then nodded quickly and turned to address his mother.

"Shall we not adjourn to the drawing room, Mama? The instrument there is far superior, and so, I must own, is the seating!"

With a laugh, Mrs Harington nodded. "Of course, my dear. Lizzy." She turned to address Elizabeth, who looked up and stopped playing as she saw people getting to their feet.

"Oh dear," she laughed, though it did not reach her eyes, something Nicholas was quick to note. "Is my playing so dire, that the room is to be vacated?"

Everyone laughed with her, but Mr Harington was the first to answer. "Far from it, my dear. You play delightfully, and we will impose upon you to continue once we are upstairs." He walked over and offered her his arm and the rest of the family followed them out into the hall, and in the confusion of noise and movement, Nicholas waited until there was only himself and Serena remaining before he pushed the door to and returned to where she still sat at the table.

"Come," he held out his hand which she took with alacrity. "Let us sit over here. We shall have very little time before we are missed."

They settled themselves on a small sofa, and Nicholas retained his hold upon her hand, raising it and pressing it to his lips for a moment. "We have had so little opportunity to be together."

Serena blushed, but squeezed his hand. "I know. I hope that things will be better once we are back at Sutton Coker."

Nicholas raised a hand and brushed a lock of hair from her cheek before bending to kiss her.

"Come, let us talk of Lizzy, before I become too distracted."

Serena, her blush intensifying, nodded, and quickly set before Nicholas what she had heard earlier that day, forestalling his immediate astonishment over the mistaken engagement by telling him further of Elizabeth's affection for Mr Darcy and thus why the situation caused such heartache for their friend. Of the rejected proposal she said nothing. Elizabeth had given her leave to share with Nicholas the intelligence of the rumour that was about and had reluctantly agreed to him being told of her feelings for the gentleman, but beyond that, she begged Serena not to go.

"And what about the inference of this overheard conversation? Does Darcy hold an interest in Lizzy? Why has no one said anything of the sort? It would be a fair prospect for her, that is to be certain, but would she care for him? She has never shown a particular preference that I have noticed." He paused and then shrugged. "But then, I have seen little of them in company with each other, so who am I to judge?"

Serena bit her lip. "All I know is that he must be told. Yet I cannot see how to effect the revelation."

"We cannot call upon the Darcys' home at this hour of night, and you know a social call cannot be contemplated on the Sabbath. Besides, even if it were so, how is such a subject to be raised?"

With a sigh, Serena recalled her friend's support of her only recently, when she herself had been equally adamant that nothing could be done to right her relationship with Nicholas.

"There must be something." She stared up at him, her eyes wide, and he shook his head at her.

"I cannot refuse you when you look at me so." He leant forward and brushed her lips with his own, then sighed. "Let me consider the matter; I am certain we can come up with something."

Their ruminations, however, were given no further time to progress, for at that moment the door was pushed open and with a mild admonishment, Mrs Harington ordered them from the room and to re-join the company, throwing Nicholas a warning look as they passed which left little impression, that gentleman bestowing a warm kiss on his mother's cheek before taking Serena's hand and leading her up the stairs to the drawing room.

Chapter Twenty Six

SUNDAY DAWNED AS FAIR AS THE previous day, and as a maid unfastened the clasps on the three long windows of the drawing room of the Harington house and pushed them open, a wave of warm air pervaded the room, a clear indication that temperatures were rising despite it only being ten o'clock in the morning.

The family's intention, following their celebratory meal which had lasted into the small hours, was to forego the morning service they had a tendency to attend in the local chapel at Lansdown and in its place attend the noontide service in Bath Abbey. Thus, having partaken of a lengthy breakfast, Serena and Elizabeth had repaired to the drawing room to await the carriages to be brought round.

Mr Harington had long had a fascination with the vagaries of the English climate. He took much pride in his ability to predict changes in the pattern of weather and, whilst not infallible, he hit his mark more often than he missed. The family had learned to indulge him in his obsession, and though the morning bade fair, he had insisted upon the use of the carriages rather than an expedition on foot, announcing at breakfast that the humidity so early in the day gave rise to the likelihood of an intensely warm day and thus the risk later on of a downpour.

Whilst partaking of their repast, the young men had argued against such a precaution on as beautiful a morning as could be observed through the breakfast room windows, but Mr Harington was adamant. Should a rain storm take them unawares later in the day when they were a good half hour's walk or more from home, they would thank him for his caution, for a thirty minute dash in the rain would soon become a week in bed with a red nose and a bad chest. It was to be avoided at all costs, and he would have his way.

Everyone had good-naturedly conceded and fallen in with his plan, and thus it was that Elizabeth currently leaned on the wrought iron railing that bounded the drawing room windows, watching for the conveyances to pull up outside, their party being of such a size as to need two rather than one.

Her reluctance to cast her eyes across the fields to Brock Street had not diminished, despite Serena's report of the previous day. The doubt lingered yet that Mr Darcy's disinterest stemmed from more than just the rumoured engagement, and thus she could not subscribe to Serena's way of thinking. She did, however, agree with her on one point: if their path crossed with any of the Brock Street party during the day, bearing in mind she would leave for Sutton Coker the following morning, it was essential to somehow find a way of clearing up the misunderstanding. Beyond that, she would just have to let the formal announcement that would surely be abroad within the next few days answer and hope that the intelligence might somehow reach Mr Darcy before he left the country.

"Lizzy."

Elizabeth straightened and turned about, and Serena studied her for a moment in silence. It was the expression upon her friend's face that indicated to Elizabeth what was on her mind, and she attempted to forestall her.

"Serena, listen-"

"No, *you* listen. For years you have been my friend – my shoulder, my adviser, my sister in my heart. Now I must return the favour. 'Tis my turn to offer counsel. I cannot but agree with what you say Jane told you: Mr Darcy will not be able to put aside his feelings for you as easily as you persist in believing."

"You have not told Nicholas?"

"Of Mr Darcy's proposal? No. I promised that I would not."

Elizabeth sighed. "Thank you."

Serena threw her a quick glance. "I think Mr Darcy needs to know more than the truth of the engagement. You must let him know how you feel about him."

Letting out a huff of frustration, Elizabeth rounded on her. "What would you have me do? We are women, tied by our sex and our station in life. I can neither declare myself, nor offer for him. I can do nothing but live in hope of him renewing *his* offer – which he will not."

"He may."

"Ridiculous. What man would offer his hand in marriage where it has once been rejected, and further, with such rudeness and false accusation?"

"Then you will have to do something that demonstrates the extent of your altered feelings, for surely he will need sufficient encouragement to approach you again. You must give him a *sign*, Lizzy."

Having attended morning service at All Saints Church, the nearest place of worship to Brock Street, the Colonel and his two cousins had returned to the house. That Darcy had been anticipating an onslaught of Haringtons, the Colonel could not deny. It was blatantly obvious in the rigidity of his stance, the flexing of his fingers and the constant flicking of his gaze from person to person, before, after and even during the short service.

It had probably been little aid to his cousin's concentration that, though none of the current family was in attendance that day, they found themselves, in effect, surrounded by Haringtons, for following Darcy's gaze, which had become fixed during the sermon upon the plaques on the surrounding walls, the Colonel had detected the name several times over. It had clearly been a place of worship for the family for many years, and how they had escaped the present day clan was beyond him.

Thus it was that returning to the house was a welcome relief all round, and soon after doing so, they ventured into the walled garden for a cup of tea and a gentle discussion over the unseasonably warm weather and their plans for the afternoon. Lady Catherine had agreed most reluctantly to Anne attending a concert in Sydney Gardens with them. She was concerned about the amount of time her daughter was spending in the outdoors, but the dry weather seemed to have convinced her it was worthy of the risk, and her only proviso had been that she too attend them, that she might keep an eye on her daughter and make sure nothing ill befell her.

This was hardly the outcome any of the cousins desired, but as the alternative was for Anne to miss out entirely on the scheme, Darcy had conceded to his aunt's demands. Thus it was that, once they had broken their fast, they gathered their belongings and climbed once more into the carriage and set off for the de Bourgh's lodgings. None of the party particularly wished to ride down to the Gardens; it would have been a pleasant enough walk, despite the rising heat and humidity. But the fact that Sydney Gardens was located at the head of Great Pulteney Street was irrelevant to their aunt. She would not have Anne arrive there in anything but a conveyance, and thus it was that they were obliged to take a set of wheels and call for their relations on the way.

⁂

Throughout the service at the abbey, Elizabeth found herself struggling to keep her attention on her prayer book or the minister's words. Conscious of the guilt of indulging in distraction when she should be focused on more righteous things, all she could think of was where Mr Darcy might be at that moment. The abbey was vast and on this summer morning, well attended, yet no countenances were familiar to her, and though she looked about continually once they had taken their places, she finally conceded that wherever Mr Darcy worshipped, it was not here.

Serena cast her an understanding look upon catching her eye as they stood for the first hymn, and Elizabeth sent her a reassuring smile and shook her head. She would not have her friends worry for her.

Eventually, the service drew to a close, and they made their way out into the sun once more, to be welcomed by the deep, resonant sound of the bells and a crush of people around them.

The Haringtons had a vast acquaintance in Bath, being semi-resident, and a great deal of conversation took place before any movement was made to leave. Unable to stop herself, Elizabeth found her attention drifting, her gaze still scouring the people thronging round the entrance to the abbey.

"Come, Lizzy."

With a start, she turned and took the arm offered to her by Nicholas, who had by now secured Serena on his other side, and they began to stroll towards the carriages. They were forestalled, however, by Mrs Harington calling them back.

"My dears! Do not be so hasty! Here is a fine plan for our afternoon!"

⁂

Mrs Harington had been delighted to learn from a friend of an outdoor concert taking place that afternoon, and she wasted little time in persuading her family and her guests that it was the perfect way in which to spend the remainder of their day. To be certain, the air was much fresher down in that part of the city, for there was a least a hint of a slight breeze, and Elizabeth had no objection at all to the scheme. To be in the outdoors was always her preference, and if she remained secluded at Marlborough Buildings, her chance of encountering Mr Darcy would be negligible.

As the afternoon had been unplanned, the Haringtons had first called in at a nearby hotel for a meal before making their way to the gardens on foot. Mr Harington had instructed his staff to await them at the gatehouse to the gardens with the family carriage and the landaulet that had been pressed into service, and after a leisurely stroll over Pulteney Bridge and along Great Pulteney Street, they had soon arrived at the Sydney Hotel, where, if sounds were anything to judge by, the concert was in full swing.

The gentlemen set off into the grounds to seek a place for them to sit and, linking arms, Elizabeth and Serena followed Mrs Harington as they made their way along the path. Despite the somewhat oppressive heat, it was a lovely afternoon. Some white puffs of cloud had bubbled up and only the slightest of breezes disturbed the leafy trees around them as they strolled towards the centre of the gardens where the bandstand was located. The music drifted to them on the air and looking around her as they walked, Elizabeth released a soft sigh. Yet another excursion, and yet again she hoped Mr Darcy would be here or at least someone from his family, that she might have a chance to put the truth before them.

After their ambiguous discourse on the previous day, she felt somewhat anxious about the possibility. The awkwardness and brusqueness of that first encounter in Bath had been vastly unpleasant. She was far from content with the current state of their acquaintance, or the misunderstanding that persisted on his part, but this did give her the incentive, even though she felt some trepidation about it, to lay the truth before him.

Soon they emerged into the circle, where all manner of temporary seating had been contrived and a large swathe of people had by this time gathered.

"There they are!" Mrs Harington waved an arm and they followed her as she made her way across the lawn to where James and Patrick had secured a small round table and several wooden seats.

Removing her shawl, Elizabeth settled herself upon one of the chairs, as did Mrs Harington and Serena, and they watched as the two men wandered off to assist Mr Harington and Nicholas who had gone in search of refreshments. She berated herself for the action, but could not stop her eyes from roving over those nearest to them, seeking familiar faces, but none were apparent. With a small sigh, Elizabeth turned back to look towards the bandstand and for a moment she let the music drift over her, closing her eyes and leaning back against her chair in feigned enjoyment. Her mind, however, would not release her so easily.

Regret for her misunderstanding of Mr Darcy's character, for being so prejudiced against him and so blinded to the truth by Wickham's lies, sadness for what might have been and how close they may have come to an understanding, had Wickham and her foolish family not intruded, washed over her. She felt so stupid, so blinkered, and yet so inexplicably sad about the loss of his regard, and this added complication merely reinforced her despair…

"Lizzy?" Eyes opening quickly, she sat up straighter and met Serena's look of concern with a rueful smile. "Are you quite well, you have gone so pale."

Elizabeth shook her head and forced a smile. "Pay me no mind. I am a little tired, that is all."

Looking as if she did not quite believe this, Serena murmured, "hmmm" under her breath before turning to answer a question from Mrs Harington.

Chapter Twenty Seven

WITHIN MOMENTS JAMES AND PATRICK returned, accompanied by a servant laden with a tray bearing tea things and a platter of fruit cake.

"We have seen Lady Gwendolyn, Mama," said James as he placed a cup on the table in front of his mother. "And she wished me to pass on her best wishes. She will call upon you in the morning before we leave for Somerset."

"The Bland-Williams are here also," added Patrick who performed the same service for Serena and Elizabeth. He dropped into the empty chair beside the latter. "Mrs Bland-Williams says she wished to send an invitation to dinner, but I told her your stay was but of short duration. She hopes to see you during the afternoon."

"And Admiral Davies has button-holed Papa as usual! Nicholas remained behind to assist in retrieving him should the service be required," added James as he placed the platter of cake in the centre of the table before seating himself. "Oh – and we saw an acquaintance of mine that I reconnected with only the other day, Mama."

Elizabeth paid little mind to James' dialogue with his mother and reached for her cup only to drop it back into the saucer with a clatter as she heard the word 'Darcy' pass his lips.

"Forgive me." Having garnered the attention of the entire party, Elizabeth could feel her cheeks colouring, but Serena aided her in mopping up the few splashes of tea that had spattered the table and saucer, and James turned back to Mrs Harington. She was not to be spared the conversation, however, for within minutes he turned to include Serena in his discussion.

"Darcy was with his cousin, whose acquaintance I made but the other day, but as they were on their way to join the remainder of their party, we did no more than exchange greetings. However, it has made me think. He has a large estate in Derbyshire, and I am certain that it is not far from Lambton. Are you familiar with the family, Serena?"

The lurch of her insides was now so customary that Elizabeth barely heeded it as she threw Serena a quick glance.

"I am not personally, no, though I know the name. But then, Papa only returned to Lambton so very recently, and I have not spent much time there as of yet."

Elizabeth picked up her cup a little more slowly this time and cradled it in her hands, appreciative of the warmth it exuded. Sipping the hot tea, she assessed her feelings. Knowing that Mr Darcy was definitely here in the gardens at least stopped her from speculating upon that very fact. It did not, however, cause her much respite, for now her mind was engaged not upon whether he was there, but where in the gardens he was at that particular moment and how she might possibly contrive to speak to him.

⁂

Seated under a hastily erected canopy, that she and her daughter might be sheltered from the sun's rays, Lady Catherine surveyed those around her with beady eyes.

"Anne, tuck that blanket securely about your legs. You must not take cold."

"Aunt, it is sufficiently warm. I am certain Anne will come to no harm."

"I do not know why I allowed you to persuade me to come, I really do not," she went on as if the Colonel had not spoken at all. "It is an odd way to be entertaining folks, by making them sit in the outdoors and be exposed to the elements."

The Colonel rolled his eyes at Darcy, who smiled before turning his attention to his sister.

"Are you quite comfortable, Georgie?"

She nodded happily, smiling up at him from the seat placed to Anne's right. "I am perfectly content, Fitz."

There was some disturbance whilst servants bustled about on Lady Catherine's barked instructions, fetching all manner of rugs, blankets and cushions from the carriage, and then retrieving a large wicker basket filled with flasks of hot chocolate, several slabs of pound cake and a bowl of fruit. Once these were all arranged to her satisfaction, she dismissed all but one servant and ordered her guests to partake.

Taking a seat on the other side of his sister but outside the canopy, Darcy looked up at the sky. Earlier, it had been a rich cerulean blue, but the clouds had steadily increased. Despite this, and the sun disappearing behind them with growing regularity, the heat did not subside, and he sighed. A storm brewed, if he was not mistaken. He glanced around at the hordes of people out enjoying the day, and could not help but wonder whereabouts Elizabeth sat, and whether or not she enjoyed herself; then, he pushed the thought ruthlessly aside. Having just encountered James Harington, he needed no further reminder of her tenancy within that family or of its permanence.

Turning down an offer of a hot drink from his sister, he accepted a tot of brandy from the Colonel, clinked glasses with him in a silent toast and knocked the liquid back, letting it run down his throat before handing the glass back.

As the afternoon progressed there came some change to the Harington party. Mr Harington had returned with Nicholas at last, and the former and Mrs Harington were soon well entertained by a stream of visitors to their small seating area and had no need of family for company. As such, the others left them well stocked with refreshments and set out to explore the gardens, enjoying the music and merriment around them as they went.

Patrick and James soon happened upon some young men with whom they were acquainted, and leaving them to it, Nicholas, Serena and Elizabeth continued in their walk. Though ostensibly acting as chaperone, it was not long before Elizabeth out-stripped her companions and, bearing in mind the public location, none of them was particularly disturbed by the fact.

Elizabeth was grateful for the opportunity to be alone for a while, though she seemed unable to cease her self-imposed task whenever out in public of late of looking for Mr Darcy's face in every corner. She longed to come across him, hoped most anxiously to be able to explain the truth of the matter in relation to the rumour that existed, but she had no notion how she might begin such a dialogue.

Thus it was, she wandered from path to lawn, aimless in her direction, but her gaze constantly seeking him.

☙

The Harington party was not the only one that had seen some alteration. Lady Catherine, who had bemoaned the growing heat for more than an hour, had finally been persuaded to return to the shade of her hearth in Great Pulteney Street. The breaking up of the party, along with the removal of the canopy and the servants, whom Darcy and the Colonel eschewed as unnecessary, did however benefit Anne. With her cousins' support, she was able to stay behind with the promise that she would be dropped home by the Darcy carriage before dusk.

Five o'clock had long passed, the hour marked by the bells of the nearest church and those of the Abbey, which resonated from the city centre nearby. Darcy and the Colonel had gone to stretch their legs, their intent being to view the new canal that had been engineered through the gardens on its way to join the River Avon further downstream, and Georgiana and Anne had been enjoying a stroll about the gardens, stopping now and again to listen to the music and occasionally visiting the stalls and barrows set up near the entrance gates and making a purchase or two.

Georgiana had been pleased to see her brother showing an interest in something, for last evening, he had appeared somewhat distracted, particularly when they had dined before returning Anne home and heading to the recital. Much as she liked Bath, she could not wait for them to leave, that they might make their intended journey to Dublin, where all possible reminders of Miss Elizabeth Bennet were behind them.

Before returning to their seats with their packages, Anne had suggested that they sit near the bandstand for a while and listen to the music, and Georgiana had happily complied, and they had soon secured a nearby bench shrouded by thick hedging.

Anne released a sigh, and Georgiana sat back on the bench and eyed her older cousin for a moment. "Are you tiring?"

"No indeed. Quite the contrary, my dear. I am enjoying the solitude."

Georgiana frowned. "But you are not alone."

Anne let out a short laugh. "You cannot imagine how pleasurable it is to escape my mother's presence. Oh, she means well enough," she waved a dismissive hand. "She thinks to protect me; yet I am in more danger of being stifled by her than under threat of anything else! I believe-"

"Anne! Look!"

Georgiana's low and urgent voice caused Anne to follow the direction of her gaze. Though she had not detected their presence, tucked away as they were beside the hedge, Miss Elizabeth Bennet could be seen walking away from them down the path that led to the rear of the gardens.

⁂

Darcy and the Colonel had eschewed the loftier view of the canal for a walk along the towpath, and as the air was a little fresher by the water and the noise less intrusive, bordering open countryside as this end of the gardens did, they lingered for quite a while, talking of the feat of engineering that it was, admiring the neatly constructed walls of the tunnels, the creative planting of verges by the towpath and the elegance of what was essentially a working waterway, as stylish here as it was functional along the stretch that penetrated Sydney Gardens.

That the topic of conversation was not entirely to his taste, the Colonel chose not to own. He could tell that Darcy wished to talk of anything, and once the subject had been exhausted, the Colonel had taken a quick glance at his pocket watch before suggesting that they begin to make preparations to depart. Leaving Darcy behind, his attention allegedly on a barge as it negotiated its way along the canal, the Colonel set off to track down his cousins and shepherd them back to their carriage where Darcy had agreed to join them directly.

He stepped through the gate into the uniform terraces of the gardens and had not gone far before he discerned both Anne and Georgiana up ahead. They were walking up one of the gentle rises towards one of the wrought-iron railed bridges that spanned the canal and, putting on a spurt of speed, he cut across a neatly tended lawn and fetched up beside them, amused at their reaction, for he had clearly surprised them with his sudden appearance.

⁂

It does, of course, behove those in such a state of mutual happiness as Serena and Nicholas to wish the same felicity upon all their acquaintance, and though he knew little of Darcy, Nicholas was sensible enough to see in him a well-respected gentleman with a somewhat quiet but pleasant demeanour, admired by their Cheapside relations and further, the object of Elizabeth's affections.

He had considered, throughout the previous evening, Serena's wish that he do something to aid their friend. A desire to concede to her plea as well as lifting some of the obvious oppression from Elizabeth's shoulders was sufficient for him to be certain that action was warranted, and thus it was that, no sooner had she disappeared from view, they turned their minds to locating where precisely in Sydney Gardens Mr Darcy or any of his party might be at that moment.

"Should we explore the labyrinth?" Serena indicated the part of the garden behind them. "If Lizzy has ploughed on ahead, then perhaps we should look where she is not?"

Nicholas's gaze roamed over the faces of those passing by. Serena was relatively unfamiliar with any of those they sought, having seen only Darcy, and that for a passing moment, and thus it was that the search was down to him, but before they had need of further reflection over which direction to take, he happened to see a familiar figure walking away from a gateway in the hedge directly opposite.

"Look." Nicholas' mutter caused Serena to turn her head.

She followed his gaze to the man but then frowned and looked up at him. "Who is it?"

"Darcy's cousin, the Colonel." They watched him for a second; he seemed to be walking with some purpose, and Nicholas, following a hunch, tucked Serena's hand through his arm and quickly led her over towards the hedge and peered through the gate.

"He is there – alone."

"He must have been by the canal all this time," said Serena softly. "No wonder we have not seen him until now."

Nicholas looked down at her affectionately. "Why are you whispering? He will not hear you; he must be at least twenty paces away." He peered through the gate once more. "And I will wager from his stance his mind is many more miles distant."

"What shall we do?"

Nicholas said nothing for a moment, merely kept his gaze upon the solitary figure. Then, he shrugged and looked back at Serena.

"We will go and speak to him."

"But what shall we say?"

Nicholas laughed, shrugged his shoulders again and then smiled at her. "I have no notion, but doubtless something will come to us at the given time!" With that, he opened the gate, which wheezed on its hinges, and waved her through before stepping onto the towpath to join her.

Chapter Twenty Eight

GEORGIANA AND ANNE HAD BEEN intent upon their target, though they had fallen some distance behind Elizabeth, for she struck a fair pace, and though Georgiana would have been able to keep in step with her, Anne did not have the same reserves, and thus it was that quite a gap had opened up between them.

As neither of them had been able to confess any particular reason for their current scheme, other than a natural curiosity, they had lapsed into silence as they walked, and thus it was that the Colonel's sudden appearance caused them both to start in surprise and simultaneously lose sight of Elizabeth.

With a resigned sigh, Georgiana turned back from searching the remaining people who were meandering through this part of the gardens and smiled at her cousin.

"Where is Fitz?"

"By the canal." The Colonel waved a hand in the direction whence he had come before casting a quick look at the heavy sky. "The air is becoming quite oppressive, and we think it would be best to return home. Darcy said he will join us at the gatehouse."

He offered an arm to each of them, and they turned to retrace the path that the ladies had just followed. They had gone but a short distance, however, when the Colonel noted the approach of two people along the path in the direction from which he had lately come and, recognising the gentleman, he frowned as his gaze flickered over the lady upon Harington's arm. His surprise over it not being Miss Elizabeth Bennet, however, he quickly concealed under a friendly smile, for they seemed bent upon greeting him, and he led his companions along the path to join them.

⁂

Elizabeth was not entirely certain of her purpose in scouring the farther reaches of Sydney Gardens, but as the time she had spent in the central areas around the bandstand had done little to aid her in her desire to meet with at least one member of the Brock Street party, she felt she had little to lose.

Her purpose had been to reach one of the small bridges that crossed the new canal and use it as a vantage point, being on raised ground, to see if she could detect any sign of Mr Darcy, his sister or his cousin. Despite this intention, however, she was rather taken aback upon reaching her destination to discern precisely what she sought: Mr Darcy, alone, down on the towpath. He stood very still, and though she still floundered for a way to open the necessary dialogue, she set off purposefully to join him.

⁂

"*Nicholas!*" Serena's voice was urgent, and she tugged at his arm as he led her towards the three people coming towards them, causing him to halt. "We have just left Mr Darcy in an apparent state of shock. Is this not sufficient?"

Nicholas shook his head. "I think not." Then, he laughed. "I am on a ride; there is no reining me in!" Seeing his companion biting her lip, he patted her arm. "Do not concern yourself so; I know what I am about."

She cast a quick glance along the path at the approaching party. "But I do not know these people, and whilst I understand that we wished to tell *someone* the truth, 'tis yet a secret in principle."

Nicholas spoke quietly as he attempted to reassure her. "This family, Serena, would have it that I am engaged, so what secret am I revealing? All I am doing is ensuring they have me promised to the right lady."

Serena nodded reluctantly, then could not help but smile as Nicholas turned her about to greet the Colonel and his companions, saying under his breath, "Besides, I cannot tolerate another evening of those mournful tunes Elizabeth will persist in playing of late!"

"Colonel! Well met!" The gentlemen acknowledged each other, and Nicholas greeted Miss Darcy before accepting the introduction to the other lady, who, it transpired, was her cousin.

He then exchanged a quick look with Serena, who looked rather apprehensive, before turning back to the others and effecting her introduction to them.

Barely had the necessary formalities been completed, however, when he added, "Miss Seavington and I are to be wed shortly."

A profound silence greeted this statement, and Nicholas was conscious of Serena retaining her breath, only to let it out in a rush as the three people before them all exchanged a confused look, and the Colonel, shaking his head as if to rid it of some notion, said, "I beg your pardon? Did you say you are to marry this young lady?"

He inclined his head respectfully in Serena's direction as he made this observation, but it was obvious from his expression that he did not quite believe the words.

Nicholas nodded. "Indeed, Sir, though it is not for public consumption as yet; we still await parental consent from Derbyshire, but my immediate family knows of our situation. It is not a private engagement."

The Colonel put a hand to his forehead and turned and walked away a few paces, and Serena and Nicholas could not help but exchange a quick smile with each other, so reminiscent was his behaviour of Darcy's but moments earlier. Miss Darcy and her cousin, however, simply stared at them both, but as the intelligence and its implications seemed to dawn upon her, the former broke into a wide smile, and stepping forward, she reached out and took Serena's hand. "I congratulate you," she turned to look at Nicholas, "*both* of you. You have my heartfelt felicitations for your future happiness."

"Thank you, Miss Darcy," Serena said with a smile. "Your sentiments are much appreciated. You do understand, though, that it is not general knowledge. We do not wish for it to get abroad until my father sends word."

"Of course not. Oh – but I cannot wait to tell my brother!" Colour flew into her cheeks at this, and she put a hand to her mouth. "Forgive me. You said it was not to be talked of, but-"

"Your brother knows, Miss Darcy." Nicholas smiled at her. "We have just this moment come from speaking to him."

The Colonel, who seemed to have come to terms with what he had heard re-joined them, shook Nicholas by the hand and slapped him on the back for good measure.

"Now that is a meeting I wish I had been privy to! Well, I wish you both all the best." He shook his head and then let out a short laugh. "You would not believe how gratified we are to meet you, Miss Seavington, and to hear of your situation." He turned to the lady in question and smiled and with a quiet 'thank you', Serena returned the gesture.

Nicholas nodded. "Then it was indeed well met, Colonel, was it not?"

"Fortuitous does not begin to describe it, Harington!" The Colonel looked to the ladies of his party and offered them an arm apiece once more. "We will leave you to enjoy the remainder of the day."

Heart pounding in her chest, Elizabeth's pace slowed as she passed through the open gate onto the towpath and neared Mr Darcy. He continued with his back to her, staring down into the water and, hesitantly, she came to a halt but one step away from him. She was reluctant to speak his name, it being so reminiscent of how she had accosted him in Berkeley Square Gardens not so long ago, but before she could determine the best way of announcing her presence, he straightened, ran a hand through his hair and turned about suddenly on his heel – so precipitously, in fact, that he almost knocked her from her feet.

On impulse, his hands shot out to steady her, and she found herself firmly grasped by both upper arms as he stared at her.

"You are not engaged." The words seemed drawn from him, as though he had no choice but to speak them, and she was consumed by relief that, somehow, he understood the truth without her having to find the words.

"No, Sir, I am not."

They lapsed into a deep silence. They were, by necessity of his having caught hold of her as she took a stumbling step aside, in close proximity, and whether he was conscious of it or not, he maintained his hold upon her arms. As she became aware of his touch through the sheer fabric of her sleeves, she could feel the warmth rise in her cheeks. Their closeness overwhelmed her, and she held her breath, her eyes fixed upon his face.

He seemed equally transfixed, and then his glance dipped towards her mouth and all rational thought deserted her as she was assailed by the memory of his holding her safe when she fell from the curricle, and the perfect conviction she had held at the time that he wished to embrace her, but before anything so untoward could happen, he seemed to realise what he was about and stepped back a pace, releasing his hold upon her.

"Forgive me." his voice was strained. "I did not expect you... anyone."

She shook her head quickly. "Indeed, Sir, there is nothing to excuse. I should have spoken; I did not mean to surprise you in such a manner."

"I was not concentrating..." he paused and searched her face as if he could not quite believe he saw her. "I fail to comprehend... I saw..."

Realising that, however he had discovered the truth, he remained confused by the misunderstanding that had arisen, she shook her head in remonstrance towards herself.

"I believe I comprehend what you observed – and what its inference was. Mr Darcy, I am most embarrassed that my freedom of manner with an old friend has led you to consider something erroneous as the truth." Elizabeth let out a huff of rueful laughter. "I was often cautioned over my exuberance as a child, and it seems I have failed to control it as an adult."

He swallowed visibly and turned his head to the side for a moment before returning his gaze to hers with an audible sigh. "I am guilty of having made an assumption; though at the time, it seemed perfectly logical. I hope you will forgive the misunderstanding."

"May I ask how it is that you now understand the truth?"

"Harington." Darcy gestured with his hand. "He was here but a moment before you arrived, with his intended." He frowned suddenly. "When we met yesterday..."

Elizabeth nodded. "Yet another misconception on both our parts, I believe. I had but hours earlier received intelligence from Longbourn of my sister's engagement to your friend. Your congratulations seemed perfectly in order to me..." her voice tailed away as she took in the expression on his face. "You did not know."

He shook his head, but a faint smile touched his mouth. "No. But then, I only wrote Bingley of my new direction but two days ago, and he is an indifferent correspondent at the best of times."

Elizabeth was gratified to see that Mr Darcy seemed genuinely pleased with the news and she could not help but smile at this proof of how mistaken she had been in her suppositions of the previous day. A silence fell upon them both once more, disturbed by nothing more than the birdsong from the nearby trees and the occasional muted voice from the garden beyond.

Then, the gentleman seemed to rouse himself, gesturing with his hand towards the gate.

"Will you allow me to escort you?"

Elizabeth nodded without hesitation. She had no desire to quit his company unless she had to. "You may, Sir, but you know not my destination. I could be bound for Timbuktu!"

He smiled at this, and they both turned towards the gate.

"Then I would take you there."

Elizabeth could not help but laugh at this piece of perceived chivalry. "To ensure that I was sufficiently distant, Sir?"

Darcy shook his head, standing back to allow her to precede him back into the gardens. "No – not at all. I should have said 'accompany' you."

They stood for a moment with their backs to the hedging and looked about. The change in the weather had clearly taken effect, and a noticeable stream of people poured back through the gardens towards the Sydney Hotel and the gatehouse. Conscious that the day now drew to a close and that these few moments in Mr Darcy's company may be her last for some conceivable time, Elizabeth sighed, before turning to address him.

"Well, as it is, Timbuktu will have to wait. I have sorely neglected my duty as chaperone to my friends."

"Then shall we take this way together for a while and attempt to seek them out?"

Chapter Twenty Nine

WITHOUT HESITATION, ELIZABETH FELL into step beside Mr Darcy. Hazarding a quick glance up at his face, she felt her heart clench inside as they walked on in silence. She had been so focused on clearing up the misconception he appeared to be labouring under. Yet now, finding she had no need to attempt such a delicate conversation, she floundered, with nothing but an intense awareness of her feelings for the man at her side. Her affection for him, a love that she still struggled to come to terms with, burned within her, and her throat ached with words she could not speak.

She was deeply conscious of him at her side, yet essaying another glance, his countenance remained closed to her, his gaze distant, as though he would be anywhere but here. With a soft sigh, she acknowledged what she had long suspected: he may have had – or even may still have – some feelings for her, but in the light of recent events, he would not be tempted to renew his addresses.

In the end, it was this reflection of the happenings in Meryton of late that gave her something to speak of and, conscious of her desire to thank Mr Darcy for all he had done, she sought to direct the conversation.

"How fares Mr Bingley, Sir? Is he well settled in Hertfordshire?"

She was conscious of his swift look towards her before his gaze returned to the direction of their walk.

"I believe so. I understand that his intention was to master the management of his estate. No doubt it has taken on a new impetus, following his recent pleasurable change in circumstances."

Elizabeth smiled, but before she could comment he continued. "But I digress. In answer to your query, I believe the air of Hertfordshire suits him very well."

"And you, Sir?"

Darcy turned to look at her, a brow raised in question. "I?"

"How did you find the air of Hertfordshire? I have been given to understand that you visited there recently."

Darcy stopped walking and perforce she came to a halt too. He threw a glance along the path, as if he wished to ascertain if he might escape her question, but then turned back to meet her gaze.

"I – I am not entirely certain..." his voice faded.

"What of, Mr Darcy? That you were in Hertfordshire or that you were not?" Elizabeth smiled at him, affecting a composure she was far from feeling. "I assure you, I have it on good authority."

"I would not have had it that you were advised by *any* authority." Darcy frowned. "Might I enquire how it is that you are aware of my presence there?"

Elizabeth turned to resume their walk, and he fell into step beside her. "I fear our conversations are forever governed by the receiving of a letter. I must own that one arrived from my father before I left Town, recounting not only your visit but some of the aftermath."

"I had hoped you would not learn of it."

"Yes. Papa did say that you had asked him to keep his counsel, but he assured me he had made no promise of the kind." She glanced up at him and, conscious that they were nearing the entrance to the gardens where she soon discerned the Harington party, she stopped, forcing him to do the same. "Why did you wish it to remain secret?"

"I – I..."

Unwilling to let him flounder and conscious that Serena's attention now seemed fixed upon them both, Elizabeth interrupted. "Well, learn of it I did, and I am pleased to have done so. Mr Darcy," she hesitated, "I cannot thank you enough for your kindness in attending to my family's... difficulty. I understand that they, and the local populace in general, are now freed from Wickham's artifice."

Darcy studied her for a moment. "I hope you will forgive my interference. I was most troubled by the disclosure you made, whilst I had the honour of dancing with you Monday last." He stopped abruptly, a look of consciousness upon his features that Elizabeth could not comprehend, unless it was a reminder of how their dance had culminated in his withdrawal from her. Had her disclosure really been such a dreadful awakening? Would he, despite discovering the truth regarding her and Nicholas, still be leaving for Ireland within days?

Discomfited, Elizabeth dropped her gaze, her insides lurching uncomfortably with the shame of it all, but before the silence between them could become too prolonged, Mr Harington's voice hailed her to come as they were about to depart. He began to usher his party towards the gates into Sydney Place, and as she could perceive the Colonel, Miss Darcy and her cousin waiting on the return of Mr Darcy, there was no alternative but to join them, and they both turned and walked on, Elizabeth desperately attempting to draw the courage to effect something that might make some alteration to their present circumstances.

"Are you to stay long in Bath?"

So deep in thought had Elizabeth been that she started and then threw him an apologetic look. "We leave for Sutton Coker on the morrow. And you, Sir?"

He said nothing for a moment. "We... that is, Georgiana and I, have booked passage on a ship that sails for Dublin this coming Thursday."

"Oh. I see." Though Serena had warned of this, hearing it from the man himself upset her, and Elizabeth sighed heavily as they came to a halt near the gate. "And – and do you expect your travels to be of any great duration?"

"A few months at the very least; possibly longer."

Turning to stand before him, she stared up into Mr Darcy's face as though she could somehow commit it to permanent memory. How she had come to love him like this, she knew not. There was a hollowness within her and a weight about her heart that she feared she would never lose.

"I believe it is time to say farewell, Sir." He bowed in response to her curtsey. "I wish you a pleasant remainder of your stay in Bath."

"Thank you, and I wish you and your companions a safe journey back to Somerset."

There was a throng of people by the gatehouse, intent upon avoiding the threatened downpour, and an array of conveyances of all shapes and sizes could be seen jostling for position along the pavement edge. An ominous rumble from the sky above was sufficient to encourage everyone further, and in the ensuing confusion, Elizabeth turned her gaze to Darcy, striving to keep her sadness over their imminent separation at bay.

Before the tightness in her throat could take any further hold, she forced a smile, determined that she would do as Serena had counselled and at least leave him with an indication of the change in her regard. She could not speak of it, but perhaps there was one thing she could do.

Elizabeth cast a quick glance over her shoulder. There was no one behind them now, and turning back to face him she took her chance, for Mr Darcy's height and breadth of shoulder shielded her from further view. Stepping quickly forward, she possessed herself of his right hand. His startled gaze met hers, but before he could utter a word, she raised his hand and pressed a kiss upon the back of it. Conscious of the heat rising in her neck, she met his eye, willing him to understand her, before offering another brief curtsey and moving past him towards where the Harington carriages stood without a backward glance.

Darcy blinked rapidly, but though he opened his mouth, no sound came. He had held his breath when Elizabeth had possessed herself of his hand, and now he blew it out in a rush before running a hand through his hair. Just then, a movement caught his eye, and he glanced to his right to meet his sister's wide-eyed stare. Clearly, she had observed the gesture that had just been bestowed upon him, and he turned around fully to stare after Elizabeth once more as she joined the Harington party who were presently making ready to enter their conveyances.

Unable to gather a single coherent thought, and refusing to meet his sister's curious gaze, Darcy offered Georgiana his arm and walked over to join the Colonel and his cousin Anne.

⁂

At Mr Harington's insistence, Nicholas attended to the hood of the landaulet, ensuring that the ladies would be sheltered should the weather break before they reached the safe haven of Marlborough Buildings, and taking advantage of the moment of privacy, knowing that there would be little opportunity for such once in the house again, Serena studied her friend as they waited on the pavement.

"You were in earnest conversation with Mr Darcy, Lizzy." The start that her companion gave upon hearing these words convinced Serena that Elizabeth's thoughts had been miles away – or perhaps, just a few yards. "He admires you yet."

Elizabeth shook her head vehemently but said nothing.

"It is apparent in his every movement towards you: the incline of his head when you are speaking – his eyes never leave you unless they must." Serena sighed. "I will never forget the look upon his face when Nicholas and I left him earlier."

Elizabeth turned to face her friend, her expression sad. "I regret disillusioning you, but we spoke of Wickham, not of love."

Serena huffed. "Well, of course you did! I never expected otherwise in the circumstances. You – well, *you* would never let the matter be until you had said what you must upon it; and he – I know him not but he would have been at your mercy."

Elizabeth gave a rueful smile. "How well you understand me. It is true that our relationship has been dogged by my persistence in talking to him of things that are often distasteful to us both."

"Dear Lizzy. You feel you must be censured for every misstep of your family. It is nonsensical."

"The only thing that is nonsensical is your persistence that anything could yet come of this. Mr Darcy made his declaration; I refused him. That is the end of the matter."

"It is not." Serena was determined to carry her point. "I believe yet that his reticence is down to failing to comprehend that your feelings have changed."

"And what if they have? Do you seriously expect a man of his stature to lower himself sufficiently to make me a second offer?"

"He lowered himself – in *his* eyes at the time," she added, at the flash in Elizabeth's eyes, "the first time."

There was, however, no opportunity for either of them to debate the matter further, for Nicholas was done with his preparations and joined them directly, assisting first Serena and then Elizabeth into the carriage before taking the driving seat, and they were soon edging their way into the steady flow of traffic. Though Nicholas had been made aware of the state of Elizabeth's feelings, Serena knew her friend would not be comfortable speaking of such things in his presence, but seeing her eyes searching the remaining people at the gates, she was certain she knew whose face she sought one last time.

Harington raised a hand as they went by, but Darcy barely registered the fact, so desperate was he for one last sight of Elizabeth. In this, he was rewarded, for she stared straight at him, and though her cheeks were quite pink, she gave him a tremulous smile as they passed by and a small wave of her hand. Instinctively, he raised a hand too but it wavered in mid-air for a moment, then fell heavily to his side. She was gone.

The Colonel eyed the congestion building near the gatehouse and then turned to face his cousins.

"I will walk Anne to her door, Darce. If we set off and try to pull over to let her out, we shall never get back into the flow again."

Seeing the sense of this, Darcy nodded and as soon as Anne had made her farewells, he escorted Georgiana across the pavement to where their carriage awaited, assisting her into her seat and then closing the door, deciding to remain outside whilst awaiting his cousin's return. It was likely only to be a matter of minutes, the gardens being but a stone's throw from Great Pulteney Street, and as he stood there, Darcy cast his gaze up at the sky. The oppressive heat remained, despite the thick clouds that now rolled overhead and a threatening rumble continued to come from the blackest of them. They would be fortunate indeed if they made it back to the house before the storm broke upon them.

He studied his feet for a moment, conscious that his cousin would be back within minutes. Nothing could hold his attention, however. All he could think on was Elizabeth, the recently revealed intelligence of her not being promised to another and her parting bold gesture. Thus it was he remained deep in thought until the Colonel re-joined him.

"Well, Darce, that was an interesting afternoon, was it not? You are almost smiling." He put out a hand to stall Darcy, who had straightened and made as if to turn towards the carriage. "So, Miss Elizabeth Bennet is free."

"Yes – yes, I know. Harington told me."

"And?"

"And what?" Darcy made an impatient gesture with his hand and threw his cousin a frustrated look before addressing him in a quiet voice, that his sister might not hear. "Fitzwilliam, not two weeks back, I was the perfect simpleton in making the lady an offer of marriage; an offer, I would remind you, that she not only did not accept, but that repulsed her. Do you wish me to repeat the error?"

"Yes, I *do*!"

Darcy said nothing, and the Colonel grunted.

"Well, you will have to pay her a call on the morrow, then."

"She departs for the West Country in the morning, along with the rest of her party."

The Colonel frowned. "Then what is your plan? You cannot sit back and do nothing. She is free; she no longer thinks badly of you; indeed, I would attest to her thinking *very well* of you but a week ago. You will wonder for the rest of your life if you do not at least try, for what have you to lose? If you do not offer, she can never be yours; if she refuses you again, then at least you will know for certain. But if there is a chance..."

Darcy turned on his heel and swung open the carriage door, but his cousin stepped close to him, hissing in his ear, "Too much time has been wasted, Darcy – this misunderstanding from Monday has done damage enough. Would you squander this opportunity that the Fates have been so kind as to extend?"

"Let it go, Fitzwilliam." He inclined his head towards his sister.

The Colonel blew out a frustrated breath and turned to step up into the carriage, but he paused with one boot on the footplate. "You were getting along famously a matter of days ago in Town – which, I might add, is more recent than the debacle of two weeks back. Has she given you no indication that she feels differently? No hint, no implication at all?"

Darcy was about to negate the matter, but the memory of Elizabeth pressing her lips to his hand not moments earlier returned swiftly, coupled with the look upon her face as she bade him farewell. With his insides swirling with anticipation, he stared at his cousin unable to utter a word.

The Colonel narrowed his gaze at him for a moment, but Darcy shook his head and, with a shrug of his shoulders, he entered the carriage, turning to sit beside Georgiana, followed immediately by Darcy, and soon they were making their way down the street towards Pulteney Bridge.

Chapter Thirty

STARING OUT OF THE CARRIAGE WINDOW, Darcy dwelled upon his cousin's words. Was Elizabeth's parting gesture a message of some sort? And if so, what did it mean? Was it just an expression of their – *what*? He knew they had forged some sort of – friendship? Bond? There had definitely been something developing between them in London, he was certain...

Yet the memory of his rejection was still fresh in his mind, and how confident had he been beforehand of acceptance? He had never even questioned it. Was he any better, but two weeks on, at understanding Elizabeth?

For himself, he knew that his feelings had grown deeper in this past fortnight. He not only loved her more, he had learned to appreciate her character – her love of her family and friends, her compassion, courage and humour – all these were of more value to him than anything that could be taught by a master. She had been his own instructor in coming to that understanding. He sighed heavily, his throat aching with unspoken words as he stared out of the window, unseeing of the Abbey as they passed it by. Yet it was a bold gesture on her part, it could not be denied – what had she meant by it?

Hope would persist in returning to him at the slightest hint of possibility. He had fallen for its seductive airs in London only to have it dashed. Telling himself that Elizabeth's being free did not mean she would be his was a hard lesson to accept, and he had doubts once more as the tendrils of hope pulsed heavily in his veins, wrapping strings around his fragile heart.

What was it his cousin had said? He would spend the rest of his life wondering what if... what if he found the courage to ask? If she turned him down once more, was his situation any the worse? He had everything to gain, and nothing left to lose. She was, after all, promised to no one.

They had made steady enough progress through the city as these thoughts chased themselves around his head, but as the carriage came to a jarring halt, Darcy blinked and sat forward in his seat.

The Colonel pushed down the window and shouted up to the coachman, then sat back down on his seat. "Some incident on the far side of the Square – an upset cart, it would seem."

Getting to his feet, Darcy opened the door and stepped out into the street; though the rain had yet to begin, its presence was in the air, but so engrossed in thought was he that he barely noticed, and he remained motionless beside the carriage until a neigh from one of the horses and a restless jangling of the harnesses roused him. Speculation was of little value. His head was urging him to discern Elizabeth's purpose, to comprehend what she had attempted to convey by taking such a daring step. His heart surged with an almost indecent hope, and he looked around, seeking inspiration, only to find his gaze drawn to the far side of Queen Square where both Harington carriages were likewise caught up in the congestion.

With sudden determination, he turned about and closed the carriage door, leaning in through the open window.

"Forgive me…" Darcy stopped. "I must leave you."

"Darce!" Colonel Fitzwilliam stared at him, but his cousin ignored him, instead meeting Georgiana's confused gaze with a reassuring smile.

"I will re-join you in Brock Street."

"But Fitz," Georgiana frowned. "It looks set to pour. You cannot be considering a walk favourable at this time."

Darcy shook his head and threw the Colonel a swift glance.

"I will be fine, Georgie. And I think a walk is precisely what I need just now. I will see you directly."

He started to walk across Queen Square towards the Harington carriages, his heart pounding furiously in his chest, and unconsciously he placed one hand on top of the one that Elizabeth had kissed and pressed it in an attempt to restore the warmth that her lips had drawn to the surface. He could picture quite clearly her expression before she had turned away: the warm colour that had flown into her cheeks, the intense look in her dark eyes… what was her meaning?

As he approached the landaulet from the side, he was able to see little of the ladies, the hood partially shielding them from view, though the rich colour of Elizabeth's shawl was easily visible folded upon her lap. The only figure he could truly identify with any certainty was that of Harington where he sat in the driver's seat.

A momentary panic seized him for a second. He had no notion whether Elizabeth would accede to his wishes and agree to take a walk, but he pushed the trepidation aside. He must speak to her, and this was his sole chance to do so.

Meanwhile, back in the Darcy carriage, Georgiana withdrew her head from the open window and stared confusedly at her cousin.

"What is wrong with him? Why is his behaviour so peculiar?"

The Colonel, who was about to take a slug from his hip flask, shrugged. "He is in love, Georgie."

"Yes – yes, I know he is. But he is very distracted. Is this because Miss Elizabeth kissed his hand?"

Choking on a mouthful of cognac, the Colonel almost fell off his seat. "She did *what?*"

"Is there any indication what might be causing the delay?"

Nicholas shrugged and then stood up on the driving board. "I cannot see beyond two carriages in front, but it looks like a spillage from the debris in the street. We shall be on our way directly, though, for I can see movement up ahead." He sat down and threw a glance over his shoulder at Serena and Elizabeth.

The former peered out from under the hood, and she threw a quick look at the sky before sitting back in her seat; the latter had quite clearly seen something that had caught her attention, for Elizabeth's gaze was transfixed, and Nicholas realised that Darcy was within feet of the carriage. A further glance at Elizabeth was sufficient to realise that she laboured under some surfeit of emotion and, suspecting that she may not have her wits fully about her, Nicholas jumped down from his seat and acknowledged the gentleman as he drew level with their conveyance.

"Darcy! Are you caught up in too? It looks as though we will be moving directly."

Though he had acknowledged Nicholas with a reciprocal bow, Darcy seemed to hear not his comment, his gaze quite fixed upon Elizabeth. Being neither a simpleton nor of mean inclination, and perfectly conscious of the impact the news he had so recently shared with the gentleman might have had upon him, Nicholas tried not to smile as he turned to face his friend, throwing Serena a quick wink as he did so.

"I believe Mr Darcy has come to see you, Lizzy."

"Miss Bennet, I-" Darcy hesitated and then swallowed hard. "Would you do me the honour of joining me? I – I intend to walk the remainder of the way, and it did occur to me that you might... I know that you are very fond of walking."

Elizabeth's mouth opened slightly, but she said nothing, merely nodded.

"You have no objection, Harington?" Darcy turned to the man at his side, who, for some reason, smiled widely.

"None whatsoever! I would, however, offer you this." He reached into the cavity under the seat where Serena sat and pulled from its depths a neatly furled umbrella which he offered to Darcy. "Elizabeth is my dearest friend, Sir." His expression sobered somewhat, and as Darcy took the umbrella from him, Nicholas held onto to it for a moment, meeting that gentleman's eye with a serious look. "I would wish to know that she is properly taken care of."

Darcy acknowledged this with a nod, and Nicholas released the umbrella into his grasp before turning to hand Elizabeth down from the carriage. He then climbed back onto the driver's seat to await the movement of the traffic, which appeared imminent.

Elizabeth came to stand before him; there was no exchange of formal greetings, for somehow it seemed wholly unnecessary, and she took the gentleman's arm as he offered it before bidding Serena and Nicholas a temporary farewell.

Turning their steps towards the rear of the Square, they walked for some little distance in silence. Elizabeth struggled for composure, both from being in such close proximity to Mr Darcy, once more very conscious of his arm beneath her hand, and from mortification over her recent action. Her usual wits had all but deserted her, but knowing they must speak of something, she began with the obvious.

"Might I enquire, Sir, why the sudden desire for a walk when you have just spent several hours on your feet in Sydney Gardens?"

"I am not certain I wish to answer you – yet."

Unsure of his implication, Elizabeth forced a laugh. "Then I assume you do not fear a soaking." She glanced up at the skies, where no hint of the sun they had earlier enjoyed remained. "I fear the umbrella will be insufficient should the storm break."

They had reached the stone steps that led up to the gravelled path, and he stopped, putting out a hand to stay her progress as she made to go up them. "You are correct. There is no time for delay." He looked down at his feet for a second, then raised serious eyes to hers. "You bestowed a kiss upon me, Miss Bennet."

There was little point in the denying it. Elizabeth blushed furiously, feeling self-conscious and altogether too embarrassed for words, but she held his gaze determinedly. "I did."

"I seek to understand your purpose. Would you tell me why?"

"You may enquire, Sir, but I fear I cannot answer without demonstrating further impertinence."

"Would it aid you if I confirm my long-held admiration for your boldness?"

"You are too kind, Mr Darcy!"

"Kind? I do not think so. Proud, arrogant, unfeeling and latterly, somewhat simple-minded perhaps. But kind? It is not an accusation you have levelled at me before."

Elizabeth could not help but smile at this. "Indeed. I am your severest critic and you bear it well." She turned and began to climb the steps, conscious that he followed her, and once they reached the top he offered her his arm again.

"I still wish to know your reason."

Elizabeth sighed as they set off along the walk and looked up at him. "I had hoped that I might have distracted you from your purpose."

He shook his head, but his mouth twitched as if he would smile. "You said it was difficult to answer. Do you not know the reason?"

Elizabeth could no longer feign ignorance, though her colour returned as she studied him thoughtfully for a moment. Then, she released a sigh and said softly, "You will think me all manner of fool, Sir. Of that I am quite certain."

Darcy shook his head. "Indeed not. Miss Bennet; there are many things I think of you, but foolish is not one of them."

"You are fairer towards me than I deserve."

"I have no desire than to be anything but. You have taught me well."

A glimmer of a smile returned at these words, but a hasty glance at the heavy sky above reminded her of the precariousness of their situation and, conscious that the walled garden of the Darcys' lodgings was even now visible at the end of the walk, she bit her lip as he continued.

"Forgive me for returning to my point. I do not wish to press you for words you would not have said, but I am certain you will understand my desire to comprehend your purpose."

Elizabeth was uncertain what she could or should say. The deed had been born of a rush of feeling for him, despair at the thought of him being gone from England, and thus her life, and her desire to give him some indication of her altered feelings. She could no more justify it than condone it. Yet it was done.

And here he was, asking her to tell him what she had felt she could not. This was her opportunity; did she not owe him that? After all he had put before her on the day he proposed, did he not deserve to know how she felt? Serena certainly believed it to be so…

As the silence between them deepened, Elizabeth came to a halt and turned to face him, removing her hand from his arm as she did so. "Well then, Sir; if you will hear it, so be it."

Chapter Thirty One

THEY HAD COME TO A STOP within a few paces of the end of the walk, and Elizabeth drew in a shallow breath, conscious of the swirling of her insides and the heat upon her face, but determined not to look away or stall in her confession.

"You did me a great honour but two weeks ago to this very day. You laid before me your heart and offered me your hand, and I rejected them both soundly and, moreover, with false accusation. I have come to discover how in error I was, that you are the best of men." Elizabeth swallowed quickly, feeling her heart swell even as she quailed at what she was about to say. "In short, Sir, I have come to learn that I regret my misunderstanding of your character, and further that I had neither the foresight nor the intelligence to realise that I might also regret the loss of your affection."

His eyes were fixed upon hers, and she found it more and more difficult to formulate the words. "In truth, Mr Darcy, I found myself reluctant to leave your company without at least expressing, in some small way, a change in my feelings towards you. The gesture's purpose was to convey this without the need for words." She stopped and laughed tremulously. "And here I am, speaking endlessly! Forgive me, but you would ask the question. I have answered you with full honesty, for I think you deserve no less in the circumstances."

Having concluded this speech, she finally lowered her gaze, feeling all the embarrassment of her confession and the onslaught of emotion that welled behind her eyes.

Before a response could be made, however, the ominous rumblings in the heavens escalated into a sudden ricochet of thunder that caused Elizabeth to jump, and she returned his concerned look with a short laugh.

"Forgive me, Sir. I assure you I am usually a little sturdier of backbone."

He nodded, but before either of them could resume their conversation, a streak of lightning flashed across the sky followed rapidly by another thunderous roar and isolated drops of rain began to fall, thudding heavily as they struck the leaves overhead and landed before their feet on the path.

Throwing a quick glance heavenwards, Darcy said nothing, taking Elizabeth's hand in a firm grasp and walking swiftly forward. They had been but steps from the garden wall that bounded the end house of Brock Street, but as they turned the corner towards the side door, Darcy stopped suddenly, and perforce Elizabeth did too. The carriage was now pulled up there, and rather than head towards more conventional shelter, he turned and drew her under the boughs of the tree that she had hidden behind only the day before.

It was as sturdy a specimen as she recalled, with a solid trunk and dense foliage; he had chosen well, for the rain, which now fell in earnest, could not penetrate its thickness and they were well sheltered for the time being, so much so that the gentleman took the opportunity to rest the unused umbrella securely against an outcrop of bark.

They stood in silence for a moment, and Elizabeth could not help but recall how she had felt the last time she had used this tree as her protector. Though the air had been cleared between them, she was conscious of the agitation within her breast that remained, due no doubt to her having been in the midst of explaining her rather improper action. To be certain, her heart pounded fit to burst, and it was only as her gaze moved across the fields towards Marlborough Buildings, where both the carriage and the landaulet could now be seen pulling up outside, that she became aware of the fact that her hand remained in Mr Darcy's grasp.

As soon as this realisation came to pass, however, she could think of little else. Daring not to move a muscle, she allowed it to rest there, savouring the warmth of it. Conscious of the heat rising in her neck as she allowed the sensation of being touched by him to wash over her, she closed her eyes, never wanting the moment to end. How long she might have stood thus, the sound of the rain beating on the leaves in competition with that of her own heartbeat, she knew not, but her eyes flew open instantly upon hearing her name spoken softly.

"Elizabeth…"

Swallowing quickly, she looked up at Mr Darcy and her breath caught in her throat. They were standing very close, for though their shelter was adequate as trees go, in order to protect two persons they had need of being relatively near, and she was quite taken with how easy this made it for her to study his features at close range. His addressing her solely by her name did not strike her as at all odd at that moment, nor did the fact that he had yet to release her hand. His intense stare caused her insides to make their customary swoop, and she lowered her gaze.

"Elizabeth…" Her name had been whispered so gently it was as if the breeze that lightly stirred their hair had breathed it. "Look at me."

Raising her head, she felt a surge of hope flow through her as she met his gaze. The look in his eyes was full of emotion, and taking both her hands in his he stared at her for a moment, before continuing, "Are you saying what I think you are saying?"

She let out a small laugh, sniffed to clear the threat of tears, and then laughed again. "I do not know. What is it that you think I am saying?"

He smiled down at her, and her heart swelled within her. "You are not helping me."

"I would not have you think that. I believe you understand me very well, Sir."

He nodded, never removing his gaze from hers, and the hold upon her hands tightened momentarily. "Then may I assume, from my understanding, that your feelings towards me are somewhat altered from what they were two weeks past?"

Elizabeth nodded quickly, and he smiled again, a gesture that she could not help responding to with one of her own.

"Are they-" he paused and swallowed visibly, and it struck her suddenly just how difficult he found this. "Are they – do you – can I dare to chance that they are altered sufficiently to allow me to hope?" He stopped and looked down for a moment, still retaining his grasp upon her hands. "Forgive me." He raised his head and met her gaze once more. "I do not wish to pressure you, but in order to fully comprehend your meaning, I must be specific. I would not have further misunderstanding between us. Do you merely regard me in better favour, or may I hope that one day there may be – more?"

Conscious that such a speech must have cost him dear, Elizabeth hesitated not in responding. "You may find the alteration in my feelings to be the work of a moment, but I assure you that I do more than regard you with greater esteem, Sir. I meant what I said: I regret the outcome of the other Sunday in all and *every* aspect."

There was a pause as he appeared to assimilate these words, and then a smile graced his face the like of which she had never seen, and unable to stop herself she smiled in return. Before she could contemplate this further, however, he spoke in earnest.

"Then, Elizabeth –" he stopped and released one of her hands, before raising his own to cup the side of her face, his gaze intent upon her. "Permit me to tell you once more how much I love you." He hesitated for the briefest moment and drew in a deep breath. "May I ask you again? Will you – would you do me the honour of becoming my wife? I promise to hold you in the dearest of affections for the length of our lives. I will have you want for nothing. Please say that you will accept my hand."

Touched beyond measure by his words, Elizabeth gulped back the rise of tears that once more threatened, albeit for a different reason. Nodding her head quickly, as speech was quite beyond her at the moment, she gave a watery laugh, but sobered immediately upon seeing the intensity of his expression as he stared at her.

"You do? You accept?"

She nodded again, and this time she smiled before raising her own hand to his face and touching it gently. "I most assuredly do, Sir. You do me great honour."

"Promise me you are happy with your decision; that I have not coerced you in any way; we are but two weeks from that awful day, and-"

Shaking her head, Elizabeth placed a finger gently to his lips, feeling all the boldness of her action, but relishing in her right to do so. "I accept your offer, Mr Darcy, for one reason alone: I have fallen in love with you, and nothing would make me happier than to become your wife."

If she had sought any other reward, nothing could have been more pleasing to Elizabeth than the expression that spread across the gentleman's countenance at that moment, but she had little time upon which to savour the moment, for he brought her close and leaning down placed a kiss upon her lips.

He drew back almost instantly, and they stared at each other, speaking no words, and when he leaned down once more she met him half way, her eyes closing as she savoured the feel of his mouth upon hers, acknowledging the solidity of his body as she pressed ever closer to him and the silkiness of his hair as she allowed herself the privilege of running her fingers through it.

When he released her lips, she swayed a little, so close had she been standing to him, and he steadied her before frowning suddenly. "You are cold."

It was true; since the rain had come, the temperature had dropped significantly, but Elizabeth could not care less, for she was perfectly satisfied by the warmth of being close to him. She was tempted to share this, but before she could speak such intimate thoughts, he had shrugged out of his coat and held it out to her, and soon she was warmly encased in it.

It smelt faintly of his cologne, and she hugged it to herself, unable to prevent a wide smile from forming.

"But now *you* will be cold."

Darcy shook his head. "No – no, I am not." He drew her close again, and she leaned her head upon his chest for a moment.

"I had a dream about you." Elizabeth felt him start as she said these words, and she quickly raised her head to look up at him.

"Please tell me it was not a nightmare."

Smiling, she shook her head. "Perhaps I did not fully appreciate its content at the time, but I have to admit I much prefer the reality."

He stared at her with narrowed eyes for a moment. "Am I permitted to know what the dream was about?"

Elizabeth's smile widened for a moment, and then she shook her head. "No. I shall do better than that. I shall show you." She placed her arms about his neck, drawing his head down and pressing her lips against his. For a second he laughed, but as her eyes closed upon the sight of his dear face, he returned the pressure of her mouth, giving her a kiss that would linger far longer than any dream.

Georgiana had repaired to the drawing room as soon as she had divested herself of her outdoor garments, and as she awaited her cousin, she hurried to the windows that fronted onto Brock Street, leaning up against the pane and straining her eyes against the rain that now fell in heavy sweeps across the pavement. Where was her brother? Had he had time to take shelter, for there was no sign of him coming towards the house from the Circus... At the sound of the door opening, she straightened up, glancing over her shoulder as her cousin entered the room.

"Do not worry, Georgie," the Colonel smiled at her as he crossed to the console table that stood between the two full length windows at the opposite end of the room. "Darcy has ample common sense. He will have taken shelter."

Georgiana sighed and walked over to the couch in front of the fireplace and picked up a book in an attempt to occupy herself until her brother reappeared, though she doubted she would pay it any mind, for her cousin's suggestion – that Darcy intended to talk further with Miss Elizabeth Bennet – had only heightened her anticipation.

She was forestalled, however, by the Colonel letting out an exclamation, and she hurried to his side where he stood at the windows that looked out over the walled garden and to the fields beyond.

"What is it? Is aught amiss?" she peered out into the garden, but could see nothing untoward. Just then, however, her eye was caught by a movement, and her gaze was drawn to where she now perceived her cousin also appeared to be looking. "Oh!"

Georgiana stared speechlessly at the sight that she beheld. Her brother was under the tree at the edge of the Crescent Fields – and he was not alone. Miss Elizabeth Bennet, who appeared to be wearing his coat, was wrapped in his embrace, and if she were not mistaken... here she leaned forward to see a little more clearly, the rain acting as a barrier somewhat, and then gasped, her hand flying to her mouth - they were *kissing*!

The sound of Georgiana's intake of breath was sufficient to draw the Colonel's attention at last, and seeing her wide eyes, hand still clasped to her mouth, he snapped to attention and swiftly placed his own hand across her eyes.

"I think that is sufficient, young one." He placed an arm across her shoulders and with his hand still resting gently over her eyes, steered her away from the window. "Go – read your book."

She walked away a few paces and the Colonel was about to turn back and check how things were progressing outside, when suddenly she flew back across the room, throwing herself into his arms and hugging him tightly.

"I am so happy for him, Richard! So happy for *them*."

The Colonel grunted. "You think that this is a good sign, then, do you?" He nodded his head towards the window as Georgiana released him and stepped back, wiping away a solitary tear from her cheek. Her eyes were shining and a wide smile had spread over her features, and he could not help but reciprocate.

"I am sure they will join us directly. Go. Find something to amuse yourself with until then."

Georgiana sighed happily, nodded and resumed her search for a book that might hold her attention, a futile practice, as all she could think of was the happiness of her brother and the fact that she was certain Miss Elizabeth Bennet was to become the sister she had always longed for.

The Colonel, meanwhile, turned back to peer out of the window, but upon discerning little alteration since he last looked, be it the steady fall of rain or the closely entwined couple under the tree, he snorted and turned away. Darcy was clearly making up for lost time, and as the lady did not seem to object to his present pastime, there was little he could do but join his young cousin and await their return to the house.

⁂

Meanwhile, in the drawing room window of the Harington residence, Serena turned away as the door opened to reveal Nicholas, and she threw herself across the room and into his opened arms.

Able at such a distance to discern little but the flash of colour that she knew to be her friend's shawl, and thus quite certain of the identity of the couple under the tree, there was one thing she had been certain of: they were most definitely wrapped in each other's arms.

⁂

Elizabeth remained secure in Darcy's arms, her head once more resting against his chest, and he sighed softly. The rain continued to pour around them, and though he knew there was nowhere else he would rather be, he was certain that they should seek more robust shelter.

"We ought to go inside, Elizabeth. This storm shows no sign of abating."

Lifting her head, she looked around at the rain-soaked fields and then glanced up at the thick, rolling grey clouds which were being hurried across the heavens by the gusty wind that had blown up, and he let out a short laugh as she began to smile.

"What are you thinking?"

She turned within his arms and placed her hands upon his shoulders, lifting her gaze to his. "I was just admiring the location. It is a beautiful place, is it not?"

Darcy could not help but laugh as he threw the foul weather another cursory glance. "Most indubitably," he agreed, and then he bent to catch her lips with his. For himself, he could think of no finer place to be just now than closely entwined with Elizabeth, fair prospect or not.

Chapter Thirty Two

THE PREVIOUS DAY'S INCLEMENT weather had passed over during the night, the storm that had arisen so precipitously sweeping eastwards across Wiltshire, leaving behind a much fresher day with blue sky and very little cloud.

Elizabeth awoke early, and for some time she lay on her back staring at the canopy overhead, her mind full of pleasant thoughts and somewhat astounded by the alteration in her spirits from the previous morning, almost unable to credit what had taken place.

Memories of the moment of Mr Darcy's proposal, of the intimacy of their embraces under the tree in the rain and the gradually building intensity of their kisses rushed through her mind, and she became conscious of a warm sensation sweeping through her body. The need to cool her cheek persuaded her to rise from the bed and, taking care not to disturb Serena, she made use of the cold water in the pitcher before dressing in a simple day dress that required no assistance from a maid and made her way down to the drawing room.

For a while, she stood at the window, one of the wooden shutters pulled aside, and stared across the fields at the end house in Brock Street, though her gaze would persist in returning, time and again, to the tree – *their* tree –a wide smile overspreading her countenance whenever it did.

Then, as it was yet so early in the day that only the servants were about, she curled up in a fireside chair, tucking her shawl about her feet as was her habit, and settled with her book, idly stroking the marker as she strove to follow the story. It was not long, however, before she abandoned the attempt, for her mind was all too agreeably engaged in dwelling upon her new situation. Though her present pleasure in such anticipation was tempered somewhat by the separation that must follow shortly upon its heels, she trusted to it being of short enough duration and to their reunion being all the sweeter for it.

With a soft sigh, she closed the book, its marker noting the very same page as when she had last put it aside, and placed it on the drum table nearby. She leaned her head back in the chair, noting the chimes of the long case clock in the corner as the latest hour passed, letting her mind drift to the previous evening.

When they had finally accepted that they could remain no longer so exposed to the elements, Darcy had made use of Nicholas' umbrella and had walked her quickly under its protection to the side door of the house in Brock Street.

Once inside, she was able to return his coat, and he had then taken her hand and led her up to a charming drawing room where they had been greeted enthusiastically by both Miss Darcy and the Colonel.

Stirring in her seat, Elizabeth could not help but smile as she recollected their reception and Mr Darcy's confusion when the Colonel had taken the immediate step of saying he supposed he ought to offer his congratulations. Miss Darcy had been so bold as to throw herself at her brother, and he had looked at Elizabeth in surprise even as he placed his arm about his sister to return the embrace.

The Colonel, seeing their puzzlement, had laughed before welcoming her into the family. He had then gestured towards the rear window down which the rain steadily poured.

"Do you forgive us?"

Elizabeth bit her lip as she recalled her embarrassment at his implication; then, she let out a rueful laugh. The Colonel had essayed no further with his teasing, and she had passed a pleasurable few hours with them during the afternoon, a note having been dispatched to Marlborough Buildings to inform the Haringtons of her invitation to take afternoon tea. Indeed, so plentiful had been the conversation and so warm and friendly her welcome into Mr Darcy's immediate family, that the cessation of the rain went unnoticed by them all, and it was only a servant coming in to light the lamps that recollected them to the passing hours.

Getting to her feet, Elizabeth walked over to the window again, her eye fixed upon the Darcys' lodgings. Both Nicholas and James had arrived at the house in Brock Street in the early evening to escort her home. Supper was imminent but, though she knew the day must end, she had been reluctant to forego the present satisfactory circumstances. The Harington men had, however, taken an arm each and marched her quite firmly away from Mr Darcy, who had come to the corner of the street to see them off, and it was only a promise from that gentleman to call as soon as practicable the following morning that stopped her from freeing herself and flying back directly to him.

Just then, a servant entered to lay a fire in the grate and, noting from the clock how far the morning had progressed, Elizabeth left the room intent upon rousing her friend.

Darcy glanced out of the side window as he made his way down to the dining room, unable to prevent his eye from straying across the fields, still wet from the onslaught of rain, the grass glistening in the morning sun. Marlborough Buildings slumbered peacefully in the distance; there was no-one about, and the only detectable movement was the spiral of smoke emanating from several chimneys. As he continued on his way down the stairs, Darcy quickly checked his watch. It was near ten o'clock, and his impatience to see Elizabeth was at its height, the more so due to their impending separation.

Pushing open the door to the dining room, he was unsurprised to see both his sister and cousin already seated at table and a servant busy filling their cups with tea.

"About time, Darce." The Colonel glanced pointedly over at the clock upon the elegant stone mantel. "My stomach is beginning to fear my throat has been cut and is making all manner of protest."

Darcy walked around to sit beside Georgiana, dropping a kiss on top of her head as he did so.

"You need make no delay for me, Cousin. I barely have time for a cup as it is."

The Colonel frowned. "To what purpose?"

Darcy did not respond as a memory from the previous evening flowed through his mind, an image of Elizabeth's face as he took his leave of her, albeit chaperoned as they had been at the time. They had both determined then that they must see each other before she left Bath, and...

The clearing of the Colonel's throat drew Darcy's attention back to the room, and he met his cousin's amused eye with forbearance.

"Miss Bennet's movements are governed by the Haringtons, and they depart today for Sutton Coker. I – we – would wish to see each other before that separation must take place."

"See?"

"We must talk. There is still much to say."

"Talking, is it?" The Colonel laughed. "It is not what they called it in my day."

Darcy threw his cousin a warning look before glancing in Georgiana's direction, but she appeared to be oblivious to her cousin's meaning.

"I believe it would be sensible to go as soon as practicable."

"But of course, Fitz!" Georgiana bit her lip, then reached out and took his hand. "May I accompany you?"

"I – I had not…"

"I think perhaps, Georgie, we should permit your brother to pay this particular call alone."

Georgiana frowned and looked over at the Colonel, who was attempting a discreet nod towards the rear window that overlooked the garden. She glanced towards it, then suddenly seemed to understand his implication, and her cheeks filled with colour.

"Oh! Of course. How unthinking of me." She turned to Darcy and smiled widely at him. "Forgive me."

Darcy shook his head. "Richard is being objectionable, Georgie. I will own that I wish to have an opportunity to speak with Miss Bennet alone if at all possible, but we can accomplish that by taking a short walk, and you are welcome to join us if Richard will walk with you?"

He glanced over at his cousin who shrugged.

"Whatever you wish, Darce. Yet I am not of a mind to forego my repast. Perhaps you should go on before us whilst we partake, and I shall escort Georgiana to make her own farewells directly."

Seeing the sense in this, Darcy nodded and, quickly finishing his tea, he soon left them to eat and made his way out of the house into the bright morning.

Alicia Harington possessed both romantic sensibility and a generous heart, conditions exacerbated by having found a mutual and lasting affection in her partner in life. She considered there to be no finer thing than being wed for love, and love alone. Thus, when acquainted with Elizabeth's change of circumstances by a jubilant Nicholas on his return from Brock Street the evening before, she had quickly understood how her guest must be feeling, knowing of their imminent departure which would sever her tie not only with Bath but also her beau.

It would be fair to say this troubled her little enough, in that it did not prevent her from enjoying a good night's slumber; however, once up and about the following morning, she turned her mind to the possibilities that may result in Elizabeth enjoying a little longer in the gentleman's company. After all, was that not the very reason why Serena had accompanied Nicholas to Sutton Coker?

Keen to aid the young people as best she could, she made her way along the hall to her husband's study, determined to persuade him to her way of thinking.

꧁

Having been shown into the elegant first-floor drawing room, Darcy walked over to the full-length windows and admired the view. He felt a little uncomfortable arriving on the Haringtons' doorstep so precipitously, a feeling exacerbated by learning that much of the household remained at table.

Yet with Elizabeth's departure imminent, he had over-ridden his conscience in the matter, and he turned away from the pleasant prospect outside, impatient for her company. As he glanced about the room, his eye caught something that quickened his interest, and he walked over to a small table and picked up the slim volume that lay there.

A rather unusual marker protruded from the pages, and he let the book fall open upon his palm, taking the interwoven stick in his other hand. He frowned as he studied it, but just then the door flew open, and he turned around swiftly, the book closing instinctively and the marker still in his grip.

"Mr Darcy; how very ungallant! You have made me lose my place."

Darcy smiled and dropped the book onto the table, stepping forward to place a kiss upon Elizabeth's offered hand. It was not what he wished, but this was not the place for liberties; he did not doubt for one moment that they would not be left alone for long.

"Good morning, Elizabeth."

The lady laughed, ruefully. "Forgive me, Mr Darcy. I have the most appalling manners." She curtsied formally. "Good morning to you too, Sir." Her cheeks were pink, but she gave him an impish look. "I trust you slept well?"

It was Darcy's turn to laugh, but he merely shook his head. "I must apologise for the hour of my call. I know that your departure is imminent."

Elizabeth's features sobered, and he felt he understood, for their parting was going to be very sweet sorrow indeed. He made to take her hand once more, but realised he still held the reed marker which he offered to her.

"Forgive me. I did not mean to remove it."

Elizabeth took it from him and slipped it into her pocket. "It matters not. I have made so little progress of late with my book, I ought to begin anew!"

Before Darcy could satisfy his curiosity further, the door was pushed open and Serena entered the room, followed swiftly by Mr and Mrs Harington and Nicholas. The necessary introductions were quickly made, and Darcy wasted little time in requesting that he and Elizabeth be allowed to take a walk; soon afterwards, they were making their way out into the sunlit morning, Nicholas and Serena following some paces behind.

Chapter Thirty Three

ONCE THEY HAD MOUNTED THE STEPS that brought them onto the broad pavement that bordered the Royal Crescent, Darcy offered Elizabeth his arm, and they walked a few paces in a companionable silence before his curiosity got the better of him, and he gestured towards her pocket.

"It is an unusual method of marking one's page. Have you – did you make it yourself?"

She shook her head. "I cannot profess to such a talent. I picked it up off the ground the other day – on my journey to Town from Kent."

Darcy blinked. "At a watering stop?"

Clearly confused as to his interest in such a morsel, Elizabeth frowned. "Yes – the inn at Bromley; I do not recall its name."

"The Red Lion."

Elizabeth smiled. "I am sure you are right. I paid it little mind, I was more intent upon stretching my legs before being once more confined to the carriage. I happened upon the neatly woven stick there and decided it would make a fine marker."

They stopped walking as she reached for her pocket and drew out the plaited stick, placing it on her palm that they might both study it, and Darcy sighed.

"It was a childhood habit, and I could not resist an attempt the other day – when I too was travelling to London from Rosings."

The implication had struck a chord with him; he had paid the woven stick no further mind, yet here it was, not only in front of him, but in the possession of the one person he would give all his worldly goods to.

Elizabeth raised her eyes to his, and he was astounded to see wetness upon her lashes.

"What is it? What is wrong?" He took a step closer to her but she gave a reassuring smile and wiped the tear away.

"Nothing, Sir. It is just..." she paused, then let out a soft sigh. "You will think me all manner of foolish, to be certain, but I am touched that I found it. I liked it very well, but now it has taken on great significance, and I shall treasure it always."

Darcy smiled. "My mother did the same. I used to paint patterns on them by way of decoration – no mean task, with the surface so narrow and uneven – and she took each one from me as though it was a precious jewel. They remain even now in one of her boxes at Pemberley; except for one-"

A strange expression filtered over Elizabeth's features, and she looked quickly at the marker again. "Which is in Mount Street."

"How did you-"

"I saw it – in the display cabinet. It took my eye immediately, not only because it was in great contrast to the other precious items therein, but also for its similarity to my recent find."

For a moment, they stared at each other. Then, Darcy smiled and reached for her hand, placing a firm kiss upon it. "I am glad that you found it, and-"

Just then, a hand clapped him on the shoulder. "You have not got far, Darcy. Is Lizzy being troublesome?"

Nicholas and Serena had caught them up, and Elizabeth rolled her eyes at the former as she tucked the marker back into her pocket.

Darcy merely smiled, but then he turned to Harington. "What time do you plan to depart?"

"My father is leaving directly – pressing business matters on the estate." He glanced at his fob watch. "As such, though the plan was to set off sooner rather than later, I think we are at liberty to leave whenever is convenient, for it is not a long journey."

"Come then, Sir." Elizabeth took Darcy's arm once more. "Let us make the most of the time at our disposal." And they resumed their walk, soon out-stripping the other couple; yet, their chance for enjoyment of each other's company did not look set to endure, for within minutes they could both detect Georgiana and Colonel Fitzwilliam turning the far corner at the opposite end of the Royal Crescent, making their way towards them.

Darcy gestured towards them. "My sister and cousin both wished to pay their respects and say farewell. I came on ahead so that we might have the chance to talk."

"Then we had best speak quickly, Sir!" Elizabeth laughed ruefully. "Or slow our pace, but then we are in danger of being caught from behind!"

With a smile, Darcy glanced over his shoulder at where Harington and Miss Seavington were walking some paces further back. "It is a neat trap, is it not?"

"Well, then, Sir. What next? I believe – I hope – our change in circumstance will postpone your planned journey to Dublin?"

Darcy threw her a quick glance. "It is no loss, Elizabeth. The distance that I believed would be mutually beneficial has no further purpose, nor has lingering in Bath with your impending departure." He smiled down at her. "I believe the best direction for my travels is Hertfordshire – unless you have any objection?"

Elizabeth shook her head, though her expression had sobered, and recalling his last dealings with that neighbourhood, he felt his own spirits waver. Placing his hand upon hers where it rested on his arm, he felt comforted by the return of her smile.

"I must speak to your father, Elizabeth. It would not do for our understanding to continue long without his being acquainted with it." He could well recall that gentleman's blatant dissatisfaction when he received intelligence of Darcy and the Colonel's extended acquaintance with his daughter.

Sensing her grip tightening upon his arm, he glanced down at her and she met his gaze with a troubled expression.

"I know it is foolish to feel so sad, when in reality I could not be happier; yet I cannot bear to say farewell."

"When do you anticipate coming home to Longbourn?"

Elizabeth sighed. "It has yet to be decided. Beyond our return to Somerset, naught has been said of the matter." The gentleman at her side stopped and turned to face her.

"Then do not go. Return home to Hertfordshire – you could travel safely under my protection, Elizabeth."

Her countenance brightened, but then she bit her lip. "I am at the mercy of the Haringtons, though I came to be companion to Serena."

"Let me speak to them. I am certain they will see the efficacy of your returning home directly."

At that moment, Nicholas and Serena fetched up beside them once more, and the gentleman looked from Darcy to Elizabeth, then frowned. "What is amiss? You both are sporting a disconsolate air that does not befit your circumstances."

Elizabeth summoned a smile, but Darcy looked from her to Harington. "I wonder if it would be fitting for Miss Bennet to travel home with us. I must visit Longbourn directly, and she would be well-attended with both my sister and her companion for company."

Elizabeth turned to her friend. "Would you have any objection, Serena? I came to be with you; I would not have you feel I have deserted you."

With a smile, Serena reached out and took Elizabeth's hand in hers. "Of course I have no objection. I shall be well looked after by Aunt Alicia, and there is talk of us travelling to Crossways in a few days' time, so there will be plenty to entertain."

"Go home to your family, Lizzy. I am certain you would wish to be with Jane also." Nicholas turned to the man at her side. "It is a capital notion, Darcy. Besides which, Lizzy is all ready to depart Bath as it is, and as she is particularly close to her father, I suspect he would wish to see her if a gentleman is to approach him for her hand."

Darcy's misgiving returned in full measure at these words, for he did not anticipate an easy ride. Yet the interview was a necessity, and the sooner it was dealt with, the better, and he nodded.

"My sister's companion returns to us this morning. If I give the instruction, we can be off by mid-afternoon."

At that moment, they were joined by the Colonel and Georgiana, and once greetings were exchanged, Nicholas turned back towards Marlborough Buildings. "Come, then. Let us return to the house and seek my parents' counsel."

Having earlier successfully canvassed her husband on the matter of keeping the young people in company with each other, Mrs Harington was quickly able to confirm their support for the scheme. Thus it was that Mr Harington left as he had come, travelling alone, and his wife postponed the departure of her own carriage into the afternoon, that she might see her guest safely on her way, with Mrs Harington vowing to dispatch Elizabeth's remaining possessions – most of which she had barely unpacked – upon their return home, a situation that suited all.

Darcy made quick work of instructing the servants in the packing up of the house, leaving Thornton to oversee matters before his valet headed for Town on a commission for his master. Upon Mrs Annesley's return, the change in plan was soon conveyed, and all that remained was for Darcy to pen a quick note for Bingley announcing their imminent arrival even as the *Express* rider was summoned, and thus all was set.

So it was that, a little after three o'clock, Elizabeth was handed into the Darcy carriage to join Georgiana and Mrs Annesley on the journey to Hertfordshire, having bid an affectionate farewell to the Harington clan and promising Serena most faithfully to write her as soon as circumstance permitted.

The journey progressed smoothly, the ladies enjoying gentle conversation and the pleasure of each other's company. Elizabeth was, at times, slightly overwhelmed by the stream of questions Georgiana had for her in relation to her home and sisters, but she answered her as openly as she could and made a poor attempt at curbing her wit at some of her family's expense, conscious that Georgiana, like her brother, sometimes misinterpreted her playful manner, though she was pleased to note that Mrs Annesley was much more attuned to her sense of humour.

The gentlemen opted to ride, the weather remaining dry for the time being, and by dusk they had reached a coaching inn just beyond Marlborough where they rested overnight.

On the following morning, the travelling party arose to break an early fast and continue their journey. With the ladies travelling inside and the gentlemen on horseback, there was little opportunity for conversation or each other's company; thus, Elizabeth and Darcy were intent upon making the most of the first watering stop.

Leaving the Colonel to order some light refreshments, Georgiana and Mrs Annesley opted to stroll around the gardens adjacent to the establishment, and Darcy and Elizabeth took themselves off for a short walk through a small wood they had espied across the road from the inn.

After ambling along for ten minutes or so, engaged in gentle conversation, Darcy suggested they turn about and make their way back, time being of the essence if they were to reach Longbourn before nightfall, and they had gone but a few paces along the path when he threw Elizabeth a questioning glance.

"You are a little quiet this morning. I trust there is nothing amiss?"

The concern in the gentleman's voice was apparent, and Elizabeth shook her head as she looked up at him.

"Forgive me, Sir. I was merely preoccupied by something that had occurred to me overnight. It has just come back to mind, that is all."

"Did you not sleep?" He hesitated. "You are not – you do not regret your decision? It was so soon after-"

Perceiving his troubled countenance, Elizabeth came to a halt, quick to reassure him.

"Not in the slightest, Mr Darcy. Please believe me; I meant all and every word that I spoke on Sunday afternoon."

He released a long breath, and she realised just how difficult it must be for him, the time being so short between the proposal that failed and that which succeeded. Boldly taking his hand in hers, she once more pressed a kiss upon it before raising her gaze to his.

"It is a pleasurable enough conundrum, nothing to disturb."

Clearly relieved, he smiled. "Then tell me, Elizabeth. What is on your mind?"

"I am unsure of how to address you, Sir, in our changed circumstances. Though I am of course obligated in company to call you Darcy – and have faith, I am quite in countenance with such a notion – yet..."

"Yet?"

Elizabeth stared at their clasped hands. She could sense his eyes upon her still and, raising her head, she met his gaze with a serious look. "'Tis quite simple. Were I to call you by your given name of Fitzwilliam – well, suffice to say, the name has long been synonymous for me with your cousin, and thus it is whom it brings to mind when I hear it."

Darcy gave a short laugh. "Point taken; perchance best avoided."

She smiled up at him then, her fingers now laced with his, and they turned to continue their amble back through the wood.

"Elizabeth, I would not have you uncomfortable. If you wish to call me Darcy in private, I have no objection."

Shaking her head, she looked up at him. "I wish for something more... more personal. Do not mistake me; I am honoured to take your name, Sir. I am, indeed, proud of all things Darcy!"

He laughed at this and shook his head. "Then, I fear the only answer is an abbreviation."

"And is there a form that I should be aware of – within the family, I mean?" She paused, then let out a rueful laugh. "If I were to take the liberty, Sir, of shortening it to 'William' – well, I must own it would not sit well with me to address you by the same given name as my cousin, Mr Collins, or indeed my friend's father!"

Darcy smiled. "Heaven forbid!"

"Then guide me, Sir! What is it to be?"

Coming to a halt once more, Darcy turned her about so that they faced each other. They were under the eaves of some trees, but steps from emerging into full view of the inn. He glanced over towards said establishment and then took her other hand in his.

"Georgiana calls me Fitz, as do my close family, though the Colonel has all manner of names that he applies whenever the fancy takes him."

Conscious of the warmth of his grasp upon her fingers and their comparative closeness, Elizabeth drew in a steadying breath.

"Then it shall be so. You are Darcy in public, but Fitz in the privacy of our own home." She stopped, conscious of warmth filling her cheeks, but then pressed on. "How well that sounds. Must we delay long to be wed?"

Darcy blinked at these words, parted his lips as though to speak, but no words came forth. Before, however, Elizabeth could reflect on her lack of modesty, she found herself swept into a strong embrace, and with little hesitation she raised her face so that the gentleman could convey in no uncertain terms just how much he appreciated the sentiment she had so recently expressed.

Chapter Thirty Four

"MAMA! THERE IS A RATHER FINE carriage coming along the drive! And two gentlemen on horseback accompany it."

Kitty's voice roused Jane, and she raised her head from the letter she was writing as Mrs Bennet got agitatedly to her feet.

"Is it Mr Bingley? You sly thing, Jane; I thought you said he had commitments that would prevent him attending us this evening." She turned on her eldest daughter, whose bemused expression conveyed her feelings precisely.

"Why would Mr Bingley take the carriage to visit us, Mama? It does not make any sense."

Waving her response aside with a fluttering hand, Mrs Bennet hurried to the window seat where Kitty was perched with her needlework and peered out in the direction of the gravel driveway.

"Why, it truly *is* a fine carriage." She frowned as she pressed her face against the glass. "Though it is rather dusty." She straightened up and turned around, raising her chin. "Your father would never send *our* carriage out in such a condition, that is to be certain."

Jane shook her head but said nothing and returned her attention to her letter. It was late in the day to be receiving a call, but no doubt the visitors would be announced soon enough, and that was sufficient for her.

Mrs Bennet turned to tidy her hair in the drawing room mirror. "Kitty, put your work away and summon Mary and Lydia. And get Hill to bring more candles – the beeswax. This instant!"

Kitty did as she was bid and soon returned with her sisters in tow, though as yet no one had been announced, and Mrs Bennet's impatience was spiralling by the second.

"If your father takes the visitors into his library, I shall never forgive him. If there are gentlemen visiting, they *must* pay their respects to me – to us. It is all very well having you settled, Jane, but I have four other daughters in need of a situation, and with the loss of Mr Wickham…"

Jane tuned out her mother's voice, having heard the lament all too frequently, and got to her feet to peer out of the window. The carriage and its escort had pulled up near the front door, and the steps had been lowered, but in the falling dusk it was impossible to discern who the callers were until someone appeared in the doorway of the conveyance and, with a smothered gasp, Jane put a hand to her mouth.

Turning around, she smiled at her mother, who was now fanning herself with a handkerchief. "Let me go and see, Mama. I shall return directly."

Letting herself from the room as Hill entered with the candles, Jane paused on the other side of the closed doors and let out a sigh of relief. Elizabeth was home!

Hurrying along the hallway to the front door, she emerged from the house into the cool evening air just as her sister rushed into her embrace with an ecstatic, "Jane!"

Having returned Elizabeth's hug, she set herself up from the embrace, quickly recognising the people stood near the carriage, and she curtseyed formally.

"Mr Darcy; Colonel Fitzwilliam; Miss Darcy."

Darcy acknowledged her. "Miss Bennet. We have much pleasure in delivering your sister safely home."

"For which I thank you, Sir; she has been greatly missed. Though, Lizzy," Jane turned to her sister. "We understood you to be in Somerset with the Haringtons. How come you to be here?"

"'Tis a long story, Jane, and I shall satisfy your curiosity directly, but we have journeyed far and my companions have yet a few miles to go for they are Netherfield bound, so let us see them on their way."

Elizabeth took her leave of the Colonel, who then led his horse over to the stone mounting block, and she turned to speak to his cousin.

Jane exchanged some pleasantries with Miss Darcy, but could not quite account for the look of suppressed excitement upon her features, or the distraction in her manner and, seeing that her attention had drifted towards her brother, Jane turned about to observe him.

She blinked rapidly; if she was not mistaken, Mr Darcy had just bestowed a kiss upon her sister's hand, and though Elizabeth's face was somewhat averted, there was deep colour in her cheeks, and she appeared reluctant to step away from the gentleman. Jane looked quickly at Miss Darcy to see if she had noticed anything untoward, but to her surprise, the girl was no longer at her side. She had dashed forward and thrown herself into Elizabeth's embrace, something that clearly surprised her sister, though she quickly returned the gesture and laughed.

"Dear Georgiana! We shall see each other on the morrow!"

The young lady stepped back and grasped Elizabeth's hand. "But I am so happy for you-" she stopped, throwing a conscious look at her brother and then another over at Jane, who narrowed her gaze, her curiosity at its height.

Darcy ushered Georgiana into the carriage and, with one long meaningful stare at Elizabeth, he mouthed something at her that Jane failed to detect, though her sister looked vastly pleased by it, and regained his mount before joining his cousin, and the party set off back down the drive.

For a moment, both girls watched its progress in silence. Then, unable to bear the suspense any longer, Jane threw her sister a quick glance. "Do you have something you wish to share with me, Lizzy?"

Biting her lip to contain a smile, Elizabeth turned and linked her arm through her sister's as they walked into the house. "Let me greet Mama, Jane. Then, we shall be at liberty to go upstairs and talk to our hearts' content."

It did not take long for Elizabeth to acquaint Jane with her news, but before she did, she expressed her own delight over her sister's engagement to Bingley and her happiness to see her beloved Jane so content.

Accepting her congratulations, Jane quickly turned her attention to Elizabeth and Darcy. Having observed her sister's growing interest in the gentleman during their time in Town, she was not overly surprised by her sister's change in opinion though she did press Elizabeth for confirmation that she was happy with her choice, such a short period having passed since her rejection of the same gentleman.

Elizabeth took little time in recounting how her feelings had changed over recent weeks and how it was that both she and Mr Darcy had come to be in Bath. She emphasised how fortunate she felt to be loved by such a man and spoke eloquently of her affection for him in return. Jane was soon appeased and thus more than content, for her only qualm over accepting the hand of Bingley had been that she would be leaving behind her dearest sister and companion in a household that would be all the more intolerable for Elizabeth with her absence.

"When does Mr Darcy propose speaking to Papa?"

Elizabeth got to her feet and walked over to the window, staring out over the parkland of Longbourn wistfully. Never before had she returned home from a sojourn elsewhere and wished she had not come. Even now, she longed to be with Darcy, no matter where he was: Bath or Netherfield, either would suffice. To be at Longbourn and distant from him, three miles or no, was perfectly intolerable.

She released a sigh, and then turned to face her sister. "I believe he intends to ride over in the morning. We have been on the road all day, and he did not wish to enter into such an interview now; besides, I think it best if I speak to Papa myself first."

"You intend to tell him you are engaged?"

"Good heavens, no – I do not!" Elizabeth laughed and walked over to re-join her sister who remained perched on the edge of the bed. "I would not wish to so fully undermine Mr Darcy; yet though Papa must know that I have revised my opinion of the gentleman somewhat since I was last at home, I feel it might be wise to relate some of our more recent encounters. Mr Darcy advised me last evening that he felt Papa was none too pleased to hear of the amount of time we had spent in his company of late when he was not aware of it. I think I had, perhaps, at best explain our meeting unexpectedly in Bath, though I am at a loss over how to account for my sudden return home!"

"I think he will be so relieved to see you, it will not trouble him!"

"Mama seemed completely disinterested, did she not? I suspect she was relieved that Mr Darcy did not call upon her." Elizabeth shook her head. "I fear the worst, Jane. She never liked him and has shown no discretion in making that known, not only amongst her own acquaintance, but even in his company. I know neither how she will take the news, nor what expression she may make of it to him."

Jane patted her consolingly on the hand before getting to her feet. "Be thankful, Lizzy, for her aversion. Her fawning over Bingley since his declaration knows no bounds. Though Mr Collins is our father's blood, not hers, you would be excused for believing the contrary."

"Oh dear!" Elizabeth watched her sister as she pulled the bell for a hot water to be brought. "I am so sorry, Jane. Is it truly awful?"

With a shrug, Jane walked over to the chest against the far wall and extracted a bathing sheet, offering it to her sister. "Bingley has the patience of a saint, but there are times when I detect that he is sorely tried. Perhaps now he has company, he will be here less; certainly, I shall be able to pay a call at Netherfield now, which before I could not!"

Elizabeth smiled and got to her feet as a servant came in with a pitcher, and Jane left her sister to refresh herself, returning downstairs to await her.

Turning towards the washstand, Elizabeth sighed. Her father's reaction to her engagement was hard to predict and, having learned more from Darcy of his last interview with Mr Bennet, she could not, even with all her knowledge of him, ascertain whether he would be pleased or disgruntled by the intelligence.

Staring into the mirror as she lowered her hands into the bowl of water, Elizabeth bit her lip. Whatever the outcome, she would do all in her power to ensure a smooth ride for Darcy the next day, and with that in mind, she made haste to refresh herself and hurried downstairs to attend her father in his library.

⁂

Bingley's greeting had been all that Darcy could wish. Their friendship being of such long-standing, the *Express* requesting that he and his family visit for a short duration had been a pleasure rather than an inconvenience, and as Bingley had been rattling around in solitary fashion since his return, he was delighted to have some company, and what was more, of the very best sort.

Darcy's letter had suggested that no mention be made of their visit prior to their arrival, a postscript that had puzzled Bingley. The knowledge that Miss Elizabeth Bennet was homeward bound, something that would bring such joy to his dear Jane, was something he was loath to keep secret, but as his friend's arrival was imminent he found himself able to comply with the request without too much struggle and instead went about engaging further household staff to assist with the influx of guests.

Happily accepting the congratulations of his visitors on his successful application for Jane Bennet's hand, Bingley had shown them to the rooms he had had prepared for them and bade them restore themselves before joining him in the drawing room for some pre-supper refreshments.

Thomas Bennet was a man of mixed parts – intelligent and educated, his greatest regret in life was the foolish infatuation that had bound him swiftly and irrevocably to Frances Gardiner. Yet the union – so dissatisfying on many levels – had its consolations. Like many a person in a less than idyllic marriage, how could he regret the progeny of the union, the lives that would not exist without its occurrence?

Contrary to appearances, he did love all his daughters, though not in equal measure and, without doubt, the depth of that love was tempered by his tolerance levels. Yet, though the younger three girls did try his patience, he loved them still, and despite his affinity for his second eldest, her mind being so much more agile, they all held a charge on him in his interest for their future.

Loath though he was to admit it to his wife, her desire to see one of them well-settled was one of her more rational notions. He was not blind also to his own failings in this regard, that had he been more sensible over the business opportunities of his estate, their dowries would not be quite so slender a morsel. His contentment in seeing his eldest well settled was appropriate to the benefit it would draw down upon the others. That it might quieten his wife's excesses, exacerbated ever since Jane had become of marriageable age, he held little hope for.

Getting wearily to his feet, he walked over to the only wall in his library that was not encased with bookshelves. Here, between the two windows, hung a collection of miniatures of his children taken over the preceding years.

As was often the case, his eye was drawn to one of Elizabeth, and he frowned. His daughter's unanticipated presence earlier that day had been sufficient surprise for one day; learning that she had been conveyed thither by the Darcys had been one he could have done without. His last encounter with that gentleman, though he had brought valuable intelligence and done them a vast service, still rankled. The memory of several weeks of that young man's taciturn manner last autumn was insufficient to be supplanted by a half hour in his company whilst discussing a particularly unsavoury matter.

Yet Elizabeth had earlier been at pains to explain that Mr Darcy – who they all knew to be a proud, arrogant and unfeeling sort – was nothing of the kind if you really knew him, and his suspicions were aroused. His daughter was hiding something from him and, coupled with her championing of Mr Darcy, he could not help but suspect that she had developed a fondness for a man who was too far above her.

As the supper bell sounded, Mr Bennet turned away from the miniatures with a sigh and walked towards the door. He only hoped Elizabeth would recover quickly from her interest in the gentleman and, though he would not deny Jane the pleasure of happiness in marriage, he could not help but regret that Mr Bingley had ever brought his friend into the neighbourhood at all.

Chapter Thirty Five

MRS ANNESLEY AND GEORGIANA HAD elected to rest for a while once they had freshened up, and the Colonel took it upon himself to visit the stables, having been concerned over his mount during the ride. Thus it was that Darcy alone returned to join Bingley, who was lounging in a leather armchair in the drawing room with a newspaper.

"Well, Darcy," he greeted him as his friend closed the door and walked across the room. "Your note was brief and to the point, but I trust you are going to enlighten me as to your present unrest!"

Darcy frowned as he took a seat. "Unrest?"

"Indeed! First of all, you make a sudden and unexplained journey out of Town on the very morning I am to depart; then I receive word from you that you are in Bath, and within days of *that* intelligence, you travel to Hertfordshire!" Bingley shook his head and chuckled. "Not that I am anything but delighted, old boy, to have you here, but the precipitance, and unpredictability, of your actions is more redolent of myself than the Darcy I have long been acquainted with!"

Bingley peered at him intently; then, he frowned. "There is something… altered about you."

Darcy stirred in his seat; he knew full well that it was his duty to speak to Mr Bennet before anyone else became aware of his and Elizabeth's understanding. Without that gentleman's consent, there would be little reason for rejoicing, after all. Yet he longed to shed any disguise and put the truth of the matter before his friend and, deciding that Elizabeth could have no objection, Bingley set to become her brother as he was, Darcy soon enlightened him over his commitment to the lady.

Though his surprise at first was such that he assumed a joke on Darcy's part, Bingley could not have been more delighted, and no small amount of questioning ensued as he tried to take in the news.

By the time the Colonel re-joined them, however, he had become accustomed to the intelligence, and his pleasurable anticipation of the close relationship it would secure between both men was paramount in his mind as he poured them all a tot of brandy by way of celebration.

Bingley then turned to the Colonel as he took a seat. "How is your mount?"

"A small wound on the fetlock. Your groom is kindly making up a poultice." The Colonel stretched out his legs in front of him. "Fine set of stables you have here."

"Thank you. I look forward to joining you both in a ride on the morrow." He turned to Darcy. "When do you propose speaking with Miss Elizabeth's father?"

"As soon as practicable. I will own to some apprehension, if our last interview with him is anything to go by."

The Colonel snorted and Bingley frowned.

"My urgent business on the day you left Town, Bingley – my cousin and I called at Longbourn to forewarn Mr Bennet about a certain unsavoury individual who appeared to have designs upon the family."

"Ah, yes. You mean Wickham, I presume." Darcy raised a brow, and his friend continued. "His fate is common knowledge hereabouts, and I am afraid that there are those in the Bennet family who are neither subtle about forecasting the details nor grateful to you for your intervention now it is known."

Darcy exchanged a resigned glance with his cousin. "Mrs Bennet never held much inclination for me, Bingley; I would imagine this interference of mine is as welcome to her as my presence ever was."

Bingley laughed. "Well, I am certain you will not lose any sleep over not meeting with her approbation. After all, Derbyshire is a fair distance." His smile faded briefly, and Darcy could understand why. To live in such close proximity to the woman would be more than he could endure. He was striving to be less judgemental and thus more tolerant, but there were things that were beyond him yet and some, he suspected, ever would be.

"So," the Colonel turned to his host. "How was it for you, Bingley? Was the gentleman hard upon you?"

For a moment, Bingley looked somewhat abashed. Then, he shook his head. "Not really. I was due a reprimand of some sort. My failure to return from Town last autumn was called under question-" he cast Darcy a quick glance. "For which I took full responsibility."

"So you felt no trepidation in your approach?"

Bingley opened his mouth, but no sound came out and then he closed it quickly. Running a hand through his tousled hair, he then gave them both a sheepish glance.

"Truth be told, I felt sick as a parrot – and was almost as green."

The Colonel let out a shout of laughter. "There you go, Darce! You are at least in very good company."

Darcy blew out a breath. "The delay does not make it any easier. Would that we had arrived at a more opportune time of day, that it could be over directly."

His cousin drained his glass, putting it on the side table. "Would you like us to accompany you on the morrow?"

"That you may delight in my humiliation?"

"No – that we might share the whipping from the gentleman's razor-sharp tongue – its lashing will no doubt be less severe if the blade must strike three targets at once!"

With a shake of his head, Darcy got to his feet, adding his empty glass to the Colonel's. "I thank you for the offer, but I think I must face him without a 'second' on this occasion."

The others stood as well, and Bingley led the way to the door.

"Well, then; let us summon the ladies and repair to the dining room. A fully-sated appetite will doubtless aid you in a good night's rest, that you may have all your wits about you for the morning."

Though she had long dismissed Mr Darcy himself as a potential suitor for one of her daughters, Mrs Bennet's aversion to the gentleman's company faded as quickly as her mind could grasp the benefit of Mr Bingley's recently arrived guests. The likelihood of their neighbour and future son-in-law now entertaining at Netherfield had increased ten-fold from when he had been in solitary occupation, and though Bingley himself was already secured, she had no intention of letting anyone else in the district get a march on her own plans when there were other single young men in town.

Elizabeth had done her best to calm her mother's effusions, but to little avail. It was in her family's interest to encourage the acquaintance, and Mrs Bennet was soon set upon arranging a dinner invitation to be sent over forthwith, that Longbourn might be the first call upon their time. That her decision was heavily influenced by discovering the presence of Mr Darcy's cousin, the Colonel, was apparent, for though he did not sport a red coat, this was far outweighed by the fact that he came from a titled family, sufficient inducement for her to consider him the rightful property of one or other of her remaining daughters.

Bored by her endless comments along this vein and full aware that his reflection over the supper table – that the second son of an Earl would hardly be in a position to take a wife with a dowry so small as £1,000 – had been completely ignored, Mr Bennet took the first opportunity to escape and, as was his wont, excused himself to return to his library.

He was followed into the hallway by Elizabeth, who bade him a quick goodnight, the journey having tired her sufficiently that she intended to repair to her room directly. Watching as she made her way up the stairs, he frowned. Her attempts over supper to persuade her mother away from ingratiating herself with Mr Darcy and his family smacked more of protecting the former than any desire to save Mrs Bennet from self-humiliation, and his misgivings from earlier returned. Was his daughter on her way to a broken heart?

He closed the library door with a snap, poured himself a glass of port and walked over to the hearth to stir the flames into further life. Mr Bennet had not taken quite so deep an aversion to Darcy as others had last autumn. He knew of the gentleman's slight of Elizabeth – how could he not, with his wife so vociferous over it – but unlike Mrs Bennet, he both found the gentleman's attitude and aloof nature quite in keeping with his expectations of someone of such high social standing. He had also heard all the rumours concerning that young man and Wickham, including his own daughter's opinions on both gentlemen – something that she clearly regretted, having since discovered how erroneous they were.

He sat down in a fireside chair, his glass cupped in both hands and stared into the flames. He valued Elizabeth beyond measure; she was, indeed, a jewel, a prize whose affections should be treasured – yet the reality stood. She was far from the Darcys' sphere, and Mr Darcy – good man or not – would never stoop to their level when seeking a wife.

These ruminations were interrupted by a brief knock on the door as it was opened, and he turned in his seat as Jane entered the room.

"Papa? I am for bed. Is there anything you need before I retire?"

"Come in, my dear. Spare me a few moments of your time." He motioned his daughter into the chair opposite as he placed his glass on the side table.

Jane smiled tentatively as she sat. "Is aught amiss?"

"I have a question for you, my dear. I know I can trust to your honesty."

Jane nodded, though her confusion clearly remained.

"Well then." Mr Bennet sat back in his chair, his hands steepled on his chest. "Lizzy's re-acquaintance with Mr Darcy – has she spoken to you of him? She seems to hold him in high regard, which is quite contrary to her view when she left for Kent."

The colour that stained his eldest daughter's cheeks was sufficient. He knew he need speak no further on the matter, that he need not put poor, innocent Jane in the position of obliging a parent by breaking the trust of a sibling. Yet he would know.

"I see. So I was not mistaken earlier when Lizzy chose to enlighten me how misled she had been in her judgement of the gentleman. She has revised her opinion, that much I heard from her own lips; but is that the end of the matter, or is there more I should be aware of?"

His eldest looked quite distressed, and his heart misgave him.

"There, there." He leaned forward and patted her on the knee. "Do not disturb yourself so. Lizzy herself left sufficient clues, my dear; you are merely confirming a riddle I was close to solving on my own. Now – run along."

Jane kissed him on the cheek and hurriedly left the room, and Mr Bennet got wearily to his feet. Walking back over to the miniatures on the wall, he stared at the one of Elizabeth he had studied earlier. The rendering had been done about three years ago and was very like and slowly he reached out and touched her dear face. So, his instinct had not been at fault. His favourite child *was* taken with a man so far above her, she was destined for disappointment.

With a dissatisfied grunt, he turned and walked over to the table containing the decanters, pouring himself a further measure of port. He had all but raised it to his lips when the door was lightly rapped and opened swiftly and, turning around, he eyed Elizabeth as she slipped into the room and softly closed the door. He did not need her to speak to know that Jane had been to her, yet speak she did.

"Papa! How could you!" She paced across the hearthrug, a shawl hastily thrown about her shoulders, then turned on her heel and paced back again. Then, she sighed and turned to face him. "You force me to convey something that should come from another."

Chapter Thirty Six

WEDNESDAY DAWNED AND heralded a further day of fine weather.

Darcy turned away from the looking glass, his dress complete, and walked over to the dresser as Thornton began his habitual tidy of the room. Picking up the small leather case, he weighed it on his palm for a moment, reflecting that his valet had made good time in his journey to Town to collect the box from Darcy's safe and restore it to his master's care – a short tenancy, for its content was destined for another at the soonest interlude.

Flicking open the lid, he smiled as the light flickered upon the dark green jewel nestled in its velvet bed. He had gazed upon it before now in such a different frame of mind – so certain of his acceptance, an altered man to the one who now held it and, conscious as he was that the person upon whom he would bestow the ring was responsible for precipitating that alteration – one that he knew he must endeavour to build upon – he felt a wave of love and gratitude sweep through him as his thoughts rested pleasurably on Elizabeth.

How he longed to see her, and how thankful he was that the Haringtons had been amenable to his suggestion that she travel to Hertfordshire under his protection. If he had been considering his impending interview with her father with Elizabeth far away in the West Country, he would have borne the wait with far less tolerance.

The chiming of the clock on the mantel roused him from such speculation and, tucking the small box into his waistcoat, he made his way out onto the landing in search of his sister and cousin.

A good night's rest was sufficient to restore Mr Bennet's usual equilibrium. The shock of Elizabeth's revelation on the previous evening had eased, though at the time he had struggled to comprehend what she was telling him. Yet her unconcealed pleasure as she recounted how her feelings had come to change for Mr Darcy, coupled with her assurance of his long-held admiration in return, was sufficient to reconcile him to a match that he had supposed could never be.

That Mr Darcy had turned out to be the hero, not the villain, of the piece he had already become accustomed to following that gentleman's visit the previous week, but now his earlier fears over Elizabeth's heart were likewise satisfied.

With his astonishment having diminished, Mr Bennet found any concern yet remaining over the union was tempered by the evidence he had seen from his daughter herself that she clearly admired the man; indeed, she professed to love him.

Mr Bennet smiled wryly. So – the great Mr Darcy was going to approach him. He shook his head in bemusement as he left the dining room, having broken his fast with his family. This had to be the most singular week in all his memory, and with that thought, he crossed the flag-stoned hallway to his library to await whatever further incongruity the morning might bring.

⁂

The fare upon the table in Netherfield's dining room had been ample to satiate even the Colonel's appetite and the morning meal had, perforce, lasted a considerable time. Soon after its conclusion, however, Bingley excused himself to speak to his steward whilst Georgiana continued at table with Mrs Annesley as they consumed a further cup of tea, and Darcy and the Colonel walked over to one of the full-length windows that opened onto the terrace, thrown open to let the morning air pervade the room.

It had been decided between the gentlemen that Darcy would make the requisite journey to Longbourn as soon as the hour was convenient for making a call and that the Colonel and Bingley would follow on with Georgiana shortly after.

With his impatience to see Elizabeth at its height, Darcy quickly checked his watch before tucking it away again. Time barely seemed to have moved on from when last he had consulted it, and he sighed.

His cousin threw him a quick glance. "You do not doubt his consent?"

Darcy shrugged. "I would not count on anything where Mr Bennet is concerned." He turned to the Colonel, lowering his voice that his sister might not overhear him. "You do recall that Miss Elizabeth rejected Collins before she turned me down. She informed me over supper at the inn the other night that, despite her mother's insistence on the offer being accepted, her father backed his daughter and refused to allow her to throw herself away – on the heir to his estate, no less."

The Colonel let out a slow whistle. "That would account for your air and countenance! I observed you both in conversation – she appeared most earnest, and your attention was quite fixed upon her, but I could tell that you were disconcerted by whatever it was that she was disclosing."

"Our perception last week that he puts the lady's happiness ahead of all else is clearly correct. All I can hope for is that I can convince him that she will be content with me."

Slapping him on the back, the Colonel shook his head. "Do not doubt your ability, Darce, to get your message across. This is just a hurdle to overcome – after all, you do have the lady's sanction, which Collins did not!" He turned to look back out of the window. "Just see it as the final step towards your future being settled."

Darcy frowned. The memory of his cousin, Anne's, words returned in full measure, of how she had no future until he was wed to another. It was adequate distraction from his present thoughts, and he glanced at his cousin.

"We must think on how to proceed with Anne. We made a start in Bath; it would be unkind of us not to continue."

"Most indubitably." The Colonel turned to face him. "Once the marriage has taken place, it would be a good thing to have Anne to stay at Pemberley."

"I do not think Aunt Catherine would permit her such a length of journey and a sojourn so far from home without accompanying her."

The Colonel grunted. "You assume Aunt will be prepared to pay you her attention once you are wed to Miss Elizabeth Bennet?"

Darcy blinked, and then frowned. "I had given it little thought thus far. I suppose there is every likelihood she will not take it well."

"Well, that is one way of putting it." The Colonel let out a short laugh. "It will be no hardship, Darce, if she severs all ties. Bear that in mind."

"But what of Anne, should that come to pass?"

"She is well of age and has her own fortune." The Colonel sighed. "Were I a better man, I would offer for her myself to free her from her cage." He threw a quick glance at Darcy. "But much as I am growing to like our cousin of late, I do not think I could be content in spending the rest of my life with her – nor she with me. But my point is, even should our aunt cut you from her acquaintance, then Anne I am certain will wish a continuance."

"Then she will need our assistance to leave Rosings."

"Indeed she will." The Colonel turned back to resume his study of the parkland. "And we will need to keep a careful eye on the bird as it flies the nest."

Georgiana, who had not really been paying attention to her brother or her cousin, frowned. "What bird?" She looked over towards the window where they stood. "Can you see a bird?"

※

Frequent though his use of the library was, Thomas Bennet was also used to being disturbed in it. Thus it was that he was unsurprised, having heard the doorbell, at the appearance of Hill some few moments later; nor was he taken aback by whom she announced.

"Mr Darcy, Sir."

Getting to his feet as the gentleman entered, Mr Bennet gave an order for tea and then waved his visitor into a chair.

"Please, be seated."

They both took up the same respective positions they had when last they met and, for a moment, silence reigned. The elder gentleman felt a slight twinge of conscience, for Mr Darcy's air and countenance were not indicative of a man at ease. Yet as he understood his reason for calling, and thus what likely caused his present anxiety, Mr Bennet felt obliged, until the gentleman had himself under sufficient control to speak his purpose, to fall back upon generalities.

"I wish to thank you, Mr Darcy, for safely restoring my daughter to me."

An inclined head was the only acknowledgement to this, but as his guest seemed to be struggling to find anything to say, completely in keeping with the taciturn and serious man that he knew him to be, Mr Bennet continued.

"We did not expect her. She wrote last week to say she would be spending some time with her friend in the West Country." He paused. "I understand she travelled home in your carriage, alongside your sister and her companion – and under the protection of yourself and your cousin."

Darcy cleared his throat. "Indeed, Sir. You are correct."

"And how is the good Colonel? Did he not wish to join you in paying a call?"

His visitor looked a little awkward for a moment before shaking his head. "He sends his best wishes, Mr Bennet, but on this occasion, I wished to speak to you alone."

Though this surprised him not, he raised a brow at the young man opposite. "Is that so?"

Darcy gestured with his hand. "Be not alarmed, Sir. I do not bring any intelligence along the lines of our last conversation."

"I am glad to hear it. One bounder a year attempting to infiltrate one's family is sufficient, I believe." He shifted in his seat, studying his guest carefully. "I trust you are well settled at Netherfield. Mr Bingley is a genial host, I suspect."

"Most indubitably." Darcy tugged at his neck-cloth as though it caused him some discomfort.

"I am fortunate in my future son-in-law. My only wish is that he lived vastly further afield." A raised brow from his visitor was sufficient to prompt him to expand upon this. "I mean no slur upon him, Sir." He waved a hand in the general direction of the window. "And Netherfield is a fine property. But though my wife is deficient in understanding at the best of times, I suspect even she would be suspicious should I tell her I intend to make a stay of several weeks with the Bingleys when they are but three miles distant across the parkland." He paused, out of patience now with trivialities. "Come then, Sir; to what do I owe the honour of your call?"

Just then, a light rap came upon the door, heralding the arrival of a servant with a tray of tea and, once they were both served with a cup and left alone again, Mr Bennet gave the young man, who, after all, was of significant consequence to his daughter, an encouraging smile. It was not reciprocated as Darcy quickly placed his cup on a small table beside his chair and got to his feet. He gestured with his hand, opened his mouth and then promptly closed it again, swallowing visibly, and Mr Bennet, who had only ever considered Darcy a controlled man, blinked in astonishment.

Then, the gentleman cleared his throat. "My purpose-" he hesitated. "I am come, Sir, to – to request the hand of your daughter in marriage."

Though he had ample daughters who were unspoken for, Mr Bennet was obviously in no doubt whatsoever which one Mr Darcy referred to. However, it was not in his nature to make things easy if there was some sport to be had, and he got to his feet as well.

"Well, Mr Darcy. I will admit to being a little taken aback. Do you have a particular preference, or shall I recommend one my four remaining daughters for you? I will lay claim to knowing them best, having been in their acquaintance just a little longer than you."

"Yes – yes, of course you do. I meant to-"

"It is a thorny one." Mr Bennet continued, ignoring the interruption. "Mary would of course, benefit from the tuition of the first-class music masters you could no doubt provide; Catherine's improvement will be in direct proportion to the distance there is between her and her younger sister; as for Lydia – well, even I would not be so obtuse as to recommend my youngest to you. So," he sighed, concealing his amusement at the gentleman's conflicted countenance. "I suppose you had best take my Lizzy."

For a moment, there was silence. Then, Darcy cleared his throat. "You knew, Sir."

Mr Bennet inclined his head. "Forgive me for making fun of you, Mr Darcy. I have been somewhat astounded by events this past seven days, and it seems there is to be no let-up." He gestured to the young man to take a seat again and resumed his own. "Though I believe this intelligence has taken the crown, so to speak?"

There was no denying the question in this statement, and Darcy nodded.

"I fully comprehend your surprise, Sir. When I last stayed in the neighbourhood, there was little indication from me, I know, of what might come to pass."

"Indeed. There is the element of the magician about you, Mr Darcy. What impression do you give to all around you, but that you find Elizabeth only tolerable, not handsome enough to tempt you, even in so little a formality as a country dance. Yet this, it transpires, is an illusion, for it now comes to pass that you admire her sufficiently to take her as your partner in life."

Darcy released a deep breath, his serious gaze meeting that of his host. "I hope you will pardon me for speaking such imprudent words, Mr Bennet. I have been fortunate in securing your daughter's forgiveness, and I can assure you my rudeness brought its just reward. The mistakes I have made of late…" he stopped and ran an agitated hand through his hair. "I have tried to correct them, but it does not excuse the making of them in the first instance."

With a gesture of his hand, Mr Bennet brushed the matter aside. "Pay me no mind, Mr Darcy. I find it hard not to give young men who come calling upon me a hard time. Surely it is a father's privilege when he is facing losing a beloved child to another. The handover of something so precious as a daughter is-" he stopped suddenly as his throat tightened upon the words. "Yes, well - suffice to say, you will I am sure generously allow me to extract payment in whatever form I wish."

"I fully comprehend, Sir. Feel at liberty to exercise your wit; I can only hope to learn from you, for though my sister is but sixteen years of age, I have already cast my mind to how I would receive any young man approaching me for her hand. I begin to see some appeal in your method." He paused. "Yet I would know, Sir, if I – if *we* may have your consent?"

"Mr Darcy, you are a man of great consequence. I am not going to refuse you, especially in the light of Lizzy's obvious pleasure in her choice. But her happiness is the point. She is the joy of my life – and there are but few of them; to see her anything but content in her marriage will break my heart. You will forgive my saying, I trust, that the attachment seems to have been rapidly formed. Whilst Lizzy assures me that her affection for you is sound, my concern is that it may not endure – on either side."

"I fully comprehend your anxiety on behalf of Miss Elizabeth, Sir. Though her change of heart appears the work of an instant, I do believe in its constancy. As for myself, I have long held your daughter in the highest esteem." Darcy hesitated, then cleared his throat. "If you will forgive me the liberty of speaking so, I hold her in the deepest of affection. All told, Sir – I love her; most ardently."

Mr Bennet eyed him thoughtfully, then got to his feet, offering his hand. "Well then, I welcome you into the family, Sir – though I doubt that you will thank me for it."

Darcy also stood, shaking his head as they clasped hands. "You do me great honour, Sir. All I wish for now is your blessing."

"Well, Mr Darcy, for what it is worth, you have it." He turned to the long table between the two windows which housed a salver filled with an array of bottles and reached for one tucked away at the back. "Loving my Lizzy shows both taste and good sense." He glanced over his shoulder at Darcy, then turned back to splash liquid into two crystal tumblers. "Good sense, however, must be questioned when it is prepared to take on a wife with such minimal dowry and a family prone to the ridiculous."

Mr Bennet walked back to where Darcy stood and handed him one of the glasses.

"You have yet to make the acquaintance of my Aunt Catherine, Sir. I think I can trade you for absurdity."

"Good. Because you will meet absurdity at Longbourn, Mr Darcy, on every occasion. It is the one given in my life, the one thing I can rely upon and the one thing I wish I could not. However-"

He broke off as Darcy started at a loud crash somewhere in the house, followed by a quickly smothered shriek of laughter and then Mrs Bennet's strident tones.

Meeting Darcy's eye, Mr Bennet inclined his head towards the door. "I will apologise in advance for what you are about to endure."

"I would endure anything for your daughter, Sir."

"Clearly." Mr Bennet grunted. "Well, I shall remind you of that in a few hours' time, young man, but in the meantime, let us raise a toast to yours and Lizzy's happiness."

Chapter Thirty Seven

ELIZABETH HAD TAKEN THE NEWS, offered by Lydia with a sneer, that Mr Darcy was sequestered in the library with their father, with a calm that belied the churning of her insides. She had exchanged a quick glance with Jane, who had smiled reassuringly at her, before returning her attention to her book once more, but she saw none of the words and instead stared at the reed marker as the man she loved no doubt ran the gauntlet of her father's sarcasm. She had hoped to have the opportunity to speak to him before he entered the library, that she might forewarn him of what her father already understood, but it was too late for that now.

She had been so happy over recent days, but she had not considered the reality of how things might stand at home. Though her mother was intent upon capturing Colonel Fitzwilliam if she could, and thus had ceased her perpetual tirade against Darcy, she still held him in little favour. Lydia persisted in her infantile defence of Wickham, and nothing Elizabeth said seemed to hold any sway.

With a sigh, she placed the marker in the book and dropped it onto a side table before getting to her feet. If only her mother knew precisely what Darcy was to become to her: a son by marriage. Darcy had told her that he wished he had either of his parents alive, that they might welcome her into their family. She had both to offer, and one was likely to take his sport with him and the other to repay his kindness to the family with incivility.

Slipping from the room, she walked to the dining room where she settled on the stool before the small pianoforte that Mary tended to practise upon and, desperate for distraction, she began to play a light air from memory, allowing the music to wash over her as she endeavoured to pass the time before she could be reunited with the gentleman.

Finally released from the library, Darcy closed the door firmly and then stood with his back to it, surveying the hallway, uncertain of which direction to go in search of Elizabeth. Glad that his duty was complete, all he desired was her company, and he walked over to an open door whence he could hear the voices of some of the younger Bennets. Fortunately, no one seemed to detect his presence in the doorway, and it did not take above a second for him to conclude that Elizabeth was not in the room.

Turning on his heel, he walked back into the centre of the hall, but just then, he became aware of the sound of music coming from a further open doorway to his right and, on peering inside, he was relieved to find what he sought.

The news of Elizabeth's engagement to Mr Darcy was broken by Mr Bennet to his wife in the privacy of his library, a wise precaution as it turned out. At first, she assumed he was in jest. When she realised he was not, silence fell – a long, blissful silence as Mrs Bennet stared at her husband in blatant disbelief. For one brief interlude, Mr Bennet thought perhaps his prayers had been answered, and that such good fortune as had recently been bestowed upon them had miraculously turned his wife into a quieter and more rational creature.

The shriek that soon followed, so piercing that even the thickness of the door was insufficient to conceal it from the rest of the household, proved him to be overly optimistic.

Keen to shield the gentleman as best she could from her mother's reaction, be it a continuance of her aversion or effusions of a highly embarrassing nature, Elizabeth willingly forsook the pianoforte upon Darcy's entrance into the room.

Going to him quickly, she was relieved by the smile that he gave her as he took her hands in his, raising one to his lips before drawing her to him briefly and dropping another kiss upon her head. "We have his consent and his blessing."

The words were softly spoken, but though Elizabeth had not really anticipated otherwise, following her confession to her father the previous evening, she released a pent up breath.

Stepping away, as she knew she must, she smiled up at him. "You were in there for such a time; I began to fear the worst!"

Darcy merely shook his head, and at the sound of approaching footsteps across the hallway, she reached out her hand.

"Come, Sir. Let us partake of the morning air."

Taking her proffered hand, Darcy placed a further kiss upon it before they made good their escape, the lady leading him through the open French doors and across a neatly tended lawn.

"How did you fare?"

Darcy threw her a quick look. "Better than I had hoped."

Elizabeth sighed. "Poor Papa. If only I had not done such an effective job in blackening your character and professing my disfavour last autumn, he would not have had to overcome such a vast hurdle."

"Do not concern yourself, Elizabeth. Your father seems adequately reconciled to the match. He even shared a glass of his very finest cognac with me!"

Raising a brow, Elizabeth laughed. "Did he, indeed? Then you are fortunate. That prized bottle rarely sees the light of day. I am not sure even Bingley was given the same privilege."

"You surmise correctly. Your father did own that he had considered offering some to Bingley at the given time, but that my friend was shaking so much he was concerned he would spill it, and he had no inclination for wasting good spirit by allowing it to be consumed by a hearthrug!"

"How very Papa that sounds!" She threw him an anxious glance. "I trust he did not make it too difficult for you."

Darcy let out a short laugh. "He had ample sport with me, Elizabeth. I see that I will have to up my game to keep apace with you both."

"Oh dear," Elizabeth bit her lip. "Was it very awful?"

Shaking his head, Darcy smiled at her as they passed through an open gate into a small but charming walled garden. As it was only early May, the flowers were barely in bud, but it was a restful place, the pale stone of the walls covered in trailing clematis, honeysuckle and wisteria, all combining to form a pleasurable backdrop for the eye at every turn.

"Please tell me he was not so mean as to tease you at such a time!"

"What do I not deserve, Elizabeth? I hardly recommended myself to him – or anyone else in the neighbourhood – on my first sojourn here. Further, he knows of my appalling mistake in considering you not sufficiently tolerable to dance with." He shook his head and sighed. "I have brought it all upon myself."

Elizabeth said nothing, leading him to a stone bench against the far wall and soon they were settled upon it, side by side, her hand still resting in his, as it had from the time they left the house. There was a small, stone fountain in the centre of the garden, and the trickling water was, for the moment, the only sound competing with the birdsong from a nearby tree.

"Are you disappointed that he understood your purpose before you had spoken?" Elizabeth glanced up at him. "I felt obliged to speak of it, for his imagination was in full sway."

Darcy shook his head. "I suspect it smoothed my passage. He does not strike me as a man who takes well to being in the dark about things – especially when they relate to you, dearest Elizabeth."

Lifting his hand, Elizabeth placed a kiss upon the back of it, and Darcy gently squeezed hers in return before releasing her. She looked up quickly, her gaze soon fixed by the movement of his hand to his coat pocket and then upon the small leather box resting on his palm.

"Elizabeth," he whispered, and her eyes flew to his.

"Though you have done me the honour of accepting my hand, I have yet to offer you a token of our engagement."

Elizabeth shook her head. "I have no desire for tokens, Fitz. Your continued affection and unchanged wishes are all I could ever hope for." She smiled impishly at him. "Though a token here would not be remiss in the circumstances." She touched her cheek and, unable to help himself, Darcy leaned forward and claimed a proper kiss in response to this, his heart swelling with his love for her.

"Do not distract me so!"

Elizabeth laughed. "But it is my duty to provide you with some levity!"

He smiled and shook his head. "Have patience. I wish to explain something to you." Darcy could tell that Elizabeth was suppressing her humour at his expense, but he pushed aside the urge to oblige her.

"When I… when I made my foolish application in Kent," he paused and raised a finger briefly to her lips as she made to protest. "I held no doubt of my acceptance. Such was my arrogance, Elizabeth, as well you know. I had this with me." He raised the palm on which the case rested. "I brought it with me once I knew from Aunt Catherine of your presence at Hunsford – though I admit I had not fully determined to approach you." He stopped and sighed. "What will you think of me – I was still gripped in a debate over whether to act upon my feelings."

Elizabeth chose that moment to mirror his gesture and placed a finger against his lips.

"Hush, my love. It does not do to dwell upon the past. We are moved beyond such trials."

Taking her hand, he bestowed a kiss upon the palm before flipping open the lid of the box and extracting the ring. Then, he held it up before them. "This was my mother's. You would do me further honour by accepting it as a symbol of my love for you."

Smiling tremulously up at him, she nodded, and he held her hand firmly in his as he slid the ring onto her finger, placing a kiss upon both when he had done.

"Your hands are so slender; I shall have the ring resized as soon as I am returned to Town."

Elizabeth looked down at her finger, studying the ring intently. Then, she raised her head, placing a hand against his cheek. "I love you so much," she whispered. "Thank you. I shall treasure it always."

She reached up and pressed her lips to his and, unable and unwilling to resist her, Darcy swept her into his embrace as they both expressed the depth of their feelings as warmly and as ardently as can be expected of a young couple in love, duly afforded all the protection a walled garden could offer.

Though proof against unwanted eyes, however, garden walls are no protection against the sound of hooves and wheels pounding a gravel driveway, and they were soon disturbed by the very same. Resting his forehead against Elizabeth's, Darcy strove to bring his breathing under control before placing a quick kiss on her cheek and straightening up.

"It would seem our moment of peace is at an end." He smiled ruefully at Elizabeth.

"For today, perhaps. But there will be others."

Reluctantly, Darcy got to his feet, drawing her up with him. "It is perhaps a timely intrusion. I do not think the colour that has washed your cheeks could be put entirely down to exercise, dearest Elizabeth."

The lady laughed as they turned to retrace their steps towards the gate in the garden wall, their slow pace reflecting their desire to remain alone as long as possible. "Likely not." She glanced up at him quickly. "Though, Fitz, it was an activity of sorts, was it not?"

He laughed also, but shook his head. "Come, enough distraction. Let us talk of something else."

"If you insist, Sir, but then you must select the subject."

Silence greeted this at first, but then Darcy turned to her with a smile. "Has today's post arrived yet at Longbourn?" Elizabeth threw him a puzzled glance. "I have become accustomed to you talking to me of letters whenever we meet. I merely wondered what today's matter might be."

Elizabeth smiled as they neared the gate. "You are learning to tease me, Fitz. But this talk of correspondence reminds me; I am long overdue in writing to my aunt, and now I have such news for her!"

Darcy grunted. "I am certain Mrs Gardiner will react to the intelligence in a far pleasanter manner than will Lady Catherine."

"Hmm, I do not envy your cousin, Anne, for she shall witness it!" Elizabeth glanced up at him, then squeezed his arm affectionately. "I still have *your* letter, Fitz. Every now and again, I take it out just to look at it. Sometimes, of course, I am merely admiring the evenness of your hand!"

Coming to a halt, Darcy turned to face her. "I cannot understand why you do not wish it destroyed. When I think of how I felt as I wrote it, I-"

Elizabeth shook her head firmly. "No, my love. It was instrumental in my coming to understand your true character, how could I not cherish it, not only for all it stands for but for what it has led us to?"

Darcy bent to kiss her one last time. They had reached the gate now, and this precious interlude was over. He motioned to her to precede him, but as she passed before him, he stayed her with a hand upon her arm.

"Once we are wed, dearest Lizzy, I shall write you a letter that will obliterate any memory of the one I handed you in Kent."

Elizabeth choked back a laugh, the colour in her cheeks returning as her gaze met his, and he leaned down to quickly kiss her lips before they turned to emerge from the walled garden, coming to a halt as they took in the sight before them.

Bingley had drawn his curricle to a halt and leapt from the bench before turning to offer Georgiana his hand. The Colonel, meanwhile, handed the reins of his horse to a garden boy who had just come running from the stable block.

Darcy sighed. "We had best join them; Georgiana will be anxious."

Elizabeth looked over as from the house came forth her father and Jane, swiftly followed by Mrs Bennet, waving her handkerchief, her voice carrying on the air towards them as she greeted Bingley with noisy affection. As a laughing Kitty and Lydia spilled from the doorway into the bright sunlight, Elizabeth laughed ruefully.

"Aye, and with good reason. Well, Sir." She glanced up at him and smiled. "Let us see how you fare; I will wager you will call for your mount 'ere long and high-tail it back to Netherfield, but if you do, be sure to take me with you!"

With that, she took Darcy's proffered arm once more, and they set off towards their families, their steps in perfect harmony as they walked across the lawn.

Epilogue

THUS IT WAS THAT, LESS THAN ONE YEAR since the name of Bingley had first been heard in the neighbourhood, Meryton society witnessed not one but two weddings, held jointly in Longbourn church.

Though the church itself was confined to close family and friends, the local populace turned out in force to greet the couples as they emerged into the fine morning, the women ostensibly to wish them well, but in many cases, more intent upon the London fashions. In the end, however, most were so taken by Mr Darcy's happy air and countenance as he looked down upon his bride, they failed to notice a single piece of lace, and it was many a long year before any of the local ladies could claim to have seen his equal for handsomeness.

Caroline Bingley was disgruntled by her brother's betrothal to Jane Bingley, and astounded and then mortified by the intelligence of Darcy's commitment to Elizabeth.

A sound talking to from her brother and, indeed, her sister, Louisa, awoke her to the reality of the situation. She must not only welcome her new sister but also extend every courtesy to Mr Darcy's choice of bride if she was to be allowed a continuance of an acquaintance with the family and admittance to Pemberley – both essential to her in her aspiration to marry well.

Their caution bore fruit and, conscious that Elizabeth, a woman whom she had derided on every level, had achieved a scale of social elevation Caroline could only hope to emulate, she quickly realised the efficacy of spending time in the Darcys' company. Yet though Darcy and Elizabeth tolerated her for her brother's sake, they were less receptive to her requests to make some stay with them than they believed the lady liked, for beyond one annual sojourn they would not go.

Eventually, Caroline tired of her endeavours in that quarter and turned her attention to a former suitor – one she had scorned, not only for his paltry four thousand a year and moderately sized property, but also for his lack of stature. In this she remained disappointed; the gentleman had since turned his eye upon another and was soon to be wed to a lady who was a far better prospect than Caroline Bingley ever could be, not only by virtue of her pleasant nature but also her lack of height.

Jane and Bingley spent the first year of their marriage at Netherfield, but when their first offspring arrived in the world, Bingley realised the time had come to purchase. Tolerant though he was of his mother-in-law, the arrival of twin grand-daughters proved such an attraction that she spent more time in their home than her own, and with his wife's willing consent, he began to cast his eye further afield in his search for a manor of his own. Following a sojourn with the Darcys, during which they had travelled to Yorkshire for a few days, his attention was soon caught by a large property with extensive acreage south of Harrogate. A deal was quickly struck, the lease of Netherfield relinquished and two very contented sisters were happily settled in neighbouring counties.

Charlotte returned to Lucas Lodge a widow. Mr Collins, intent upon his traps – his desire to free the Hunsford garden of rabbits had become his obsession – had become entangled in some reeds whilst attempting to set one and had toppled into the pond. It was a rather shallow affair, insufficient to drown a mouse, let alone a parson of mean stature, but the water was rank and, having swallowed some of it, he was taken with a putrid fever from which he never recovered. Charlotte was philosophical about having to return to the family fold, but one thing she had gained from the interlude: within a few weeks of her return to Hertfordshire, she gave birth to a child, a daughter whom she named Felicity.

Mr Collins, as fate would have it, had a younger cousin, but though they shared a blood line and thus a surname, there the similarity ended. Francis Collins was tall of stature, with a keen mind. He was a medical man with a sound reputation and a successful practice in Town, and though he made the journey to Hertfordshire to meet with Mr Bennet in relation to the entail, he made it clear that he was in no rush to take over the running of Longbourn, for his work was his life, and he trusted that Mr Bennet would remain in sound health for some time to come, offering his services to ensure that it would be so.

Mrs Bennet, who struggled to comprehend how anyone could prefer a profession over the life of a gentleman, found the whole situation unfathomable. Further, though his features were plain enough, his air and countenance were striking, and she had three daughters as yet unwed. Thus, she frequently invited Dr Collins to make some stay with them, and though he obliged with accepting the invitation, he was less malleable when it came to choosing a wife. Spending much of his time when in Hertfordshire at Lucas Lodge with his niece, it was inevitable that the lady who finally stole his heart was the child's mother, and so it was that, despite all Mrs Bennet's efforts, Charlotte Lucas remained destined to one day be mistress of Longbourn in her stead.

As for Charlotte herself, she still firmly believed that happiness in marriage was entirely a matter of chance for, as luck would have it, her second chance gave her precisely that.

Georgiana Darcy displayed no eagerness for an establishment of her own, being more than content to help her beloved sister, Elizabeth, in raising the growing brood at Pemberley, ably assisted by Mrs Annesley – Martha – who had remained with the family to be of like assistance and who grew to become as close to Elizabeth as another sister. There came a day, however, when a neighbouring estate was in probate, and the heir, whom it had taken substantial time and effort to trace, finally arrived from the continent.

Georgiana first met Theodore Vanderzee when he paid a courtesy call on the Darcys one autumnal day in the fourth year of their marriage, and both he and Georgiana fell swift and hard, so much so that the banns were read by the end of November, and they were wed on the Feast of St Stephen.

As a ship's captain, Theo had been used to travel and was reluctant to settle in one place. Though he was more than happy to find safe harbour with Georgiana, they often sailed over the water to the new colonies of the Americas where they spent considerable time. His estate was carefully managed by an able steward, with Darcy acting as overseer, though there would always come a time when Georgiana grew homesick for the peaks of Derbyshire and the love and company of her brother and his wife, and they would return to their estate for a few months, much to Darcy and Elizabeth's delight.

Anne de Bourgh finally found an establishment of her own. Having made the acquaintance of one Frederick Eastman at Georgiana's wedding, a wealthy widower from Shropshire with two teenage sons, they struck up a fast friendship. She felt all the appeal of gaining a life and home of her own with no pressure to produce an heir, and he was taken by her lack of pretension and amused by her acidic turn of phrase.

Lady Catherine, once she was given to understand the source of Mr Eastman's wealth to be inherited rather than earned, had been somewhat pacified. Though she was still displeased with Darcy, her desire to visit Pemberley and see for herself how his wife fared overcame this in time, and with her daughter on her way to being settled herself, she found that the notion of being alone in the vast house at Rosings held little appeal. Shropshire was a long way from Kent, and if she wished to be welcome in Derbyshire, she was obliged to curb her forthrightness. It would be untrue to say that her personality underwent any significant alteration. Her manner remained superior, her attitude towards those whom she considered socially beneath her never improved, but in Elizabeth she found a niece whom she could tolerate.

The good Colonel resisted all attempts to wed him to an heiress at first, despite necessity and familial pressure. He spent as much leisure time as his commission would permit at Pemberley, for in Darcy and Elizabeth and their children he could find no better company. Yet the pleasure he derived from being around the little ones, such an antidote to the trials of his profession, was what inevitably led him to seek a wife, for he longed for a family of his own.

The Fitzwilliams, with their wealth and status, were an attraction to any lady of fortune seeking social ascension, and once it was seen that the second son was in the marriage mart, it was not long before a young lady with a generous dowry, a pleasing manner and sufficient intelligence to render her good company was presented to him.

Miss Rowena Hamilton had a kind heart hidden under a brusque manner. She was quick to criticise, but equally quick to apologise; indeed, she did all things expeditiously. Within a month of making the Colonel's acquaintance, she had set a date and within just under a year of marriage, the lady presented him with a son, Henry.

She then promptly surrendered her tenancy on this world, leaving him saddened by her loss, but not heart-broken, for though he had been content, it was not a love match. The same could not be said for his child, however, whom he adored. Having now sufficient income from his late wife's fortune, he relinquished his commission in order to care for Henry – known within the family as Harry – and initially Colonel Fitzwilliam took up residence at Pemberley, where he found solace, company and ready hands to assist in the raising of his son and demonstrated little interest in socialising or any inclination for finding a mother for his child. Thus, the thunderbolt, when it came, struck him before he could take evasive action.

The Colonel had taken great comfort from the companionship that had developed over time between himself and Martha Annesley. They were of similar age, and the lady not only understood the sadness of losing a spouse but had been an officer's wife. Thus it was that one day, as little Harry took his first tentative steps from the Colonel's arms across the lawn into Martha's embrace, so went his father's heart.

This steadfast affection refused to leave him, despite his attempts to rid himself of it; he knew not what to do about it nor how the lady herself considered him, though he was often seen walking the grounds deep in conversation with her. Elizabeth – who was privy to the lady's long-held love for the Colonel – had a suspicion that before long her husband would lose patience with his cousin and point out what was staring him in the face, and thus she looked forward to there soon being another wedding in the family.

Mrs Bennet, despite gaining two fine sons in law, showed no sign of improvement. Silly she was and silly she remained. Mr Bennet took great pleasure in visiting with his two married daughters, and found that he was well satisfied at home, for Colonel Fitzwilliam, having witnessed the lady of the house disturbing her husband once too often as he attempted to share a post dinner port with his guests in his library, had fastened a couple of heavy-duty bolts upon the door, ensuring that it was only accessible from the inside once secured.

There had been teething problems at first (Mrs Bennet's persistent hammering on the door and complaints shouted through the thick wood were hardly conducive to the peace such a barrier promised), but as with all things, it did not take long before the lady tired of her histrionics, and so it was that, whether at home in Hertfordshire, or visiting his eldest daughters for any length of time, he was certain to find a fair amount of peace.

With Serena and Nicholas, Darcy and Elizabeth remained on the most intimate of terms, for Darcy grew to really love them, and they both were ever sensible of the warmest gratitude towards the persons who, by drawing Elizabeth to London and thus into Darcy's circle, and then onwards to Bath, had been the means of reuniting them.

The End

About the Author

Cassandra Grafton has always loved words, so it comes as no surprise that writing is her passion. Having spent many years wishing to be a writer and many more dreaming of it, she finally took the plunge, offering short stories to online communities. After that, it was a natural next step to attempting a full length novel, and thus *A Fair Prospect* was born.

She currently splits her time between North Yorkshire in the UK, where she lives with her husband and two cats, and Regency England, where she lives with her characters.

http://www.cassandragrafton.com

https://www.facebook.com/cassie.grafton

https://twitter.com/CassGrafton

Made in the USA
Lexington, KY
30 June 2013